GIRL NEXT DOOR

DOOR

KAREN KING

bookouture

Published by Bookouture in 2024

An imprint of Storyfire Ltd.
Carmelite House
50 Victoria Embankment
London EC4Y 0DZ

www.bookouture.com

ISBN: 978-1-83525-615-2
eBook ISBN: 978-1-83525-614-5

GIRL NEXT DOOR

BOOKS BY KAREN KING

Psychological Thrillers

The Stranger in My Bed

The Perfect Stepmother

The Mother-in-Law

The Family Reunion

The Retreat

Romantic Comedies

Snowy Nights at the Lonely Hearts Hotel

The Year of Starting Over

Single All the Way

PROLOGUE

Rachel

When I was younger I really wanted to fly. I often sat at the window watching the birds, their wings outstretched as they soared, and I longed to be able to join them. Mum loves to tell the story of how she once found three-year-old me standing on the garden table, flapping my arms wildly then jumping off, hoping to fly up into the sky. Instead, I hit the ground and hurt my leg. I never tried again, but I still sometimes wondered what it would be like. If I could have one superpower, it would be flying.

Especially now. Because right this moment I'm hurtling through the air and there is nothing I can do to stop the fall. Nothing I can do to ease the inevitable crash to the ground. If only I could flap my arms, fly back up to my bedroom then climb inside to safety.

But I can't prevent the inevitable.

Nobody can save me...

Nausea and sheer terror consume me as, almost in slow motion, I plunge to the hard, off-white slabs below. Even though it's all happening in an instant, I can feel the coolness of the air as I speed through it, see the ground coming ever closer, hear the traffic from the road in front of the house.

Regrets flash across my mind. I wish I'd been kinder to Ben, not cheeked my mum so much, realised how amazing my life was.

Most of all I wish I'd spoken out, told someone what was going on.

But it's too late now.

I'm going to die.

Suddenly a feeling of peace comes over me and I am no longer afraid. I close my eyes and brace myself for the inevitable thud as my body meets the concrete.

1

THREE MONTHS BEFORE THE FALL

Vanessa

'What's for lunch? I'm starving,' Jacob says as he ambles barefoot into the kitchen, his dark hair tousled, dressed in his usual trackie bottoms (grey today) and a tee shirt (black).

'Ham and cheese toasties.' I take the sandwich toaster off the shelf and plug it in. 'And you wouldn't be so hungry if you'd bothered to get up in time for breakfast,' I tell him, but I'm only teasing. I don't mind the boys having a lie-in at the weekend. We had a takeaway and watched a movie last night, as we often do on Fridays, so it was late by the time we turned in.

'Great. Can I have two?' he asks as he goes over to the fridge, takes out a big bottle of chocolate milkshake and pours himself a glass.

'Sure. Can you give Lucas a shout, please?'

Just then Lucas walks in, blond hair flopping over his eyes and dressed in black sliders, jeans and a tee shirt with the name of his favourite band splashed across the front. He's only a few months older than Jacob but he's in the year above him at school, and those few extra months seem to make him more self-assured. He reminds me so much of Aaron, his dad.

'Two for me as well,' he says as he opens the fridge and takes out a can of Monster, his favourite energy drink. I worry about how many of those he drinks, but then are Jacob's milkshakes any healthier?

'Pass me the cheese and ham, please,' I say as I take the bread out of the breadbin.

Lucas hands them to me, then pulls the can ring and takes a gulp. 'Dad's been busy.'

'It's a nice day so he wanted to get out in the garden.' I glance out of the large, double-glazed window to where Aaron is mowing the lawn. Our three-year-old daughter, Chloe, is playing in the sandpit at the top of the garden. Her blonde hair is finally long enough to put into little pigtails and she looks so cute.

I love our garden. It's not very big but Aaron and I have worked hard on it together, creating colourful flowerbeds around the lawn. Sunflowers, roses and hollyhocks grow along the fence that divides our garden from next door. The fence is high enough for privacy but low enough not to block out the sun – not that we have to worry about our privacy at the moment. The house next door has been empty for a couple of months, ever since our former neighbours split up and it was repossessed.

Aaron stops the mower and wipes his forehead with the back of his hand. It's a beautiful May day, the sun is shining and the sky is clear, so he's wearing just a black vest top and denim shorts cut below the knees. As my eyes rest on him, a warm glow floods through me. He's so handsome, with his dark cropped hair, sexy designer stubble and lithe body, but above all he is a thoroughly decent person inside and out, and I feel so lucky to have met him. To have a second chance at a loving, happy family, after what happened with Ricky. I brush the memories of that terrible time away and turn to the boys.

'Let's eat outside,' I suggest. 'It's a shame not to make the most of such a gorgeous day.'

'Okay,' Jacob says through a mouthful of milkshake. 'Want me to lay the table?'

'Please.'

'I'll make a jug of squash,' Lucas offers.

As I wait for the toasties to cook, I glance out of the window again and see the boys walk over to our big wooden table. Aaron waves and Chloe spots them and runs over, her arms in the air, wanting to be picked up. Lucas puts the jug of squash down before he picks her up and swings her around, her giggles bubbling through the air. Jacob sets the plates, cutlery and tomato ketchup – the boys love to dip their toasties in it – on the table then goes over to talk to Aaron.

At a glance you'd think Aaron and Jacob were father and son, with their short dark hair and brown eyes, but only Lucas and Chloe are Aaron's, biologically anyway. Chloe is sister to both boys and is the one who binds the family together. With her big blue eyes and blonde curls, she takes after me – although my curls are the bane of my life. They're so wild and unruly, I always keep my hair short.

Toasties done, I pile them onto a plate and take them outside. 'Lunch is ready!' I call.

We all sit down and tuck in, chatting over each other amicably as we share our news. Lucas's teacher has given him top grades for his IT coursework, Jacob's English teacher praised his essay, and Chloe pipes up to say she can count to twenty so we all listen to her and clap when she manages it successfully.

Suddenly a football zooms over the fence and lands on the lawn. Chloe giggles, scrambles off her chair and runs over to pick it up. I'm surprised when a thatch of black hair appears at the top of the fence and a young boy, who looks about six, peers over. It looks like we finally have neighbours. 'Sorry, can I have my ball back please?' He must be standing on something to see over the fence, as it comes to Jacob's and Lucas's shoulders.

'I want to play with it,' Chloe says, now clutching the ball.

'Okay, we can play catch if you like,' the boy offers kindly.

At that moment, the neighbours' back door opens and a teenage girl steps out and glances over the fence at us. She is slim and pretty with long, curly dark hair and deep brown eyes; she's dressed in short denim dungarees with a red tee shirt underneath, and a big sunflower on a chain dangling over the front. 'Ben, you should be more careful!' She smiles over at us. 'Sorry! We're moving in today. My folks sent Ben into the garden to keep him out of the way.'

'That's okay.' Jacob gets to his feet and goes to Chloe, coaxing her to give him the ball, while Lucas saunters over to the fence.

'Hi, I'm Lucas.' He's standing sideways, looking over the fence towards the back door at the young girl, and I can see the disarming grin he gives her. Aaron sees it too and winks at me.

'And I'm Jacob.' He is beside Lucas now.

'Hey, I'm Rachel.' She goes over to the fence and takes the ball Jacob offers her, then looks questioningly at them both. 'Are you brothers or friends?'

'Step-brothers.' Lucas grins.

'Rachel, will you...' An older version of Rachel comes outside and pauses when she sees us. She has to be her mother – they look so similar – her hair is tied back in a ponytail and she's wearing a long, colourful top over some leggings. She looks harassed and I immediately want to help. I know how stressful moving house can be.

'Hello! It's good to have neighbours again.' I get up and join the boys at the fence. 'I'm Vanessa – everyone calls me Ness – and this is Aaron, my partner, his son Lucas and my son Jacob, and our daughter Chloe.' I point to everyone in turn. 'Do you need any help unpacking? Ben can come over here and play in the sandpit with Chloe, if you like.' Ben might be older than Chloe but he looks young enough to enjoy the sandpit.

'Can I, Mum? Please?' Ben asks eagerly.

Our new neighbour nods, looking relieved. 'That's very kind of you. I'm Suzy, lovely to meet you all. My husband Carl's brother is helping us but there are a lot of boxes to take out of the van – it would be great to have a hand if that's okay with you?'

'Of course, we'll all help,' Aaron offers. 'Won't we, boys?'

Lucas and Jacob nod eagerly.

'We'd really appreciate that, thank you so much,' Suzy says.

'And how about I make everyone a drink? Tea, coffee or something cold?' I ask.

'Oh, that would be lovely. Three coffees please, we all have one sugar and milk.' Suzy gives me a grateful smile. 'Thank you all so much.'

So Ben and Chloe play in the sandpit while Aaron and the boys go to help our neighbours and I make drinks for everyone. I'd been hoping that someone with a child of a similar age to Chloe would move in next door, so they could play together, and am pleased to see Ben is already playing nicely with her.

Later, when everything has been unloaded off the van and Carl's brother has gone home, we invite Suzy, Carl and Rachel around for a drink and a bite to eat. Carl is a bear of a man, stocky with long ginger hair and a beard, while Suzy is delicate and petite, she and Rachel could almost be sisters. She works in a clothes store in the town centre, she tells us, and Carl is a builder.

'Do you work?' she asks.

I nod. 'I'm a freelance editor, I work from home, and Aaron is a video game software developer.' I'm surprised when

Vanessa mentions where they used to live in Sutton Coldfield, it's about an hour's drive away.

'What made you move to this area?' I ask.

Suzy and Carl glance at each other and I wonder if I shouldn't have asked but then Carl says that he was offered a job in Cheltenham.

'It was too good an opportunity to pass and we all fancied a change of area,' Vanessa added.

We all sit chatting for a while, and the conversation flows smoothly. They seem such a pleasant family and I really hope we're all going to get on well. It will make such a big difference to have neighbours again, especially ones with children of similar ages to ours.

'Are you going to Springfield, Rachel?' I ask. Springfield is the local school our boys attend.

'Yes, I'm in Year 9, the same class as Jacob.' Rachel smiles at Jacob. 'Jacob and Lucas are going to walk to school with me and Jacob said he'd introduce me to some of the other kids.'

'That's very kind of you both,' I tell the boys, pleased that they're looking out for Rachel already.

'I don't mind being seen with two Year 9s. Got to look after the little ones.' Lucas reaches out and playfully musses Jacob's hair.

'Gerrof!' Jacob says with a grin, pushing Lucas's hand away. 'It will be us looking after you, old man.'

When our new neighbours leave to carry on unpacking, we all go inside. 'Let's see if we can finish that side quest in *Kryakdon*,' Lucas challenges as they race up to their rooms.

'I'm thirsty,' Chloe says, tugging at the leg of my jeans. 'Can I have some juice?'

'Of course, sweetie,' I say, smiling as I hear the loud shouts from upstairs announcing that the boys are immersed in their game.

Aaron and I are so pleased at how well the boys get on. I'd

heard a few horror stories about blended families but we've been living together for four years now and everyone is happy. Jacob and Lucas hit it off right away, and when I discovered I was pregnant with Chloe, Aaron suggested that we all live together and I happily agreed. Aaron and Lucas were living in a two-bedroom apartment, so it made sense for them to move into my rambling four-bedroom house.

Jacob's dad, Ricky, has been off the scene for years, and Aaron's late wife, Amanda, died when Lucas was eight. Jacob went out of his way to make Lucas welcome, letting him share his toys without any fuss at all, and we soon became a close family. The boys are like brothers and they adore their little sister, Chloe. Next year we're planning to get married abroad: just me, Aaron, the boys and Chloe. I can't wait.

Everything seems so perfect. Little do I know that, thanks to our new neighbours, my family is about to fall apart.

'I'm off, then, see you later,' Aaron says on Monday morning.

I look up from coaxing Chloe to eat more cereal and am surprised to see him wearing his light-blue suit – he doesn't usually dress so formally for work. He flexi-works between the company office and home, although he's been working from home a lot over the last few weeks while the office is being refurbished. 'You look smart. Are you meeting an important client?' Aaron sometimes accompanies his boss to a meeting to explain the new software, he's top of his league in video game development and I'm very proud of him.

'Yes, we're hoping to get a big contract.' Aaron bends down to kiss me, his lips pressing softly on mine.

I lift my hand to touch his cheek. 'Good luck.'

'Thanks.' He goes over to Chloe and kisses her on the forehead. 'Bye, petal.' Petal has been his special name for Chloe ever since she was born and he declared her lips looked like two flower petals.

'Bye, Daddy.' She waves to him as he heads out the door, then dips her spoon back into the cereal, tipping up the bowl. I sigh as cornflakes and milk flow over the table. She's hardly eaten any of it, as usual. I glance impatiently at the clock on the wall as I grab some kitchen roll to clean up the mess. It's gone eight and the boys aren't down yet. They're pushing it, they're supposed to be meeting Rachel in twenty minutes.

I heard them earlier, going in and out of the bathroom. Usually, they come down in their pjs, grab some cereal and take it back up with them, often leaving the bowls in their bedrooms when they go off to school despite my repeated reminders to bring all cups, bowls and plates back down again.

I clean up the cereal, give Chloe a cup of milk then go out into the hall. 'Boys, you'll be late for school!'

'Coming!' Jacob shouts.

He bounces into the kitchen a couple of minutes later. I take in his newly washed hair and the strong smell of aftershave – Aaron's, I realise. His school shirt is open at the neck, sleeves rolled up and cuffs upturned, and his eyes are sparkling, a smile playing on his lips. He doesn't usually look so spruce.

Before I can say anything, Lucas strides in nonchalantly, his fair hair flopping over his face and curling behind his ears – he really should get it cut. We are expecting an email from the headmaster ordering it any day. He is wearing his shirt out and open-necked, like Jacob, but there is something about the way Lucas wears it that makes him look more suave. He is wearing Aaron's aftershave too, unlike Jacob he hasn't used the one Aaron keeps in the bathroom for everyday use – he's used the expensive one I bought Aaron for Christmas, which he keeps on the dresser in our bedroom. Lucas must have sneaked in and used it. It is on the tip of my tongue to repri-mand him, but I stop myself. Aaron might have given him permission.

I'm fairly sure that the reason both boys have made such an effort is because of Rachel, our pretty new neighbour.

'Well, you two look smart,' I say, lightly. 'You don't usually spruce up this well for school.'

Lucas flushes and goes over to the cupboard to take out a bowl, and Jacob shrugs. 'It's no big deal.'

They gobble down their breakfast in record time then leave together for the ten-minute walk to the school.

I look out of the window, watching them stroll down the path to the back gate, where they stand chatting and waiting for Rachel.

A few minutes later she joins them and their faces light up. It looks like Rachel has made quite an impression on them both, I think in amusement.

Well, she is a very attractive girl – I'm sure that she will have plenty more boys flocking around her in the class. Meanwhile, if her presence gets mine up, dressed and out of the house on time, that has to be a good thing.

Right?

Chloe clutches my hand, chattering away as we walk to nursery on Tuesday morning. It's a gorgeous day and she is wearing her favourite yellow shorts and daisy-print tee shirt. I hummed and hawed over wearing shorts too but plumped for white crops and a summery top. I decide I'll work outside for a while later this morning, it would be good to feel the sun on my arms instead of being cooped up in the study. On the way home from drop-off, I pop into the local minimart for a couple of things, bumping into Suzy at the till – she's got her hair pulled back and is once again wearing a long tee shirt over leggings. We say hello and I wait behind her as she scans her groceries.

'It's so kind of your boys to take Rachel under their wing, she's nervous about starting a new school,' Suzy says.

'She's bound to be, but it's a nice school, I'm sure she'll soon settle in. And the boys are getting on so well with her already,' I reply as Suzy pops her bread, milk and cheese into a cloth shopping bag. 'Has Ben started at the primary school okay?'

'Yeah, he couldn't wait. It's all so exciting at his age though, isn't it?' She taps her card on the machine and stands to one side. 'Are you heading home now?'

She's waiting to walk back with me, I realise. 'Yep. I'm going to have a much-needed cup of coffee before I start work, though. Fancy joining me?'

Her face lights up. 'That would be lovely, thank you. If you're sure you're not too busy.'

I have a load of editing to do today, but I can definitely spare half an hour or so to talk to my new neighbour. 'I won't be starting work until I've had a coffee, and then half a dozen more through the day,' I tell her.

'I envy you working from home, although I'm not sure I'd have the discipline myself,' she remarks as we leave the shop and head off down the tree-lined street, past the big detached houses that lie back off the road. 'What sort of editing work do you do?'

'I edit women's fiction for a big publishing company,' I tell her. 'I'm only actually meant to work four days a week, the days Chloe goes to nursery, but sometimes I take on extra work.'

'Well, I only work four days too so if you ever have to work on my day off, I'd be happy to look after Chloe for a couple of hours,' she offers.

'That's really kind of you, thank you. And if you ever need Ben picking up from school, just let me know,' I say as we turn the corner into our street, past the block of terraced houses to the semi-detached ones – our houses are the final two, with Suzy's being the corner house.

We chat away in my kitchen as if we've been friends for years. One cup of coffee runs into two and it's halfway through the morning before I know it. Suzy glances at the clock, then quickly stands up, grabbing her bags. 'Gosh, look at the time. I didn't mean to keep you this long, I'm so sorry!'

'Don't be silly, it was really nice to talk to you,' I tell her. And it is true; I like Suzy, she's warm and funny, we have really clicked. 'We must do this again.'

'Definitely, but coffee at mine next time,' she says as she leaves through the kitchen's French doors.

I manage to get a surprising amount of work done over a few peaceful hours in the garden – interrupted only by a quick call from my sister, Hazel, who I tell all about our new neighbours – before it's time to fetch Chloe from nursery.

We walk home the back way and find Jacob, Lucas and Rachel standing at the gate, clearly just home from school. Chloe runs to them and Rachel bends down to talk to her before she scoops her up into her arms. Chloe looks delighted, giggling as Rachel tickles her under the chin.

What a lovely girl, I think.

A little later, when I go out into the garden to get the washing in, I hear voices above me and look up to see the boys sitting on Jacob's bedroom window ledge. They're talking to Rachel, who is sitting on her window ledge too. The windows in our house and next door are the same design, made of three parts: one on each side that opens wide outwards, and a fixed centre piece so the kids have to lean over and twist to the side to speak to each other.

They're all holding on to the window frames, but it looks very precarious. 'Be careful, you could slip. Go back inside!' I shout.

'Don't stress, Mum. We're fine,' Jacob calls down.

It worries me though, and when I tell Aaron about it later, he agrees that it's dangerous and we have a word with the boys. They roll their eyes and shrug.

'We're not stupid, we hold on,' Lucas says.

Aaron crosses his arms and gives him a stern look. 'It's still very irresponsible. What if Chloe sees and copies you? What if she falls?'

The boys do look worried at that; they adore Chloe.

'Okay, we'll make sure we keep our bedroom doors closed so she can't get in, and we'll close the windows after us,' Lucas concedes.

I pipe in, 'Better still, don't sit on the ledge at all. If you slip and fall onto those slabs, you could die.'

'Looks like the boys are both a bit infatuated with our new neighbour,' Aaron says a couple of days later, his voice laced with amusement as he stands at the kitchen window, sipping a mug of black coffee.

I walk over and glance out of the window too. The boys are standing at the gate: Lucas flicking his hair back, Rachel laughing and Jacob clearly hanging on to her every word. Aaron's right, they are both smitten, and Rachel is revelling in the attention. Who could blame her? She's only just moved in and already she has two lads vying for her attention, accompanying her to school and back, practically worshipping the ground at her feet.

'Well at least it gets them up and out of bed in the morning. I've never seen either of them look so smart.' Jacob and Lucas's sense of style is normally teenage-scruff, their bedrooms are a tip, clothes are discarded and thrown on chairs only to be worn again whether they are crumpled or not. But so far this week they have showered and worn clean clothes every day. 'Let's enjoy it while it lasts.'

Aaron is working from home today, so he goes into the

converted garage, which serves as our study. Chloe isn't at nursery because it's a staff training day and I've officially got the day off, but I'm hoping to catch up on emails later. First, I take Chloe to the park and then do some shopping, it's too nice a day to be stuck indoors.

When the boys return from school, Rachel in tow, I'm sitting at the kitchen table answering some emails and Chloe is beside me colouring.

'Is it okay if Rachel hangs about here to listen to some music?' Lucas asks.

'Of course,' I say.

Rachel pulls out a chair and plonks herself down beside Chloe. 'Wow, you're colouring sunflowers. They're my favourite!'

Chloe's face breaks out into a big grin and she points to the sunflower dangling from a chain around Rachel's neck. 'Sunflower.'

'Clever girl!' Rachel tickles her tummy and Chloe giggles. 'Can Ray colour with you?'

Chloe nods and passes her a yellow crayon.

'Coke, milkshake or Monster?' Jacob asks, opening the fridge.

'Iced water please,' Rachel replies, beginning to colour the picture with Chloe.

'Let's put some music on and sit out in the garden,' Lucas suggests.

'Sure.' Rachel stands up. 'Want to come with us, Chloe? Leave Mummy to work?' She holds out her hand and Chloe scrambles off the chair.

'Oh, thank you,' I say, grateful for the chance to answer the emails in peace.

Every now and again Rachel's or Chloe's laughter floats through the open window, bringing a smile to my face.

I've just finished my work when Aaron comes out of the

study. 'Fancy a cuppa?' he asks then glances around. 'Where's Chloe?'

'Rachel came home with the boys and they've taken Chloe out into the garden with them,' I reply.

'Shall we join them? I could do with some fresh air,' Aaron suggests, taking the jug of blackcurrant squash I made up earlier out of the fridge.

I stretch and get up from the table. 'Good idea. Although I suspect they'll go off when we go out there.'

We put the jug of squash, glasses, Chloe's plastic cup and some biscuits on a tray, then add another bottle of water for Rachel and take it outside. The children are sitting on the blanket I laid out for Chloe earlier. Chloe is on Rachel's lap and they're listening to music from Lucas's phone, which is perched on a stand on the table.

'Anyone want a snack?' I ask.

'Oh, look, Chloe.' Rachel gets to her feet and holds her hand out to Chloe. 'Shall we get a drink and a biscuit?'

Chloe clutches Rachel's hand as they go over to the table.

'You're so good with her,' I say as she holds out the plate so Chloe can choose a biscuit.

'She's such a little sweetheart. I've always wanted a little sister,' Rachel replies.

Then I notice Ben looking over the fence.

'Come and join us, Ben,' I tell him.

'I'm okay, thank you,' he says politely, and then he turns to Rachel. 'You said you'd play *Minecraft* with me.'

'I know. I'll be home soon,' she replies, and he scowls a bit and disappears back into the house.

'It's so cool that you both work from home. What sort of software design do you do?' she asks Aaron.

'Video games,' Aaron replies.

She listens in fascination as he tells her about the new computer game he's working on. Teenagers are always intrigued by Aaron's job, and the boys' friends often question him about it.

'I'd better go now and play that game with Ben,' Rachel says finally as she gets to her feet. 'Thanks so much. See you tomorrow, guys.' She waves to Jacob and Lucas.

The boys race to the gate, Lucas gets there first and swings it open. 'Too slow!' he says triumphantly to Jacob, who shrugs.

'Thanks.' Rachel steps through, and with another wave, she strolls home.

'She's a ray of sunshine, isn't she,' Aaron says.

'Yes, and she's really good with Chloe.' I pick up the tray. 'I'm so glad that they've moved next door.'

I bump into Suzy on the way back from nursery the next day and she invites me in for a coffee. 'How's it all going?' I ask as we walk into her huge kitchen that overlooks the back garden. I'm not surprised to see the sleek, fitted cupboards, built-in cooker and modern hob and other appliances – the previous neighbours were a young, high-flying couple.

'There's still a lot to do,' she says as she switches on the coffee machine. 'You know what it's like when you move, you feel like you'll be unpacking boxes forever. The kids seem to have settled though, thank goodness, and Rachel seems more herself. We were worried about her... You know what it's like with teenagers...'

'Yes, it can be difficult to start a new school at Rachel's age, but I'm sure she'll be fine. At least she knows Jacob and Lucas. And she's a lovely girl, she'll make friends easily,' I reassure her.

'Let's hope they're the right friends,' Suzy replies.

A couple of weeks later, I'm in the lounge when I see Rachel go past with a girl with long fair hair. They look really chummy as they chat together.

'Rachel's made a friend then, I saw them together yesterday,' I say to Suzy over the fence when we're hanging out our washing the next day.

'That's Amy. She seems like a nice girl.' Suzy pegs a tea towel on the line. 'I'm so pleased at how well Rachel is settling in now.'

'That's great, it's important for them to be happy at school, isn't it?' I pick up my empty basket. 'I'd better get back to work. I've got to finish editing this book before I pick up Chloe, and Aaron is working at the office today.'

'How about I pick her up?' Suzy says. We cleared it with the nursery for Suzy to pick up Chloe if I'm busy, and with Ben's school for me to pick him up. It's such a big help to have Suzy next door.

'That would be great, thank you,' I tell her. 'I'll have a coffee brewing for you when you come back.'

When they get back, I put some cartoons on for Ben and

Chloe in the lounge while Suzy and I have a coffee and a chat in the kitchen, and a little while later, Jacob, Rachel and Lucas pile in.

'Can me and Rachel use the conservatory please, Mum?' Jacob asks. 'We're working on a project together.'

'How come you aren't doing it with Amy?' Suzy asks Rachel.

'Mr Pembroke put us into pairs and Jacob's my partner. He said if he put two girls together, they'd chat too much, and two boys would mess around.'

'He's got a point,' I reply. 'Yes, of course, you can use the conservatory.'

Suzy puts her empty coffee cup down. 'Come on, Ben. Time to go,' she calls.

Jacob grabs a can out of the fridge and goes out just as Ben comes in from the lounge, Chloe tagging behind him. Then Chloe sees Rachel and goes running over to her for a hug, her arms outstretched.

'Hello, sweetie.' Rachel picks her up and cuddles her tight, and Chloe gives a wide, toothy grin over her shoulder. It's like Rachel is the big sister Chloe has never had.

For the next week, Jacob and Rachel work hard on their project for an hour or so every night. Lucas waits until they look like they're finished and then brings them some drinks, which is so considerate of him. I'm glad they have the project to work on, as it seems to have brought them closer together. I don't think I've ever seen Jacob look so animated and upbeat.

Then on Friday, Jacob says they should be finished tonight. And as they work away, I glance over at them, bending over a piece of paper on the coffee table in the conservatory, their heads almost touching. I notice Lucas standing in the dining room, watching them. He turns and grins when he sees me, then saunters into the kitchen, hands in his pocket.

'Time they had a break,' he says, tucking two bottles of sparkling water under his arm and one in his pocket. One of the pluses of Rachel moving in is that the boys now drink a lot of water, rather than the energy drinks and Coke they used to prefer. He takes the bottles into the conservatory and hands one to each of them, perches on the arm of a chair and whispers something to Rachel. She throws back her head and laughs.

I watch them all with a smile on my face, it's so good to see them getting on so well. Then Lucas reaches out his hand and moves a wisp of hair away from Rachel's face. Her chestnut eyes widen as they lock on his and a shy smile forms on her lips. For a moment they both gaze at each other, with Jacob looking awkwardly between them, then Rachel quickly gets up and starts putting the papers away, her head bent over the table and her long hair covering her face. Lucas smiles triumphantly at Jacob and my heart skips a beat.

It's obvious that Rachel and Lucas are attracted to each other.

So where does that leave Jacob?

On Monday morning, Lucas and Jacob come down to grab a bowl of cereal each then disappear back to their rooms. There's been a bit of an atmosphere between them all weekend and Rachel hasn't been around, which is unusual.

I'm wondering if this has got something to do with the look Lucas and Rachel exchanged on Friday. It would be understandable if Jacob felt a little jealous.

'I'll take this into the study; I need to start early,' Aaron says, pushing his chair back and picking up his mug of coffee. He's working from home today, which means he'll be in the study, where he has his state-of-the-art computer which no one is allowed to touch. He's paranoid it will get broken so the kids are banned from going in there unless one of us is in there too. I have a desk too, but as Chloe isn't at nursery today, I'll have to use the kitchen table. It isn't officially a workday for me but I have a bit I want to get through, and if I bring a box of toys into the kitchen, she will hopefully play nicely without needing too much from me.

I'm loading up the dishwasher when Lucas comes rushing downstairs and out the back door. Surprised that Jacob isn't with him, I go to the kitchen window and watch him walk briskly to the gate, where Rachel is waiting. She smiles at him and glances questioningly down our garden path as if looking for Jacob. Lucas shakes his head and says something to her, then they go off to school together, side by side. A knot of unease forms in the pit of my stomach, and I turn around as Jacob shuffles into the kitchen, head down.

'Lucas and Rachel have gone ahead,' I tell him.

He shrugs. 'Up to them.'

As I watch him walk down the path alone, I can't help myself worrying. The boys have always gone to school together. And now it seems that Rachel has driven a wedge between them. It's what I've been dreading since I realised they both fancied her.

I tell myself that it's only a crush. Lucas and Rachel will both probably be infatuated with someone else in a couple of weeks. Or Jacob will. And then hopefully things will go back to normal.

'Mummee.' Chloe clutches my jeans. 'I want you to play with me.'

I bend down and scoop her up. 'Mummy and Daddy have to work, so let's go and get you some toys to play with.'

She nods eagerly. We go into the lounge and I let her choose what she wants to put in her playbox: her colourful bricks – of course – and her farm animals. She has some big crayons and a colouring book in the drawer in the kitchen, so that should be plenty to occupy her for a couple of hours.

Then I boot up my laptop and open my work folder while Chloe sits near me on the soft brown rug, her tongue sticking out between her teeth as it always does when she's concentrating, building a tower with her bricks.

A few minutes later Chloe shouts, 'No!' and I look up to see the tower of bricks collapse. She's over-balanced them. She frowns and starts to build them again, I can see that they're going to topple. 'Shall Mummy help you?' I ask.

She shakes her head. 'I'll do it.'

I know it's best to leave her to it otherwise she'll have a tantrum. She might only be three, but Chloe is fiercely independent, and if I'm not careful, we'll end up in a battle of wills. I try to choose my arguments with all the kids, believing that if you let the things that don't really matter ride, kids will listen when you say no because you don't do it very often.

Chloe can be very headstrong, not like Jacob, who was shy and sensitive as a child, always wanting cuddles and looking for approval although he had some terrible tantrums. *How much of that was because of Ricky?* I wonder. Even now Jacob erupts like a volcano when pushed into a corner.

'No!' Chloe shouts again as the bricks topple. She hits them with her hands, her face twisted in frustration.

'Why don't you play with your farm?' I ask, and, getting up, I take it out of the box and help her set it out. Her face breaks into a smile as she starts to play with the tiny plastic animals, and I heave a sigh of relief. She plays happily until lunchtime, and afterwards Aaron says he'll take her to the park as he hasn't got much on this afternoon. Which is brilliant, as by the time they return I've finished the edit and sent it back to the publishers. I glance at the clock. The boys will be home soon.

But Jacob comes home first, alone.

'Didn't you want to wait for Rachel and Lucas?' I ask him as he kicks his shoes off in the hall.

'I'm not being a third wheel,' he mutters.

'So are they...' I stumble for the word to use. 'Are they seeing each other?'

'Yeah.' Jacob gives a dismissive shrug. 'Don't worry about it, I'm not bothered.'

I can see that he is bothered though. He clearly feels like he can't even walk to and from school with them anymore. I want to reach out and hug him, like I used to when he was a little boy.

'You're all so young.' I stumble to find the words. 'There's plenty of time for girlfriends.'

Jacob gives me a scathing look. 'Oh Mum, save me the lecture. I've told you, I'm not bothered. They're welcome to each other.' He pours himself a glass of milk then goes up to his room.

A while later I look out of the window and see Lucas and Rachel walking along the path, hand in hand. They stand talking at the gate and I wonder if Rachel will come in, as she often does, to say hello to Chloe but she carries on home.

'Jacob's been home for ages. Did you two have to stay back at school for something?' I ask.

Lucas shrugs. 'Jacob carried on ahead.'

I can't help myself feeling saddened and uneasy at this turn of events. Lucas and Jacob got on well from day one. It's awful to see them being like this with each other now.

I mention it to Aaron when he comes back from the park with Chloe, and he kisses me on the forehead. 'Look, I don't think this is anything we should worry about, it will settle down soon enough. Teenage romances rarely last long. No doubt Rachel and Lucas will tire of each other and then things will go back to normal with the boys.'

I try to absorb his words, but it's hard to ignore the worm of apprehension wriggling in my stomach.

7

The boys go to school separately for the rest of the week, and Rachel doesn't come around at all. So when Suzy pops in for a coffee on Friday morning, I mention that Chloe misses Rachel. 'I hope Rachel doesn't feel awkward coming over because she and Lucas are...' I falter a little, wondering if Suzy knows, and if I'm making too much of it.

She looks worried. 'Lucas and Rachel? Are you saying they're a thing?'

'It's only been a few days. Nothing serious.'

Suzy frowns. 'I hope not. Carl won't like it. He thinks Rachel is too young for boyfriends.'

'Like I said, I don't think it's anything serious, but I can see that Jacob likes Rachel too and is feeling a bit shut out. So I wondered if that's why Rachel hasn't been round. I only mentioned it because Chloe is asking after her, and I don't want Rachel to think she has to keep away.'

'Why would she think that?' Suzy rests her hands on the table and leans forward, her eyes narrowed. 'Are your boys arguing over Rachel, then?'

I feel a bit embarrassed now. This is sounding far worse than it is. 'No, not really. You know what teenagers are like.'

'I do, only too well.' She sighs. 'I'll have a word with Rachel tonight and find out what's going on before Carl catches on.'

I find it a bit odd that she's so worried about Carl finding out. I realise that Rachel is only fourteen but surely it isn't that big an issue? Some men are overprotective with their daughters, I remind myself. I hope Rachel doesn't get into trouble; I almost wish I hadn't mentioned it.

Jacob is quiet all through dinner that night, refusing to meet Lucas's eye and studiously concentrating on his meal. I can see that he's upset but Lucas and Aaron seem oblivious to this as they chat about a new computer game. It's a conversation that Jacob would normally join in with.

'There's a Games Fayre in Birmingham in August,' Aaron says. 'I could get you both tickets. Do you fancy that, Jacob?' He glances over at Jacob, who nods slowly, and I'm grateful to Aaron for including him.

'Yeah, great. Thanks,' Jacob mumbles without looking up.

'Can you get a ticket for Rachel too?' Lucas asks.

Jacob mutters under his breath as he jabs a chip with his fork. 'She can have mine. I don't fancy it after all.'

'Surely you can all go together,' I venture.

'What, and spend all day watching them holding hands and being all soppy with each other?' he snaps in a sudden outburst, then puts two fingers in his mouth and makes a gagging sound.

Chloe giggles and copies him, leaning over her plate as if she is going to throw up.

Aaron frowns. 'That's enough, Jacob. Watch what you say and do in front of your sister, please. She's copying you.'

'You're just jealous that Rachel prefers me to you,' Lucas retorts.

Jacob pushes his plate away and stands up, shoving his chair back. 'Doesn't bother me, she's welcome to you.'

'That was a bit insensitive, Lucas,' I say gently when Jacob has gone out. 'You'd probably feel put out too if it was Jacob and Rachel who had hooked up.'

'He's the one acting immature, not me!' Lucas snaps, then he storms out of the room as well.

'We need to talk to them,' I say to Aaron as I put my knife and fork down, my appetite gone. 'I hate all this tension.'

'Best to leave it alone, I think. Jacob will get over it,' Aaron says.

I glare at him. How would he feel if Lucas was the one being left out?

'That's not fair. You're making it sound like this is all Jacob's fault and he's sulking over nothing. He must feel very hurt and rejected,' I point out as I clean Chloe up. She's been playing with her food while we've been distracted with the boys, and there's a mess everywhere.

Aaron sighs. 'Look, it's just a bit of teenage rivalry, no need to make a big deal out of it. And to be honest, I'm surprised with Jacob's reaction, it was quite extreme. He's not good at handling rejection, is he?'

I jerk my head around to face him. 'What do you mean by that?'

Aaron draws a breath slowly, trying to de-escalate. 'Look, let's not fight over this. Fancying someone and them not feeling the same way back is a fact of life for everyone. And Jacob needs to learn to deal with it. We don't want him reacting like...' He stops as if realising he's said too much.

But it's too late, and I'm furious. I know exactly what he was going to say. How dare he? 'Like who, Aaron? Like Ricky?'

'Slow down, I didn't mean anything, Ness... but you are a bit overprotective with Jacob. You can't make everything right for him, you can't shield him from life.' He starts to collect the dirty plates off the table and load the dishwasher, keeping his back to me.

Chloe is looking at us with worry evident in her big blue eyes, so I hold back the words that are on my tongue. We try not to argue in front of her.

'Let's get you to bed, darling.' I pick up Chloe and take her upstairs, Aaron's words ringing in my mind. How dare he compare Jacob to Ricky? Lucas would be just as hurt if Rachel had chosen Jacob over him, and if Jacob was pushing him away.

A short while later, I come back down to find that Aaron has gone for a run. He goes running a couple of times a week but never on a Friday evening – Friday is usually our family movie and takeaway night only now we're all at loggerheads. Aaron always says that running clears his head, and it certainly seems to have done the trick this time as he comes back with a bunch of white carnations. They're obviously from the garage forecourt, but it's the thought that counts.

'I'm sorry I snapped at you, love. Please, let's not fight. It'll all blow over and the boys will soon be friends again.'

He holds out his arms and I go into them, the tension in my chest easing immediately. I hope he's right, but I wish Rachel had remained friends with both boys instead of choosing one over the other.

Until recently I'd been so happy with our neighbours, and the children were getting on so well. Now it seems that the pretty new girl next door is causing real problems between the boys.

And even worse, cracks have appeared in my relationship with Aaron.

8

It's a gorgeous Sunday afternoon, the sun is shining and Chloe is playing in the garden while I water the flower pots.

'Ray!' Chloe squeals, running over as she spots Rachel walking past.

'Hello, sweetie,' Rachel says, leaning over the gate.

Chloe holds out her arms and Rachel picks her up and gives her a cuddle. Chloe snuggles into her, tracing the big sunflower logo on her tee shirt with her finger. 'That's pretty!' she says.

Rachel looks at me warily as I walk over to them. 'Good to see you, Rachel. We've all missed you.'

Her face breaks into a big smile. 'You too. I've missed this little one,' she says as Chloe cuddles into her. 'It's just a bit... you know.'

I nod. I do know. 'You're always welcome,' I tell her.

Rachel kisses Chloe on the cheek, then puts her back over the gate. 'I'm going to see my friend Amy, darling, but I'll play with you soon,' she promises.

Chloe waves and runs off to play with her picnic set.

A few minutes later, Suzy comes out and calls me over.

I glance at Chloe, who is playing happily, and walk over to the fence. 'Everything okay?' I ask.

'I wanted to let you know that I've had a talk to Rachel, and she assured me that it's not serious between her and Lucas, they just enjoy each other's company.'

'Well, that's good...'

'She's got nothing to do with the fallout with Lucas and Jacob, by the way. You know what teenage boys are like,' Suzy continues. 'She's stopped coming around because she doesn't want to be piggy in the middle.'

I can see that Suzy is worried by all this, and I wonder if it's because of Carl. He seems fairly laid back, but I've heard him shout a couple of times and I think he has a bit of a temper.

Not everyone is like Ricky, I remind myself.

'I understand. I've actually just spoken to her and told her she's welcome anytime. She's on her way to see Amy,' I add.

'That's good.' Suzy looks relieved and we chat for a while, arranging to have a coffee the following morning when we're both free.

I go inside feeling a bit more reassured. I've got to leave the boys to sort it out. It's not really that big a deal, is it? Siblings often fall out, especially in their teens. I think of all the fights Hazel and I had. Especially over my borrowing her clothes, I remember with a smile.

Hazel is two years older than me, and when she started work she treated herself to some gorgeous clothes, which I often borrowed when she was out, hoping to get home before her and sneak them back into her wardrobe without her knowing. I didn't always succeed and she would get so mad at me. We're really close now though, and will do anything for each other.

I decide that I'll ask Hazel around for coffee too tomorrow, it's her day off work and she hasn't met Suzy yet. I think they'd get on like a house on fire, and Hazel will be pleased to see me making some local friends – I've been quite isolated since Ricky.

I guess I threw all my energy into making sure Jacob was okay, and even though Hazel likes Aaron well enough, she has always said it's important to have female friends, not just the support of your partner.

The next morning, Hazel comes armed with a chocolate fudge cake from the local bakery and hits it off with Suzy right away as they exchange horror stories about difficult customers – Hazel is the manager of a large department store in Worcester town centre. I make coffee while Hazel gets out plates and cuts the cake, then we chat away. We discuss the situation with the boys and Rachel briefly, but mostly we don't mention the kids at all. It's refreshing sometimes to have conversations that don't revolve around them, particularly given the anxiety they've caused me lately.

'She's nice,' Hazel says approvingly when Suzy goes. She puts the kettle on for another coffee. 'Look, Ness, try not to worry about the kids, it'll all sort itself out.'

Which is basically what Aaron said.

However, the tension between the boys increases over the course of that week. Lucas is out a lot with Rachel, while Jacob is holed up in his room. When Lucas is in, the boys avoid each other. They won't even eat at the same table together unless we put our foot down, and even then they don't speak to each other and leave the table as soon as they've finished.

The atmosphere in the house is so strained and I'm not sure what to do. Chloe feels it too, I can tell she does although Aaron seems happy to ignore it. He's in the study a lot, or at work, and he's going out for increasingly frequent runs, so it's probably easier for him not to absorb the tension in the house. But it really gets to me.

. . .

A couple of weeks later I'm in the garden watering the flowering baskets when Lucas comes home without Rachel. He slams the gate closed behind him, fury etched all over his face, and I glance up at him. 'What's the matter, Lucas?'

'Nothing,' he growls and storms off down the path.

Then to my surprise, Jacob and Rachel come along, chatting animatedly to each other.

Is this why Lucas is angry?

'Where have you been? I was waiting for you for ages!' Lucas snaps as he walks back outside and marches up the path towards them. I wince at the wary look in Rachel's eyes. Lucas didn't have to be so bolshy.

'We had to stop behind to talk to the teacher about our art project,' she explains.

Jacob is very talented at art and even won a prize a little while back. There was a piece in the local newspaper about it, I was so proud of him.

'We did look for you when we came out, Mason said you'd already left,' Rachel points out, a little defensively.

Lucas shrugs. 'You could have texted and told me, but no worries.' He smiles at Rachel. 'Shall we all go to the park when we've got changed?'

Rachel hesitates. 'Jacob and I need to finish our project. He was going to come around to mine later so we can spend a couple of hours on it. If you're okay with that?' She gives Lucas an anxious look.

'Sure. Fine.' He shrugs again.

'We can always go to the park after,' she says, as if trying to pacify Lucas.

'Don't worry about it, I've arranged to meet some mates there.' Lucas walks back into the house, leaving Jacob and Rachel exchanging puzzled glances. I put the watering can down and give them a reassuring smile.

'You can work on your project here if you want, like you did before,' I offer, knowing that Ben has been off school ill and that Suzy might have her hands full. 'What exactly is it about?'

'Symbolism,' Rachel tells me and they both start explaining the ideas they have, it's obviously a topic they're enthusiastic about.

Then Lucas comes back out, dressed in jeans and a tee shirt, hands in pockets. 'Laters,' he mumbles as he saunters past them.

Rachel relaxes. 'Okay,' she agrees. 'I'll go and get changed. I won't be long.'

Jacob and I go inside. He changes into his trackies and Rachel joins us in a few minutes, dressed in denim shorts and a tee shirt.

'Want a drink before we get started?' Jacob asks her.

'Great, thanks. Sparkling water, please,' she says.

Jacob passes her a bottle from the fridge and gets one for himself, then they both head upstairs, which surprises me as they usually sit in the conservatory.

'Leave the door open,' I shout after them.

'Oh, Mum,' Jacob groans.

'I mean it!' I tell him.

I go upstairs a little later and see them both sitting on the bed, poring over Jacob's laptop. Then Rachel looks up. Her face is red and her eyes are a bit swollen.

'Are you okay, Rachel?' I ask, suddenly very worried. She looks so upset.

'Yes, we've been watching a film for our project and it's a bit sad,' she says, wiping her eyes. She doesn't sound or look convincing and I'm pretty sure it's not a film she's crying over.

I want to question her further, but it feels like prying. And she's not my daughter; it's not up to me to question her.

Something is going on though. Something she doesn't want to tell me about.

9

Rachel and Jacob work away on their art project for a couple of hours, and when she goes home there is still no sign of Lucas.

'Can you text Lucas and tell him dinner will be ready in half an hour?' I ask Aaron as I put the potatoes on to boil.

'What is it?' Jacob asks.

'Sausages and mash,' I tell him. The boys like that so I hope we can all sit around the table and have an enjoyable family meal, regain a sense of normality, how we used to be. Although Lucas sends a thumbs up to Aaron's text, he isn't home when dinner is ready.

I haven't had a chance to ask Jacob what Rachel was crying about earlier. I want to broach the subject casually, so that he doesn't think I've been spying on them. It strikes me that I haven't seen Amy around for a while. Have the two girls fallen out? Is that why Rachel was so upset?

'Where's Lucas got to? I'm about to dish up,' I tell Aaron.

'Don't worry about him. Put his dinner in the micro, he can warm it up.' He gets the plates out of the cupboard and lays the table.

'We always all eat together as a family,' I protest. Aaron knows how important that is to me.

'I know, Ness, but the boys are getting older now. We need to give them space and a bit more freedom,' Aaron replies.

I guess he's right. And maybe if we hadn't had all the recent upset with the boys, I wouldn't have minded but I don't like the fractures that have begun to appear in our family.

We're nearly done with dinner when Lucas finally gets home. 'Can you please wash your hands then sit down and join us? You're very late,' I reprimand him, annoyed that he hasn't apologised yet.

'I'm not hungry.' Lucas scowls.

'I've taken the trouble to cook you a meal. The least you can do is eat it,' I tell him, my voice sharp, looking over at Aaron for support.

'Make sure you eat it later, we don't want food wasted,' Aaron tells him lightly.

Lucas nods and stomps upstairs, and I'm furious with Aaron but don't want to argue in front of Chloe.

'Finished,' she says.

I look at her plate: she's eaten her sausage and most of her potatoes but as usual left her vegetables. I take her spoon and scoop up some peas. 'Eat a little bit more, then you can watch a cartoon,' I coax.

She pulls a face then obliges.

'I'll put the TV on for her,' Jacob offers. He helps Chloe down from the chair and holds her hand as they walk out of the kitchen.

I'm still fuming as we start to clear up in silence, and we've almost finished when we hear the boys shouting. We dash out into the hall.

'You don't own her, you know!' Jacob yells.

Then we hear a crash, and we run up the stairs, with Aaron in the lead and me hot on his heels. My hand flies to my mouth. Lucas is sprawled out on the hall carpet, at the top of the stairs. Jacob, his lip bleeding, is standing over him, his face red, his fist clenched, obviously about to punch him.

'Jacob! What the hell do you think you're doing?' Aaron hurtles up the top two steps.

Lucas scrambles to his feet and lunges at Jacob, but Aaron has reached him now and pulls him away, standing between them. 'Calm down! Both of you!'

'It's obvious that Lucas started it. Look at Jacob's lip.' I hurry over to Jacob to see how bad the split is, but he pushes me away.

'I'm okay, Mum. Stop fussing!'

'What's all this about?' Aaron demands. 'Why are you fighting?'

'He's sneaking around with Rachel when he knows I'm going out with her,' Lucas says, wiping his hand across his mouth, his eyes spitting fire.

'They're in the same class, Lucas, of course they're going to talk to each other and work on projects together,' I point out, shaken by the fury on both their faces.

'You really need to control yourself, Jacob. You could have seriously hurt Lucas,' Aaron says sternly.

'You've got to be kidding,' Lucas scoffs.

'Lucas threw the first blow,' I point out.

'And Jacob knocked Lucas to the floor and would have carried on hitting him if we hadn't arrived.' A muscle twitches in Aaron's jaw. 'Both of you go to your rooms and calm down. Now!' he orders.

I've never seen Aaron so angry before. And although he sends both boys to their rooms, I can see that he is angrier with Jacob. I admit it did look bad with Jacob standing over Lucas like that. Even so, couldn't Aaron see that Jacob's lip was bleeding? He'd only been sticking up for himself.

Either way, the boys have never fought like this before, and it scares me. I can't help wondering what would have happened if Aaron and I hadn't been at home. How far would they have gone? Would one of them have ended up being very badly hurt?

That day was the start of the divide between Aaron and Lucas, me and Jacob.

That was the day we became them and us.

10

THE DAY OF THE FALL

'Shall we go to the park?' I ask Chloe. It's a lovely day and I want to enjoy some time with her, she's back at nursery tomorrow.

'Yes, please,' she says, nodding and scrambling to her feet. 'Can I go on the swing?'

'Of course you can,' I say with a smile. I hold out my hand and she grabs it with her soft, tiny one. I wonder whether to take a cardigan for her as the weather is a bit unreliable for August, and in the end I decide to take it just in case. I look longingly at the pushchair; it would make the walk so much easier if Chloe would agree to sit in it. 'Shall we take the pushchair?' I mentally cross my fingers.

She shakes her head adamantly. 'I want to walk,' she insists.

I sigh but know that it will be pointless to take it, I'll only be pushing it there and back empty. Chloe has refused to go in her pushchair ever since she could toddle. I should be pleased that she's so independent and happy to walk, I remind myself.

It's slow progress: Chloe holds my hand tight and stops to look at every flower and bug we go past. I don't mind though, it's good to spend some time out of the house. Lucas and Jacob are out at the Games Fayre, which Aaron got them tickets for, and hopefully they will be gone for the day. I can't stand the tension when they're both in.

We spend a lovely hour at the park, Chloe plays on the swings and the small slide. I chat to a young mum who has brought her twins to play. They look about four and are dashing around like whirlwinds but she seems very calm and collected.

'I struggle to cope with one, never mind two,' I tell her admiringly.

'It's got easier now they aren't babies, the first twelve months were a nightmare,' she tells me. 'Have you only got the one child?'

'No, I've got a son too, he's fourteen now and a stepson a little older so I'd forgotten how time-consuming little ones are. Mind, teenagers are frustrating!'

'So I've heard,' she says with a smile. 'Thankfully I've got years before I have to cope with that yet.'

We chat for a while, then the woman gathers her twins and with a cheery wave says she'd better set off home. Chloe decides she wants to go home too. She's tired and walks slow but won't let me carry her. Miss Independent.

We meet Suzy on the way – she has her dark hair up and is wearing a smart navy skirt and blue printed blouse, so I'm guessing she's been to work. I'm glad to have bumped into her, I haven't seen much of her this last week or so and I wondered if something had happened to upset her, so am relieved when she smiles and slows her pace to walk with us. 'Ben was the opposite, always wanted to go in the pushchair,' she says. 'I don't know which is worse!'

I smile back. 'Have you just finished work?'

'Yes, early shift today because of stock-taking, and my feet are killing me.'

We chat easily as we walk along, enjoying the ease of each other's company.

Then we turn the corner, and my heart kangaroo-jumps into my chest.

An ambulance and a police car are parked at the end of the street, right in front of our houses.

'Oh my God! What's happened?' Suzy screams, running down the street.

In a panic, I lift Chloe up into my arms and run too, ignoring her loud protests to be put down, my heart pounding.

Has something happened to one of the boys? They could have returned while we were at the park. Please, God, don't let any of them be hurt.

As I get nearer, I see that Suzy and Carl's side gate is open and two police officers are standing outside it.

'Carl! What's happened?' Suzy screams as she runs into the garden.

'It's Rachel,' I hear him say, his voice ragged. 'She's fallen from her bedroom window.'

11

'Rachel!' I gasp, shock searing through me at Carl's words. With trembling hands, I instinctively clutch Chloe closer. She protests and wriggles but I'm not going to put her down. I need to hold her, protect her. Keep her safe.

The police officers are standing to one side now and the paramedics are bringing Rachel out on a sort of folded stretcher. I've seen them in the hospital dramas I often watch, so I know that it's a scoop stretcher and is used if the paramedics think the patient has a back injury. I'm hoping that's a precaution rather than a reality.

I can't see from here if they've supported Rachel's head and neck but I'm sure they have, back and neck injuries are so common with a fall like this. I think she must be alive as her body isn't covered with a blanket, but she could be paralysed, her brain damaged.

I can't bear it.

Suzy is following them, her face completely devoid of colour. Carl is standing at the gate, and Ben is clutching his hand, crying.

I go over to my friend. 'Oh Suzy, I'm so sorry. Is she... okay?'

It's a stupid question but I don't know what else to say. I step forward and hug her tight.

Tear-filled eyes meet mine as Suzy, her face etched with worry and pain, stammers, 'She's breathing but it doesn't look good. What if...?'

She swallows, unable to finish the sentence. I want to comfort her, reassure her, but how can I? What can anyone say at a moment like this?

'Let me look after Ben so Carl can go to the hospital with you,' I offer.

She nods gratefully. 'Thank you, and I'll phone my mum, she'll come and collect Ben as soon as she can,' she adds. Her voice is quivering, and she takes shaky breaths as she speaks.

I hold out my free hand. 'Come on, Ben, we'll sort out a film for you to watch.'

He looks anxiously at his mum. 'I want to come with you and Dad.'

'It's not the place for you, love.' She squeezes his shoulder reassuringly. 'Please go with Ness, Nanny will be here soon and she'll look after you.' She kisses him on the cheek and pushes him gently towards me.

'Come on, Ben, Mummy and Daddy need to be with Rachel right now,' I coax.

Unsure what to do, Ben glances at me then back at Suzy, but her attention is on Rachel, who's lying on the stretcher and being carried into the back of the ambulance. I can imagine the thoughts that are going through Suzy's head. I know how I'd be feeling if that was Jacob, Chloe or Lucas lying there.

What if Rachel dies?

I push the awful thought away and hold out my hand to Ben. 'Nanny won't be long.'

He reluctantly takes my hand and clutches it tight. Suzy and Carl are now getting into the ambulance, and the paramedics are attaching wires to hook Rachel up to machines. I've no idea what they are but they are obviously necessary to keep her stable.

Or alive.

Suzy turns back to me then, using the cuff of her thin patterned top to wipe away the tears which are rolling down her cheeks and spilling off her chin. 'Please pray for Rachel,' she says.

We're not religious, either of us, but I understand. She's desperate, she wants any help she can get. 'I will,' I promise.

I want to step into the ambulance and hug her again, she looks so pale and distraught, but the medics close the ambulance doors and a few minutes later they are off, blue-lighting down the road. I stand there, watching them, still in shock.

Ben starts to sniffle and Chloe wriggles in my arms. 'I need a wee wee.'

'We'd better get you to the toilet then.' I put Chloe down to get my key out of my pocket, then usher them both inside. Chloe runs straight to the loo and I take Ben into the lounge and turn the TV on.

'Sit down and watch the cartoon, Ben. I'll be back in a minute, I need to see to Chloe,' I tell him. Chloe has recently started to go to the toilet by herself – there is a step and a child seat in the downstairs loo which she uses but I still like to check on her. Ben obediently sits down on the edge of the sofa. He looks completely in shock.

I feel shaken up myself at the thought of that poor girl plunging to the ground.

Will she survive?

It didn't look good, with all those wires and the urgency on the paramedics' faces. I know that even if she comes round, there's a good chance she might never walk or talk again.

And I can't stop thinking that it could be Jacob or Lucas lying there in that ambulance.

When Chloe is finished, I take her into the lounge to join

Ben on the sofa before going to fetch them some biscuits and cartons of strawberry milkshake. When I return, Ben has his arm around Chloe, and they're both watching a Disney film on the TV. I give them their snack and sit beside them, my stomach in knots, my hands trembling around my cup of tea as I constantly check my phone in case Suzy texts with an update.

It's about an hour later when Glenda, Suzy's mum, comes to collect Ben. I've met her a couple of times and have never seen her look anything but elegant and immaculately made up, as she is today, but her silver hair is all over the place, her brown eyes are red-rimmed and her face pale.

'I had such a shock when Suzy phoned me. I had to sit down and get myself together.' The words are tripping out of her mouth. 'What a dreadful thing to happen, I can't believe it.'

'It's awful. Is there any more news?' I ask as I let her in.

'All I know is that Rachel's in a coma,' she says, and I gasp, my hand flying to my mouth as she continues shakily. 'She's broken her wrist but we're lucky she didn't break her neck or back. We all just have to hope she comes around soon. The longer she's out...' Her voice trails off. She doesn't need to finish the sentence.

I give her a hug, lost for words, before Glenda follows me into the lounge. Ben turns around as we go in and jumps off the sofa, running over to her. 'Nanny! Is Rachel okay? She fell out of the window.' He looks terribly distressed.

Glenda crouches down and hugs him. 'I know, darling, but the doctors are taking care of her. She will be all right, don't worry.' Then she stands up and turns to me. 'Thank you so much for looking after him.'

'Of course, it's no problem at all. I wish I could do more. If you need anything, I'm here,' I tell her. 'And please let me know as soon as there's any news.'

I can see the fear in her eyes, the same fear that is making me feel sick to my stomach. 'I will,' she promises. 'Hopefully there will be some good news soon.' She tousles Ben's hair. 'Come on, Benny, let's get you home.'

The time drags when they've gone, and I long for Aaron or the boys to return home, to have someone to talk to. It's all so awful. I wonder whether to call or message them, but this isn't something I want to tell them over the phone. I'm hoping that Rachel will come round soon, then at least I can tell them that she will be okay.

Chloe is playing happily with her doll's house now so I go out into the garden to get the washing in, leaving the back door open in case she wants to join me. As soon as I step outside my eyes are drawn to Rachel's bedroom window. The side window is wide open as it often is. My eyes dart a few metres across to Jacob's bedroom. His windows are closed, and so are Lucas's.

I put the now-dry washing into the basket and go inside to sort it out into separate piles. After checking in on Chloe, who is still playing happily, I take it upstairs to put the towels in the airing cupboard. Then I spin around as I hear a noise coming from Jacob's room.

'Jacob?'

I knock on the door then turn the handle. 'Jacob, are you in there?' I open the door and enter gingerly.

I step back in shock when I see Jacob sitting on the bed. His back is against the wall, his head resting on his arms, which are folded across raised knees. Sobs are wracking his body.

12

'Jacob!' I cross the room, stepping over all the clutter on the floor, and sit on the bed, wrapping my arms around him. 'What's the matter? Is it Rachel? Did you see what happened?'

He lifts his head, wipes his eyes on the hem of his tee shirt and nods his head.

I'm stunned. If Jacob saw Rachel fall, why didn't he run down to get help or phone the police? I suppose he must have been in shock; he still is. He's trembling, and I hold him tight. 'That must have been awful for you to witness,' I say softly. 'How did it happen? I thought you were out for the day. Were you talking to each other from your windows?'

He shakes his head agitatedly and gulps. It's clear that he's struggling to speak. Perhaps he's blaming himself for not being able to save Rachel, but there is no way he could have reached out and grabbed her, their bedroom windows aren't close enough together. I know I must reassure him about that, but right now I need to know what happened. I wait patiently for him to get himself together.

'The Games Fayre was boring, so I came home. I haven't been back long,' he stammers. 'I went up to my room and had my headphones on. I was playing a game, then I thought I heard a scream outside.' His eyes, wide with terror, rest on my face. 'So I ran over to the window.'

'Go on,' I say, stroking his hair.

'It was horrible, Mum. I saw Rachel on the ground.' He shudders. 'She was just lying there like a broken doll.' He looks utterly traumatised.

'Oh, love...'

'I didn't know what to do,' he continues. 'Then Carl came running out; he must have heard her scream too. I wanted to go down and see how badly hurt Rachel was, but I couldn't. I couldn't move.' His voice cracks. 'Is she okay? She isn't...?' He can't bring himself to complete the sentence, but I know the missing word is 'dead'.

'No, darling, she's alive but she's in a coma. They've taken her to hospital and the doctors say she's stable, that's a good sign. Hopefully she will come round soon.'

Jacob looks relieved. 'I can't get the scream out of my head, it was so horrible, she must have been terrified, and when I saw her she was totally still...'

'Do you know what made her fall?' I ask gently.

He shakes his head, his eyes wide.

I glance at the clock on his wall. Hours have passed since Rachel fell. Hours in which Jacob hasn't known whether his friend was dead or alive. I can see that he is terribly upset so why didn't he come down when he heard me come in?

A thought creeps into my mind. I don't want to ask it, but I must.

I place my hand reassuringly on his and try to keep my voice calm, gentle. 'Jacob, were you leaning out of the window talking to Rachel when she fell? You can tell me, it's okay. Even if you were, this is not your fault.'

'No! I wasn't!' He pushes my hand away and glares at me. 'I knew you'd think that! I didn't go anywhere near the window! I logged on to my game then I heard the scream.' The stream of words is gushing out of his mouth and he's biting back tears.

He's telling the truth, I know it.

Jacob is starting to calm down a little so I get up and go over to the window, noticing that the latch isn't closed properly. He must have opened it when he heard the scream and leant out to see Rachel's body lying twisted under her window. I guess he closed it then, reeling from what he'd witnessed.

I open the window wide and look out, over the low fence into next door, and my gaze rests on the paving slabs below Rachel's window. There's a smudge of red on them and it makes my stomach churn. I can almost feel the poor girl's terror as she plunged down to the hard ground, and Jacob's horror when he saw her lying there.

How many people survive comas? And even if Rachel does come through, will she ever be the same again?

Jacob, too, could be permanently damaged by this; he's such a sensitive soul. Witnessing something so awful at such a young age could have a lasting impact on his psyche, and he's already been through a lot in his short life.

Whatever happens with Rachel now, I know I need to keep a close eye on my son. I need to make sure he's okay.

13

Suzy

I'm frozen in shock as the ambulance speeds to the hospital. The siren is screeching, the machines are whirring and the paramedics are talking to Rachel, telling her to hold on while her eyes are closed tight, her face is paper-white and her hair is matted with blood.

I can't believe this has happened. Things seemed to be finally looking up. Me and Carl had been worried about Rachel starting a new school, especially so late in the school year. She is so vulnerable: she might put on a happy, upbeat face to the world, but underneath that she's so insecure, always fretting that she doesn't look right, act right, that no one likes her.

I dreaded telling her when Carl had been offered a job with a big building firm in Cheltenham, as I thought she might not want to move away, luckily Rachel was delighted. It was almost as if she'd been happy for the chance to make a fresh start.

I noticed that she'd been a bit withdrawn in her former school, not spending as much time with her friends, apart from Meg, and I wondered if there had been a fallout. Teenage girls can be so cruel to each other, but Rachel would never tell. She keeps her own counsel and rarely opens up about what's bothering her, although I knew that something was wrong, so I was relieved at how easily she took the idea of the move. She's settled in well here and seemed to be thriving. Ben, on the other hand, although he was excited to start at a new school, seems to be struggling to make friends.

Now look at her, lying motionless, wired up to all sorts of machines, with me and Carl praying that our little girl is going to survive.

What on earth happened?

I haven't had time to talk to Carl yet. He's sitting beside Rachel, his eyes fixed on her face, as if willing her to wake up. Then he raises his head and his eyes meet mine. I can see the abject pain in them.

'I don't know how this happened, Suze,' he whispers, answering my unspoken question. 'I was in the kitchen making lunch when I heard a blood-curdling scream outside and I knew right away something terrible had happened. I ran outside and saw Rachel lying sprawled out on the ground. I went straight to her and checked her pulse. I... I thought she was dead, then I saw she was still breathing, although it seemed so faint. I didn't know if I was about to lose her or what I should do.' He shakes his head and swallows as if the memory is too awful to recall. 'I wasn't sure if I should put her in the recovery position, I was scared to move her, which turned out for the best as the paramedics told me that if I had, it could have been fatal.'

I reach out and squeeze his hand. Then I look at Rachel's motionless body, her eyes closed, long black lashes spread out like fans.

'Please don't let my little girl die,' I whisper, tears falling down my face. I can't lose her. If she dies, part of me will die with her.

14

Vanessa

'Mummy!' Chloe shouts. It sounds like she's standing at the bottom of the stairs. She's obviously tired of being on her own but doesn't want to come up and join us.

'I'll be down in a minute, darling,' I call. I don't like to leave Jacob alone in this state but I need to go to Chloe. 'Why don't you come down too, Jacob? Don't shut yourself away up here.' I want to stay and talk to him, he looks so fragile and scared. I think of how he and Lucas have been arguing over Rachel. They'll be devastated if the worst happens to her.

It won't. She'll be all right. She has to be.

'I will in a minute,' he promises.

'Mummy!'

'Coming!' I squeeze Jacob's shoulder reassuringly then stand up. 'I'm sure Rachel will come round soon and will be perfectly fine,' I say although I'm not sure at all. An image of her wired up to those machines in the back of the ambulance and Suzy's and Carl's ashen faces flashes across my mind, and I'm hit by a wave of nausea.

Modern medicine can do marvellous things, I remind myself. It is amazing what people recover from nowadays. Rachel will pull through.

Chloe is sitting on the bottom step, waiting for me, and she gets up as I come down the stairs. She's sucking her thumb, her eyes big and round, and I know that seeing Rachel being carried off in the ambulance has worried her. 'Everything's all right, sweetheart,' I reassure her. I hold my hand out to her. 'Do you want a drink?'

She nods, her thumb still in her mouth, and we both walk into the kitchen. I pour her a beaker of fruit juice and put the kettle on for a coffee. Then I make us all some sandwiches, cutting Chloe's into quarters so she can eat it more easily. I call Jacob down even though I feel too upset to eat and I'm sure he does too, but we have to keep up our strength. I sip my coffee as Chloe tucks into her food hungrily, and I wait for Jacob to join us.

I'm wondering whether to go up and check on him when he shuffles in and grabs a can of Coke before joining us at the table. Chloe is quiet so I talk to her about our trip to the park, wanting to distract her. Jacob sits in silence, his shoulders hunched, twisting his earlobe as he always does when he's worried. He picks at his sandwich, and I nibble half of mine. We're both on edge waiting to hear news about Rachel.

I'm trying to decide whether to phone Aaron and Lucas when the doorbell rings.

Jacob lifts his head, and I can see the panic in his eyes. I guess, like me, he's wondering if it's bad news. 'Maybe it's Glenda,' I say, pushing back my chair and hurrying out into the hall.

When I open the door, I'm surprised to see two police officers standing there. I recognise them from earlier, they were at the scene of the accident.

'I'm PC Wallis and this is PC Daskal,' the male officer says. 'We're looking for Jacob Dawson' – the policeman checks his notepad – 'and Lucas Paige. We understand they are friends with Rachel West, the young girl next door who was involved in a tragic incident earlier. Are they at home?' With his fair hair and clean-shaven face, he looks barely old enough to be a police officer. The policewoman next to him is older and looks quite stern. I don't think she'll suffer fools gladly.

'Jacob is here, but Lucas is still out,' I reply. 'Come in.'

As the police officers step into the hall, I wonder how they can talk to Jacob without Chloe overhearing and getting upset.

'Let's talk in the lounge,' I say. 'I'll have to put the TV on to distract my little girl.'

'That's fine,' the policewoman replies. 'It's only an informal chat. There's no need for you to be with him if you prefer to look after your daughter somewhere else.'

'No, I would prefer to be with Jacob. He's pretty shaken up. He heard Rachel scream so he ran over to the window, and saw her sprawled out on the ground.'

'That must have been a shock for him,' the policeman says, his eyes sympathetic.

I show them into the lounge and tell them to take a seat on the comfy dark blue sofa before I go back to the kitchen.

'A couple of police officers want to talk to you about Rachel's accident,' I tell Jacob, gently.

He rubs his eyebrow with his finger. 'Why? I didn't see anything!'

'I know, but we live next door so they're trying to find out what happened. It's nothing to worry about,' I reassure him as I pick up Chloe.

Jacob follows us, hands in his pockets and head down, and it seems to me that even more colour has drained from his face as he sits down opposite the policeman. 'Is Rachel okay?' he stammers, his voice low.

'Rachel fell,' Chloe says, looking worried, her wide eyes fixed on Jacob's face.

'I know, darling, and we need to talk to the police, so you sit and watch your cartoon.' I switch the TV to a kids' channel then settle Chloe in the armchair, giving her a teddy to cuddle, while trying to listen to the police officer's reply.

'We don't know, Jacob. She's in a coma and we're waiting for further reports.' The policeman takes a pen out of his pocket and looks down at his notebook. 'Now, can you tell me exactly what happened? Take your time,' he says.

Jacob is staring down at his hands, twisting his fingers together. He's clearly struggling.

'I didn't actually see anything.' He keeps his eyes fixed on his knees as he slowly relates what he told me earlier.

'Rachel's your friend, isn't she?' the policewoman asks after a pause.

Jacob nods.

'So why didn't you go out to check how she was, after you saw her on the ground?' Her voice is gentle but firm and both police officers are watching Jacob's face. I get the distinct impression that they think he knows more than he's saying.

Jacob bites his lip. 'I was too shocked to move. I couldn't believe it.' He looks up, his eyes clouded over, and he blinks back tears. 'Then her dad came out and called an ambulance... I didn't know what to do. Her dad was there and dealing with it.'

'I understand,' the policewoman says with a nod. She pauses and shifts in her seat, her gaze going from Jacob to me and back again.

'The thing is, Jacob, right now we are not sure Rachel's fall was accidental.' She hesitates again then asks, 'Was she upset about anything? Do you know any reason why she might want to hurt herself?'

'What? You think she jumped? That she tried to kill herself?' Jacob looks horrified and he shakes his head vehemently. 'Of course not! She wouldn't!' he says emphatically. I can hear the tremble in his voice and his eyes are panic-stricken.

My nails are digging into my palms as I watch him. Could Rachel really have jumped out of that window? She always seems so happy and bright, like the sunflowers she loves so much.

Then I recall walking in on her crying a few weeks ago, and Rachel saying they'd been watching a sad film. I hadn't believed them at the time so I mentioned it to Suzy, who seemed concerned, saying that Rachel had been quiet and moody lately and she was a bit worried about her. Clearly Rachel had been upset over something.

Surely it couldn't have been anything so terrible that it would lead to her taking her own life? And if Jacob knows what it was, why isn't he speaking up now?

15

Jacob is shaking, his knuckles white as he grips his knees. He looks as if he might keel over any minute. This is too much for him to deal with. I really wish he hadn't come home early and heard Rachel scream and seen her body lying on the ground. He's too young and sensitive to handle something as horrible as this.

'I agree with Jacob, I'm sure this was a tragic accident. Rachel must have been leaning out of the window and slipped,' I tell the policewoman.

'She would have had to be sitting on the windowsill rather than leaning out,' the policeman counters.

An image of Rachel perched on the windowsill, looking down at the ground below, willing herself to jump bursts into my mind. I shut my eyes tight to block it out then snap them open as the policeman asks another question.

'Are you sure you can't think of any reason why Rachel would jump, Jacob? Was she worried about anything?' He pauses. 'Maybe she was being bullied by someone?'

Jacob hesitates before shaking his head emphatically. 'No, she wouldn't jump. No way.'

I instinctively reach out and touch his arm as I hear the anguish in his voice. 'This is a lot for Jacob to deal with. Could we end it there, please?'

The policeman puts away his notebook. 'Of course. I understand that this is very upsetting, but we need to understand why this happened.'

'We'll be back later to talk to Lucas,' the policewoman says. 'Meanwhile, if you recall anything, anything at all that could help explain what happened to Rachel, Jacob, please let us know.' She nods. 'We'll see ourselves out.'

After the police leave, Jacob sinks his head into his hands. 'They've got it wrong, Mum.' He raises his head and tears are spilling out of his eyes. 'Rachel wouldn't jump. She wouldn't,' he repeats.

'I don't think the police really think she did, love, but they have to consider every possibility. I'm sure Rachel will regain consciousness soon, and then she can explain everything.' I put my arm around him and he nestles into me, like he did when he was younger. He doesn't usually let me hug him anymore, but today he does. He's had an awful shock. I think about Lucas, he will be upset too. At least he didn't see Rachel lying on the ground though, blood seeping through her wavy brown hair.

I think that image will stay with Jacob forever.

Poor Suzy and Carl, they must be devastated. I'll text Suzy later and ask if there's anything I can do to help. I wish Aaron and Lucas would come home, I long to have someone to talk to. It's all so awful.

I put *Finding Nemo* on the TV for Chloe and make a cup of tea for me and Jacob, spooning two sugars in for him as he looks like he's still in shock. He sips it, lost in his thoughts, and then he goes upstairs.

Cradling my tea, watching the steam spiral up in front of me, I feel helpless and desperately worried about my son. The last thing I feel he should be doing is shutting himself away, but I don't know how to reach him.

I text Suzy, offering her my support and asking her to let me know as soon as there's any news. She replies a few minutes later.

She's still in a coma. My little girl. Oh God, Ness, what if she doesn't come round?

I imagine her and Carl sitting by Rachel's side, holding her hand, willing her to regain consciousness, willing her to live. I message back:

She will. She'll be fine. Sending you a big hug XOXO.

I just wish I believed it.

16

I desperately want to talk to someone about what's happened, but Aaron still isn't home, so I call Hazel.

'Hi, sis, how are you doing?'

At the sound of her warm, confident voice I feel my shoulders relax. 'Oh Hazel, something terrible has happened.' She listens quietly as I tell her about Rachel's fall, and Jacob seeing her on the ground. 'He's in such a state, Haze, and poor Rachel. She's in a coma, it's unbelievable.'

'Oh no! That's terrible. Suzy and Carl must be devastated. And Jacob, this must be really traumatic for him.'

'I really hope she didn't jump,' I say. It would destroy Suzy if she thought Rachel had been so desperate that she didn't want to live anymore. 'Poor Suzy and Carl, they must be going through hell, seeing their precious daughter lying in hospital, wondering if she will ever come out of the coma. I can't help thinking it could be Jacob, or Lucas. You never know what teenagers are going through, they keep so much themselves.'

'I know, I'm worried about when Zara is older too, the teenage years are such a minefield. All we can do is keep talking to them, make sure they know that they can come to us,' Hazel replies.

She is right, but if Rachel did jump, then she must have been in a terrible place mentally, and Suzy and Carl hadn't picked up on it even though I'm sure they did try to talk to her, they seem like wonderful parents. I hadn't seen how much pain Rachel was in either, and I saw quite a bit of her, or at least I hadn't realised just how bad things were when she was upset that day. Could I have done something to prevent this?

'Rachel was crying about something a few weeks ago,' I admit to Hazel. 'She said they were watching a sad film but now I wonder...'

'Did you tell Suzy?' Hazel asks sharply.

'Of course, and she said that she'd talk to Rachel. I haven't mentioned it again because I didn't want to pry.'

'It might be worth talking to Jacob again. Maybe she confided in him.'

'If she did, I don't know if I'll be able to get anything out of him, but I'll try. He's in a right state at the moment, as you can imagine.'

Hazel pauses. 'He's been through a rough time lately, too. Is he still asking about his dad?'

'Yes, but I'm trying to fob him off. I've never told him what happened between us and I'd rather him not know.'

'I understand why, and I agree that he doesn't need Ricky in his life, but he's fourteen now, Ness, he has a right to know about his father. You don't have to go into too many details, just enough to satisfy his curiosity. Once he learns what his father did, he won't want to know him.'

I know that Hazel is right. Jacob hasn't seen his father since he was five and has never asked about him all these years.

Not until recently, since he and Lucas have been clashing over Rachel, with Aaron always jumping to Lucas's defence.

I've wondered if this has made Jacob feel isolated, that maybe that's why he's been wanting to know about his dad.

Well, Ricky is the last person he needs, especially now.

'I'll talk to him when all this is over, he has enough on his plate right now.'

'True. Don't leave it too long though. And don't dress it up, Ness. You have to make sure he understands why you've kept Ricky away from him.'

The thing is, I don't want Jacob to know what his father did. I don't want him to know anything about Ricky. But Hazel's right, I have to tell him now he's started asking. So I promise that I will, and we chat a bit more before she has to go.

I feel better after talking to Hazel, I always do. She was the one who got me through when Ricky and I split up. I truly think I'd have gone under without her. Ricky made it impossible for me to have many friends, and even now I don't have anyone very close to me other than Hazel, and more recently Suzy. It took a while to build up my confidence after Ricky, and working from home means I don't meet many people. Then I met Aaron, and all our spare time has been spent together.

I look at the clock. It's almost five-thirty, Aaron should be home from work soon, and then Lucas will be back from the Games Fayre.

I don't know how I'm going to break this awful tragedy to them. I can't help feeling guilty for not speaking to Rachel more and trying to find out what had upset her. If it was something she didn't want her mother to know, then she might have confided in me and perhaps this could have been avoided. Even though I could never have predicted this happening.

I need to learn a lesson from this, to keep my family close, make sure they're all safe and that the boys know that they can talk to me about anything, Chloe too when she's older. Especially now, because I am sure Jacob knows more about this than he's saying.

If Rachel confided in him about something, then he'll be reluctant to tell, he's loyal like that, but I need him to know that sometimes you have to break a confidence to keep someone safe.

17

The front door opens and Aaron shouts, 'Only me!'

'Daddy!' Chloe scrambles off the sofa and rushes out into the hall to greet him, and I follow her.

'Hello, petal.' Aaron scoops her up in his arms.

'Rachel fell,' she tells him sadly. 'Jacob is sad.'

Aaron turns to me, shocked. 'What's happened?'

'Rachel's in hospital, she fell out of her bedroom window and is in a coma. We don't know if...'

'Jeez.' Aaron's jaw drops, his face ashen, he gently puts Chloe down and she runs back into the lounge to play with her toys, then listens as I fill him in on everything. Relating it all again makes me well up. Poor Rachel. And Suzy and Carl.

'I can't believe it! What an awful thing to happen.' His voice is shaky as he reaches out to me, hugging me tight.

I'm so glad he's home, it's been horrendous dealing with this by myself all afternoon. 'Jacob is in a terrible state,' I say.

'He's bound to be.' Then Aaron frowns. 'How come he was home, anyway? Didn't he go to the Games Fayre?'

'Yes, but he was bored so he left. Lucas is still there so he doesn't know yet. I couldn't tell him on the phone, it's too upsetting.'

'Of course.' Aaron is shaking his head in disbelief.

'The police want to talk to him,' I continue. 'They've already talked to Jacob. I guess it's because they're friends with Rachel and go to the same school, so they might know if anything was troubling her.'

'What a terrible thing to happen.' Aaron pulls his phone out of his pocket. 'I'll call Lucas now and ask him to come home.' He dials then sighs in exasperation. 'Straight to voicemail. Why doesn't he ever answer my calls?'

Jacob is the same, it drives me crazy. He will never answer a call from me, he just lets it go to voicemail and then sends a short text: *What?*

Aaron leaves a message asking Lucas to come home as soon as he can. Then he gives me a worried look. 'Rachel and Jacob weren't sitting on the windowsill talking to each other, were they? We've warned the boys about that.'

I shake my head. 'I asked him. He said he'd only just come home and put his headphones on right away to play a game. Then he heard a scream from outside, so he went over to his window.'

'Do you believe him?'

'Of course I do!' I say, feeling my cheeks flush. 'He wouldn't lie over something so important.'

'He might not like to admit it if they were talking at the time. If Rachel is seriously injured or dies, he might feel responsible.'

Suddenly Jacob shouts from the top of the stairs, 'That's right, blame me, as usual!'

Aaron sighs. 'Jacob, I—'

'Forget it!' Jacob storms back into his room and slams the door.

'Must you?' I demand angrily. 'Jacob is upset enough

without you accusing him. He assured me that he was playing his game when it happened. And I believe him.'

'Stop shouting.' Chloe runs out of the lounge, her face puckered as if she's about to cry and puts her hands over her ears, and I feel awful. She hates shouting or any loud noises.

'Sorry, petal.' Aaron picks her up again, pecks her on the cheek and carries her into the kitchen.

I follow, taking a deep breath to calm myself down. I'm so annoyed with Aaron, not so much because of what he said – hadn't I thought the same myself? – but because Jacob overheard him. My son looks so fragile since the incident, all I want to do is wrap him up in cotton wool and keep him safe. Like I've been trying to do all these years, ever since we got away from Ricky.

'Rachel is hurt,' Chloe says in a small voice.

'I know, sweetheart. The doctors at the hospital will make her better soon.' Aaron kisses her on the forehead and puts her down on a chair at the table. He's saying the words to comfort her, just like I did to Suzy, because Rachel has to be okay. The alternative is too unbearable to think about.

Aaron glances over at me guiltily. 'Sorry, Ness, but it was the obvious conclusion.' He shakes the kettle to check the water level and switches it on. 'I need a cuppa. Want one?'

I feel like I'm swimming in tea, but I nod. 'Yes, thanks.'

I put a couple of biscuits on Chloe's plate and give them to her, to distract her a little, and she picks one up and starts munching it.

A few minutes later the back door opens and Lucas comes in.

'I just called you,' Aaron admonishes him.

'Yeah, but I was almost home so there was no point replying,' he says nonchalantly. He looks from one to the other of us and stiffens. 'What's the drama?'

'It's Rachel,' Aaron tells him gently. 'She's had an accident.'

Lucas's eyes widen and he reaches out to grip the back of the chair. 'What's happened to her?'

I fill him in while Aaron makes the tea, taking an extra cup out of the cupboard for Lucas. I see him spoon sugar into it as I did for Jacob.

Lucas listens quietly. 'She will be all right though, won't she?' he asks in a wobbly voice. I can see the fear in his eyes. If Rachel doesn't recover, I don't know how either of the boys will cope.

'It's early days yet but she's in the right place, and her mum and dad are with her.' I reach out and touch his arm lightly. 'The police want to talk to you and ask a few questions.'

His brows knit together. 'Why? What's it got to do with me?' His voice is shaking. 'I've been out all day.'

'It's just routine. They've already questioned Jacob,' Aaron reassures him, handing him the mug of tea.

Lucas takes it, nursing it in his hands. 'Was Jacob home then?' he asks.

Aaron hands another mug to me and we sit down at the table at either side of Chloe, who is now tucking into her second biscuit, but Lucas remains standing.

'Yes, he saw her on the ground after she fell.' Every time I say that, I realise how strange it is that Jacob saw what had happened to Rachel, but when I came home, he didn't come down to tell me, he stayed there, hunched up on his bed. Scared.

Because of the shock, I tell myself.

I know how it sounds though, how suspicious it looks, and I wish that Jacob hadn't come home early. That he'd been far away, like Lucas, when Rachel fell.

Now not only does he have to deal with the trauma of what he saw, but everyone is going to wonder if he knows something about the fall that he's not telling us. Something he doesn't want anyone to find out.

18

Suzy

We've been sitting here for hours, waiting for news. The doctors are with Rachel doing tests and all me and Carl can do is wait. We drink countless cups of weak coffee from the hospital vending machine, pace the floor, check our phones, and all the time I want to shout and scream but I daren't, because once I start I won't be able to stop. I can't crumble. I have to keep strong for Rachel and Ben. And Carl.

The image of my beautiful girl sprawled motionless on the ground below her bedroom window will be etched on my mind forever. When I saw my daughter lying there as if she was dead, my heart stopped beating for a moment and I froze to the spot. I wish I hadn't been out at work, that I'd been at home. Then perhaps I could have prevented this happening.

I'm worried about Ben too, he must be in a terrible state. Carl said that thankfully our son hadn't seen Rachel fall, he'd come outside afterwards when the ambulance arrived. He's only six, so who knows how this will affect him? I want to be with him and reassure him, right now though Rachel needs me more. I'm glad Ness offered to take him home with her until Mum arrived, she's a good friend and I know that she will look after Ben as if he is her own.

'She must have been sitting on the window ledge talking to one of those lads from next door,' Carl is saying. 'It's the only thing that makes sense.'

'She couldn't have been, Ness told me that Jacob and Lucas were out,' I tell him. 'She must have slipped, but why would she be sitting on the window ledge in the first place? It doesn't make sense.'

'I don't know. Maybe she saw a friend and was talking to them?' he suggests.

I think this over; it's a possibility. Our house is on the end of the street and the pathway runs along the side of it and around the back.

'Unless...' Carl gets up and paces around, his agitation contagious. 'Maybe she was tidying her bedroom? Maybe she was leaning out to clean her window?'

It feels like he's reaching for any excuse, but I can't make sense of it either. My daughter is in intensive care and I have no idea how badly hurt she is. I want answers. I want to know what caused my precious child to fall on the paving slabs in front of the kitchen window. I want to know what's going to happen to her now. I have no idea about the extent of the injuries she has, if she will ever walk or talk again. I'm trying not to think about the worst-case scenario. I'm praying silently for a miracle: that Rachel will open her eyes, and everything will be okay.

Carl runs his hand through his hair. 'Why won't they tell us what's wrong with her? We've been waiting for bloody ages.'

Anger is Carl's way of dealing with things that he can't control. He doesn't get violent, but the shouting and anger are bad enough to deal with, so there's a lot I haven't told him. This move was supposed to be a fresh start for us all, yet barely three months later Rachel is in a coma.

The doctor comes out and my heart plummets.

I know from the compassionate way she looks at us that it's not good news.

I clutch Carl's hand and take a deep, shuddering breath. 'Rachel, is she...?' I whisper.

'She's stable but still in a coma and there is some swelling on her brain, I'm afraid. There doesn't seem to be any internal damage, and we are all hoping that she will wake up soon. I must warn you though that the chances of that are low in these cases. And we won't know for sure about any lasting damage, particularly on her brain, until she comes around,' she adds softly.

The chances of that are low.

It could be worse, there could be no chance at all. She could have broken her neck, been killed outright, I remind myself. At least she's alive, and it's possible she might pull through.

A few hours later, the police come to talk to us. They want to know if Rachel was worried about anything, if she was under pressure, unhappy.

'I don't think so, she seemed content in her new school, she made friends there.' I screw my eyes tight to stop the tears from falling as I realise why they're asking. What they're suggesting. They think she jumped.

I shudder and close my eyes, Rachel's desperate scream pulsating in my head. I didn't hear it, but I can imagine it and it haunts my thoughts.

I remember the pain in her voice a few months ago when it all got too much for her: *I can't cope, Mum! I don't want to be here.*

I thought it was over, that she was happy, settled. Then another memory snakes into my mind: Ness telling me that she'd caught Rachel crying.

I asked Rachel about it and she laughed it off, said they'd been watching a sad film. And I believed her because that's what I wanted to hear.

'She wouldn't jump! She must have fallen, it was an accident!' Carl is insisting to the police.

He is right, that's the only explanation. I have to believe that Rachel fell by accident because I simply can't bear to think otherwise.

My phone rings and I glance at the screen. 'It's Mum,' I say. It's a bit strange that she's calling as she's been texting while we're at the hospital, not wanting to disturb us in case we're talking to the doctor.

'Suzy, love, I had to call you,' Mum says when I pick up her call. Her voice is quivering, she sounds strange, afraid. 'I'm so sorry, darling, but I've got some terrible news.'

19

Vanessa

'I'm going to bathe Chloe now and get her to bed before the police come back to talk to Lucas,' I tell Aaron after dinner. 'I don't want her hearing anything else, she's already so upset.'

'Good idea. I can deal with them if they arrive before you come down,' he assures me.

'Okay, Chloe looks exhausted, so I think she'll be asleep in no time.'

Chloe raises her arms to be picked up, and she leans her head on my shoulder as I carry her up the stairs. She's so tired that I decide to leave her bath for tonight and put her straight to bed. It won't hurt for one day.

As I reach the top step, I hear the boys talking in Jacob's bedroom. The door is closed but the voices are loud, angry. I pause, wondering what they're arguing about, then I catch my breath when I hear Lucas say, 'This is all your fault.'

'Don't blame me!' Jacob sounds furious, defensive. 'You were the one who—'

'No way!' Lucas interrupts him before I can hear what Jacob was about to say.

If I wasn't holding Chloe, I would open the door and demand to know what they're talking about.

It's obvious they know something about Rachel's fall. What are they hiding?

Chloe whimpers and I cuddle her closer, not wanting her to make any more noise because it will alert the boys that I've heard them. I can tell by the deathly silence that it's too late. This is too serious to ignore but I need to get Chloe to bed and calm myself down so that I don't go in all guns blazing.

There could be a reasonable explanation for what I overheard.

I'm desperately hoping there is.

Chloe is fast asleep by the time we reach her bedroom, so I decide not to risk waking her by undressing her. I slip her shoes off and slide her under the duvet, and she snuggles up, her eyes still closed as I kiss her softly on the cheek. 'Night, darling,' I whisper. I close the rainbow and stars curtains that match her duvet cover, switch on her unicorn night light and leave the door slightly ajar in case she wants to come into our bed in the night – she often does if she's had a bad dream.

Then I quietly cross the landing to Jacob's room quietly. His door is firmly closed, and I wonder if Lucas is still in there – I haven't heard him go out. I pause to take a deep breath, telling myself to handle it carefully and not to raise my voice. I don't want Chloe to be woken up. Without bothering to knock, I open the door and stand in the doorway. Jacob is sitting on his bed and Lucas is standing in front of him, they are both facing the door as if they were expecting me.

'What's Jacob's fault, then?' I ask, keeping my tone soft, neutral. I need to let them know that they can talk to me. Tell me anything. Even things they think I don't want to hear.

A furtive look passes between them before Jacob says sullenly, 'He's blaming me for what happened to Rachel.'

'Yeah, because you're always sitting on the windowsill talking to her,' says Lucas.

'So are you,' I remind him. 'And Jacob wasn't talking to her today.' I shift my glance to Jacob. 'Were you?'

He shakes his head vehemently. 'No! I already told you. I didn't see or hear anything until she screamed.' He shudders and tears spring to his eyes.

I step forward to comfort him, but he pushes me away and angrily wipes the tears with the back of his hand. I step back and turn my attention to Lucas, who looks defiant. 'So why are you saying it's Jacob's fault?'

Lucas tosses his hair out of his eyes and glares at Jacob. 'They fell out. Jacob wouldn't answer Rachel's calls. I reckon she knew he was home and he was ignoring her, so she was shouting across to him when she slipped.'

'That's not true! Stop making this my fault! You're the one who caused the argument,' Jacob yells. He gets up and pushes past me, hurtling down the stairs.

I brace myself for a cry to come from Chloe's room, thankfully she doesn't murmur. She was so exhausted, she's crashed out.

'What's going on? And I want answers fast! What did Jacob and Rachel fall out about exactly?' I ask Lucas, although I think I know. Anyone could have seen that Jacob and Rachel were growing closer over the last few weeks, then suddenly this week they weren't talking anymore. Perhaps Rachel has moved on to someone else. I don't blame her, she is young, still finding her way. Attraction can be fleeting at this age.

He puts his hands in his pockets and shrugs. 'I dunno. Ask him.' Then he walks out too, into his own room, and slams the door shut.

Unease slithers into my mind as I stand in the now empty bedroom. They know something. I can sense it.

Is Lucas right? Was Rachel leaning out of the window to try to get Jacob's attention?

And when I heard Jacob say, *Don't blame me, you were the one,* before Lucas interrupted him, was he going to say that Lucas caused the argument? Or was it something else that they don't want me to know?

My mind is whirling and I sink down on Jacob's bed, trying to make sense of it all.

'What's up?' Aaron peers around the doorway. 'Jacob has just run out into the garden like a bat out of hell.' He sits down on the bed bedside me. 'Have you and him had words?'

I shake my head then repeat the conversation I overheard.

'Look, if what Lucas said is true, then it shows Rachel didn't jump on purpose. Jacob might blame himself, but at least it was an accident.'

'What did Jacob mean by saying that about Lucas? What did Lucas do to cause a fight?'

Aaron shrugs. 'Who knows? Perhaps Jacob and Lucas fell out because Rachel decided that she likes Lucas more? Either way, Lucas can't have had anything to do with Rachel's accident. He wasn't even in.'

I get up from the bed and look outside. Jacob is staring up at Rachel's bedroom window, tears streaming down his face. He looks so young, so desperate.

'I need to speak to Jacob, he's taking this really badly,' I say. 'I'll only be a few minutes.'

Jacob turns as I open the back door and make my way over to him; his eyes are red raw and his face all blotchy. 'Sorry,' he mumbles, 'but I'm sick of everyone accusing me. Why won't anyone believe me?'

'I believe you.' I stand beside him and rest a hand on his shoulder.

He fixes his gaze on Rachel's bedroom window. 'I can't get her scream out of my head, Mum. And seeing her sprawled out on the ground. It was horrible. She must have been so scared.' Tears spring to his eyes again and he balls them with his fists to try to stop them falling.

'Oh, darling.'

He tears his eyes away from the window and stares at me. For a moment I think he's going to say something then he turns around and heads back to the house, his head bowed. We've always been so close and now I feel like I can't reach him. It frightens me. He's upset, traumatised. Rachel was – is – his friend.

I close my eyes and lean back against the wall.

What if Jacob is at risk too? It's clear Rachel's fall has devastated him, and the boys are definitely hiding something. How can I keep Jacob safe if he won't confide in me?

20

The police arrive a little later that evening, only it isn't the uniformed police officers from earlier, it's two plain-clothed detectives.

'Evening, Mrs Dawson, I'm DC Millet and this is DS Byron.' The tall, stout, clean-shaven man shows me his ID, and the woman beside him – petite and friendly looking – does the same. 'Are Jacob and Lucas at home?' he asks. 'We need a word with them.'

'Has Rachel woken up?' I ask hopefully.

'I'm afraid not but there have been further developments and there are a couple of things we need to clear up,' DC Millet says.

'Two of your colleagues already spoke to Jacob,' I point out.

'Well, we'd like another word,' he says.

His firm tone makes me feel nervous. Why are there detectives dealing with this now? It feels like an investigation into a crime, like they think the boys are to blame.

'May we come in for a few minutes, Mrs Dawson?' DS Byron asks pleasantly.

'Yes, sorry, of course. Go through to the lounge, first door on the right.' I step back to allow them to walk in, and I follow them through. Aaron is sitting on the sofa, and he looks at us questioningly.

'These detectives want to speak to the boys,' I tell him. 'I'll go and fetch them.'

I feel a little annoyed as I go up the stairs. The boys are really upset about Rachel, and Jacob has already been questioned. Why should he have to go through it all again? I remind myself that the police are simply trying to get to the bottom of what happened to Rachel, they probably just want to chat about Rachel's state of mind. I can't be selfish when my boys are fit and healthy and Rachel is lying unconscious in hospital.

I knock on Jacob's door then open it and am surprised to see Lucas in there too after the ruckus earlier. They're sitting on the bed talking, but go quiet as soon as I walk in.

'Can you two come down, please? Some detectives are here, they want to talk to you about Rachel.'

I see a look of panic pass between them both. 'It's nothing to worry about,' I reassure them. 'I think they want to know if Rachel was troubled over anything. The police asked you that earlier, Jacob.'

They are as white as ghosts as they stand up. Then with a final look at each other, they follow me downstairs. They sit on the sofa next to Aaron, facing the detectives, and both look so young and scared, my heart goes out to them.

DC Millet takes out his notebook. 'I'm sorry to say that we have very good reason to suspect that Rachel's fall wasn't an accident. Nor did she jump.'

I inhale sharply. The boys look at each other, then at Aaron. You could cut the tension in the room with a knife.

DC Millet flicks a look at DS Byron, who gives him a little nod before he turns his attention back to us. 'We believe Rachel was pushed.'

My stomach flops, my mouth goes dry. *Pushed!* Are they seriously saying someone tried to kill her?

After a heavy pause, Aaron breaks the silence. 'That seems rather far-fetched. Why do you think that?' he asks slowly.

DC Millet consults his notebook again, then looks over at Jacob and Lucas. 'Rachel's little brother Ben has told us that he saw someone running out of her room after she screamed.'

That means someone must have sneaked into the house next door, crept upstairs and pushed or thrown Rachel out of the window. Why on earth would anyone do such a horrible thing?

I guess that's why the police want to question Jacob and Lucas. The boys would probably know if Rachel had fallen out with anyone, or if someone had a grudge against her.

The boys are sitting like a pair of statues, hands clasped in their laps. They're terrified.

'Can Ben identify this person? Sex? Hair colour? Size? Did he know them?' Aaron asks calmly. I always admire how he deals with situations like this, he's so rational – which actually drives me mad sometimes, but right now it's what's needed. I'm too panicked to think straight, I don't know what to say.

DS Byron takes over the questioning now and her face is impassive as she looks from Jacob to Lucas. 'I'm afraid not. Ben is sure that it was a teenage boy, but he couldn't see his face or hair because he was wearing a black hoodie.' Her words hang heavily in the air, and I feel like we're all holding our breath, waiting.

Then she looks at each boy in turn, her gaze penetrating, her tone even as she asks, 'Do either of you have a black hoodie?'

My eyes meet Aaron's and I see my own fear mirrored there.

Both Jacob and Lucas have a black hoodie, and I'm pretty sure the detectives already know this.

21

Aaron finds his voice first. 'Of course they have black hoodies, what teenage boy doesn't?' he demands. He's keeping his voice steady, but one of his feet is jiggling on the floor, and I can see the whites of his knuckles, his hands clasped on his knees. 'Look, what exactly are you insinuating?'

'We're simply making enquiries, Mr Paige. It's our job to establish what exactly happened to Rachel. Especially as the lass can't tell us herself.' DC Millet's piercing grey eyes sweep us all in turn but his gaze rests on Jacob for a little longer. Then he looks at his notebook again. 'Mrs West said that there was a bit of... tension between Rachel and your boys.'

I'm staggered. Why would Suzy say that? Surely she doesn't think that Rachel's fall had something to do with Jacob or Lucas? They would never harm Rachel, they adore her. I swallow, my eyes shooting to Aaron's face. His lips are pressed tightly together.

'They are all friends, they hang out together a lot,' he replies calmly, and I'm impressed again by his ability to keep his emotions under control.

'Yes, but we understand that the friendship had been

strained lately,' DS Byron says. 'Mrs West said Jacob and Lucas have been competing for Rachel's attention, and Rachel's friend Amy said that Jacob and Lucas came to blows over Rachel in school a couple of weeks ago. Several other students have backed this up.'

This is the first I've heard of the fight but a quick glance at the boys' guilty expressions tells me this is true.

This doesn't mean they would hurt Rachel though.

Honestly, I feel betrayed by Suzy, who I have come to regard as a close friend. Why is she making it sound like one of my boys would be capable of such a terrible thing? It's true that they have argued a lot over Rachel, there's no use denying that, but neither of them has ever been anything but kind towards her.

'They're teenagers, so of course they occasionally fight, but they would never hurt anyone.' Aaron's voice is firm and convincing.

'Of course they wouldn't!' I add adamantly. 'Can't you see how upset they are about this?'

'We're just trying to confirm what others have told us.' DC Millet's voice is sharp. 'I'd like to ask the boys a few questions now.'

'Perhaps we should get a solicitor,' Aaron suggests.

'There's no need for that, it's all very informal, we just need to clear up a few facts,' the DS says. 'Let's start with you, Lucas, as Jacob already gave the police his version of events.'

'I've been out all day. I didn't even know about Rachel's fall until I came home,' Lucas stammers.

'Even so, you may have seen something before you went out that could help us. Or perhaps Rachel confided something in you?' DS Byron says. 'Although, I understand that you both fell out with Rachel recently?'

Aaron darts a puzzled look at me, obviously he was unaware of this too.

Lucas shakes his head. 'It was nothing. Just a stupid disagreement. We're good.'

'Has Rachel settled into school okay? Is there anyone else she's fallen out with?' DS Byron asks.

'Not as far as I know, I'm not in her class,' Lucas replies. He looks at Jacob, who seems to be avoiding his gaze.

The boys are polar opposites of each other in this moment. Jacob looks nervous and scared, whereas Lucas looks more confident, as if he has nothing to hide. That's what I'd expect of them though. Jacob is always anxious – he's like me – whereas Lucas is more sure of himself – like Aaron – but the police officers don't know that.

I hope they don't look on Jacob's demeanour as a sign of guilt.

Please, God, don't let either of them have anything to do with this.

I shake the thought from my mind.

'Now, Jacob, you saw Rachel on the ground after she fell.' DC Millet looks pointedly at Jacob and my heart sinks. 'Can you run through the moments that led up to that again, please, and what you saw?'

My heart lurches at the anxiety on Jacob's face, and I recall how shaken he was when I opened his door.

Slowly, hesitatingly, he recounts exactly what he told me.

'That must have been very upsetting for you.' DS Byron's voice is gentle, sympathetic.

Jacob nods. 'I couldn't believe it,' he mumbles. 'I kept staring at her, expecting her to get up but...'

'You didn't call an ambulance though? Or go round to see how she was?'

He shakes his head. 'Her dad came out...' His voice falters.

The detectives ask a few more questions about Rachel's friends, and any other boys she knew and invited to her house.

Jacob and Lucas are keeping their replies short, I notice, and they're still avoiding looking at each other.

I know it's just a precaution; the police must look at every possibility. And I know that the black hoodie means nothing. As Aaron said, most teenagers have one. Besides, Ben knows both Lucas and Jacob, and hoodie or not he would recognise them.

So, who was the lad Ben saw coming out of Rachel's bedroom?

And what exactly are our boys hiding?

22

Aaron

I still can't get my head around it. Rachel was so young and full of life – is, I correct myself. She's not dead. And she's not going to die. She can't.

I try to focus on the questions the police are asking Lucas and Jacob. Obviously they're the prime suspects. Both are besotted with Rachel, arguing over her as if she is their property when it is up to her who she chooses. And it doesn't have to be one of them. I've told them that so many times, Rachel is free to go out with anyone she wants.

Thankfully Lucas is keeping calm, just as I'd told them both to do. It's lucky that he was out and didn't come back until ages after Rachel's fall, so he has a clear alibi. Jacob is very much in the frame though, and he knows it. He's upset and angry, adamant that he didn't see anything, that he'd been in his room playing a video game when he heard Rachel scream. Jacob is mostly a laid-back lad, but when he gets fired up, he's off like a rocket. I've had to pull him off Lucas a couple of times recently, it's like a red mist comes down.

Lucas, meanwhile, is more level-headed; he thinks before he acts.

When the detectives ask them if Rachel had fallen out with anyone at school or if she'd been upset about anything, the boys shake their heads and I notice that they don't look at each other. I wonder if the detectives notice this too.

'I think you'd be better off questioning Rachel's girlfriends, Detective,' I say. 'Rachel isn't really likely to confide in the boys if anything or anyone is troubling her.'

'Yes, we'll be doing that, thank you. We already had a phone conversation with her friend Amy before she and her family left for their holiday in Spain. She was very helpful.'

The sentence feels loaded, and the detective leaves it hanging in the air for a moment before turning to me. 'And what about you, sir? Can you tell us your whereabouts for today?' he asks.

This catches me off guard, I hadn't expected to be questioned.

'I thought you were looking for a young lad?' I say, confused.

'It's just routine, sir. We'll be doing door-to-door questioning of everyone in the street. Someone might have seen something. And we don't actually know for certain that it was a young lad Ben saw running out of Rachel's.'

'Of course.' I try to keep my breath steady, and I inform them that I was at work in Redditch.

'Do you go into the office every day?' the female detective asks.

'I work at home sometimes too,' I reply.

Then the detectives ask Vanessa and me if we see a lot of Rachel, and if we had noticed anything different in her behaviour.

'She pops in quite often and she's usually very upbeat, although she did seem a bit subdued last time I saw her,'

Vanessa says. She turns her head to me. 'You talked to her a bit, didn't you? I think you said she was worried about a project she was working on?'

DS Byron shoots me a penetrating look. 'Really? Does Rachel often confide in you, sir?'

I wish Vanessa hadn't said that.

'She asks me computer-related stuff sometimes, for her IT coursework,' I reply evenly. 'She doesn't "confide" in me, why would she? I had no idea that she was upset about anything.'

Finally, the two detectives have finished their questioning, and the DS puts away her notebook. 'Well, that's all for now, but if any of you remember anything, no matter how small or insignificant it seems, please let us know.' She's looking at the boys as she says this.

'We will,' Lucas says, and Jacob nods earnestly.

The detectives get up and head over to the door, then DC Millet turns back. 'Oh, we'll need both your black hoodies, please, but don't worry, we won't keep them long.'

Lucas and Jacob look horrified.

'Why?' The question bursts from my lips. I'd been trying to keep my cool, but now I'm outraged.

The detective absently scratches his neck. 'Ben is adamant that he saw someone in a black hoodie leave Rachel's bedroom after she screamed. And we found a trace of blood on the windowsill – as if Rachel struggled and scratched her arm. It's possible there could be blood on the hoodie that person was wearing, so we need to rule Lucas and Jacob out. We'll return the clothes to them as soon as we've finished conducting our tests.'

'Mine's in the wash,' Lucas says. 'I fell over playing football yesterday and it got muddy.'

The detectives exchange a look.

'That's okay, we don't mind if it's dirty,' DS Byron replies.

Vanessa looks worried as the two boys go out to get their

hoodies, and I give her a reassuring look, hoping she can't see the panic in my eyes.

The boys come back down, holding the hoodies. Jacob looks pale, and his hand is shaking when he offers his to the DS, who is now wearing latex gloves. She puts each hoodie in a separate clear bag and seals them.

'When can they expect them back?' I ask.

'We'll be as quick as we can. Thanks for your help. We'll see ourselves out.'

Lucas and Jacob go straight upstairs to bed when the detectives leave, and I fetch us both a glass of wine before I sit next to Vanessa, putting an arm around her shoulder. She looks so anxious and there's some blood on her bottom lip from where she's been biting it. 'I don't like this, Aaron.'

'It'll be okay, I promise. It's all routine stuff,' I tell her. 'Nothing to worry about.'

I am worried though. Very worried.

23

Vanessa

I sip my glass of wine slowly, my hand trembling. I haven't drawn the curtains in the lounge yet – it's dark outside and I can see a crescent moon, the sky clear and studded with stars. I'd have enjoyed that once, and the peace and quiet of the evening with Chloe asleep and the boys in their rooms, but now everything seems strange and unsettling. I can't believe that Aaron is managing to stay so calm while I feel like I'm in a nightmare.

'I wish I could trust that it will be okay, like you, but everything is getting worse. Our boys are being treated like criminals,' I say to Aaron, my voice shaky. 'And they must be worried sick about Rachel. I can't believe that the police think she might have been pushed. Who would do such a thing?'

The enormity of what's happened hits me in a sudden wave. I put my glass down and wine slops over the edge, blood-red dripping onto the coffee table. 'What if she dies, Aaron?' I don't say the thought that flashed into my mind, that one of our boys could be suspected of *murder*. I can't voice it. It's as if saying it aloud would make it real, and none of this feels real.

How have our lives changed so much in such a short time, just one day?

What about poor Suzy and Carl? They must be beyond distraught. They might lose their daughter.

Aaron has his arm around my shoulders, and he pulls me in, easing me into a hug. 'Try not to stress, love. It's all only hypothetical. The police are just trying to build a picture. They must know that Ben would have recognised the lad if it had been one of our boys but they have to explore every option, it's their job.' He drops a kiss on my forehead. 'Hopefully Rachel will regain consciousness soon. Then she can tell the police exactly what happened.'

'I hate to think of that poor girl lying there, comatose, with Suzy and Carl sitting by her side not knowing if they'll ever talk to her again.' I rest my head on Aaron's chest. 'Suzy must be going through hell, wondering if her daughter will ever wake up, and if she does, will she be able to walk, think clearly, live her life?'

Tears fill my eyes as I imagine it being one of my kids lying there, and how anguished I would be. I long to go to the hospital to comfort Suzy, help her in some way. I'll send her another text later, telling her that I'm thinking of her and to let me know if I can do anything.

Aaron holds me tight and strokes the back of my head. 'It will all be okay, Ness. Remember that the police have to question anyone connected with Rachel.'

He's right, of course. And if someone really tried to kill her, then they must be found.

I ease out of Aaron's hug, wipe my eyes and nod. 'I'll text Suzy and let her know we're thinking of her.'

I feel better when I've sent the text. I don't expect Suzy to reply, she will be focusing on Rachel, but I want her to know that we're there for her and thinking of them all.

'I think I'll go around and see Glenda and find out if she has any news, or if she needs help with Ben,' I say. Poor Glenda must be worried sick, and Ben can be a handful at times, just like Jacob was at his age.

'It's getting late, why not leave it until the morning? Glenda probably wants some time to come to terms with all this, and you've had an awful day. You could do with relaxing a bit. Let's have another glass of wine and try to unwind,' he suggests.

I don't know about another glass – I could do with a whole bottle right now. Aaron is right though: I should leave checking on Glenda until the morning. Ben will be in bed and she probably won't want to be disturbed. I bet she's on tenterhooks waiting for news from the hospital.

'I guess you're right. I'll call on her in the morning when Chloe has gone to nursery,' I say as I sink down onto the sofa.

Aaron gets up and goes into the kitchen, returning with the bottle of wine. 'It will all come right,' he says as he tops up my glass.

'I really hope so. That poor girl. She's so sweet and good-natured, so natural and kind with Chloe too.' I take a sip. 'She always took an interest in my work – and yours too, didn't she?' Rachel had gone into the study a couple of times to talk to Aaron, I saw them bending over the computer screen as he showed her what he was working on.

'Yes, she had a lot of questions, she's a bright spark, that's for sure.' Aaron sits down beside me. 'Try not to worry, Ness. She's in the best place.'

'I can't stop thinking about her,' I tell him. 'I saw her lying on that stretcher.' I shudder and he holds me tight again.

Aaron is my rock. But even his arms can't take away the horror that someone tried to murder our neighbour's daughter.

And that our boys seem to be the prime suspects.

24

THE DAY AFTER THE FALL

The wine helps me sleep deeply that night and I wake up feeling more positive. I check my phone but there's no reply from Suzy yet, which isn't surprising as her attention will be focused on Rachel. I can only imagine how she must be feeling after what Ben said about someone in a black hoodie running out of Rachel's room. And Carl, he was at home at the time. He'll blame himself, he'll think he should have heard something. Maybe Suzy blames him too.

Despite this, I'm still clinging to the hope that it was all an awful accident.

When I return from dropping off Chloe at nursery, Aaron is holed up in the study – he was already down here when I woke up. I pop my head around the door and say, 'I'm going around next door to see if there's any news, or if Glenda needs any help with Ben. I won't be long.'

He glances up from his computer and nods silently, then turns his attention back to the screen. There are deep shadows under his eyes and he's still in his dressing gown. I think he must have slept really badly, the stress is getting to him too, even if he doesn't want to admit it.

I knock on the front door and Glenda comes out, pulling a thin cream robe around her. She looks exhausted, her eyes raw from crying, her skin sallow and her silver hair tangled. She appraises me briefly, barely making eye contact.

'I was wondering if there's any news?' I ask her tentatively. 'If Rachel has come round yet?'

She shakes her head wordlessly, as if she's too exhausted to speak, and turns to go back inside.

'I'm so sorry, you must all be really worried. Please let me know if I can help in any way. Perhaps I could look after Ben while you go to the hospital or run an errand,' I say quickly before she can close the door.

She spins around, and suddenly her eyes are cold and accusing as they fix themselves on mine. I step back as if I've been slapped across the face. 'There's no way I will leave Ben with you,' she says, her voice low and bitter. 'Suzy told me that your boys had a massive argument over Rachel, that they wouldn't leave her alone. Always fighting over her. I bet it was one of them Ben saw running out of her bedroom. They wear black hoodies, don't they?'

I'm wounded by her venomous accusation. It's so cruel and unfair but I fight the urge to retaliate. Glenda's in shock, traumatised, I remind myself, she's lashing out at me because I'm here.

'Yes, as do most teenage boys,' I stammer. 'Besides, Ben knows Jacob and Lucas. He would recognise them.'

'Oh, really? How? He didn't see the lad's face, only his back as he ran down the stairs after pushing my granddaughter out of the window, the coward,' she snaps.

'Glenda, please. Jacob and Lucas would never harm Rachel. They're her friends.'

'She can do without friends like those two! Suzy said Rachel came home from school crying the other week. Your boys have been putting pressure on her to choose one of them above the other.' She looks me up and down as if I'm something horrible she's stepped in, her eyes full of pure hatred. 'I'll thank you not to come knocking again. And make sure you warn your boys that they haven't got away with this. The police will get to the bottom of it, mark my words.'

With that, she slams the door in my face.

I stare incredulously at the closed door. This can't be happening. She can't seriously suspect Jacob or Lucas of trying to kill Rachel?

I head back home, my thoughts swirling and conflicted. Except for that one occasion when I saw her crying, I hadn't realised that Rachel had been so unhappy. Suzy hadn't said a word, not that we'd seen much of each other lately, we'd both been so busy, but Suzy had been fine when we last had coffee together a couple of weeks ago, and I'm sure she would have told me then if she'd been worried about her daughter. Until yesterday, I'd only seen her once since that coffee – I bumped into her in the supermarket last week and she mumbled a quick hello then dashed off saying she was busy.

I didn't think anything of it at the time but now I wonder if Suzy was deliberately avoiding me. Was it because of the way the boys have been arguing over Rachel? Surely that shouldn't affect us, not our grown adult friendship. It's not like it would be unusual for a couple of boys to squabble over a pretty girl.

Did Suzy really believe Jacob and Lucas were upsetting her daughter? I'd told her about the time when I'd seen Rachel crying, and it was like a cloud had come over her. Later she'd told me that Rachel had assured her she'd just been upset about the film, but I wasn't so sure about that. Perhaps she'd had a row with her dad. I'd heard Carl bawling at her a few times, and Suzy said he didn't want her going out with boys. Maybe Suzy didn't want to admit to trouble behind closed doors?

Anyway, whatever it was that had upset Rachel so much, I am sure my boys were not involved. It can't just have been their teenage crushes that were impacting her so much, something else must have been going on. It is awful for Jacob and Lucas to be dragged into it like this – they are devastated enough over what happened to Rachel without being blamed for it too.

And to think I had been so pleased when our neighbours had moved in.

I could never have imagined that my precious family would soon be torn apart, all because of the sweet, bubbly girl next door.

25

I go into the kitchen to make a cuppa, my mind still in turmoil. Glenda's words have really upset me. It makes sense now why Suzy hasn't replied to my message. I know she's in pain and I want to support her, but how can I do that now that I know she thinks my family is to blame?

I poke my head into the study, where Aaron is still busy working. 'Want a cuppa?'

'Thanks. Yeah, I think I'll take a quick break.' He comes into the kitchen. He still hasn't changed out of his pyjamas and dressing gown, it's not like him. 'How was Glenda?'

'Quite nasty, actually. They're all blaming Jacob and Lucas, after what Ben said. Suzy told Glenda that the boys have been making Rachel's life a misery the past couple of weeks.'

'It'll be the grief talking,' Aaron says reassuringly. 'Is there any sign of Rachel coming around?'

I shake my head. 'Still in a coma. And it seems that Suzy is convinced it was Lucas or Jacob in her bedroom yesterday. Aaron, we've got to find out who it was. It's the only way we're going to clear their names.'

Aaron leans against the sink and rubs the back of his neck as

I spoon our teabags into the bin. 'The police will do that,' he reassures me. 'It's a pity Jacob didn't go round to check on Rachel when he saw her fall, though. He might have seen the scumbag running out of the house. Then he could have given a proper description to the police.' He sighs. 'I hope he doesn't feel guilty about that.'

'He was in shock, Aaron!' I reply defensively. 'How would you feel if you saw one of your friends fall crashing to the ground?'

'I know, sorry. I didn't mean anything by it.' He gives me a peck on the cheek. 'Try not to worry, I'm sure the police will find this boy soon. See you in a bit, I'm going for a shower.'

He heads up the stairs carrying his mug and I throw the teaspoon angrily into the sink, fuming that he has turned this on Jacob again. *I hope he doesn't feel guilty.* Why would he feel guilty? None of this is Jacob's fault.

Hazel agrees with me when I give her a call later to update her. 'Jacob's reaction was a perfectly normal one, Ness. The police won't find any of Rachel's blood on either of their hoodies, and they'll find out who Ben saw. The boys will be in the clear soon. How is Jacob?'

'You know Jacob, he keeps a lot to himself, but I can tell that he's really upset. He thought a lot of Rachel – thinks,' I correct myself. 'I honestly don't know how he'll cope if she...' I can't bring myself to say the words.

'You're all bound to be affected by this, especially the boys.' Hazel is silent for a moment then she says, 'I'm guessing with all this going on you haven't spoken to Jacob about his dad?'

It had gone right out of my mind. 'No, and he hasn't asked any more either. Best to leave it until we know how Rachel is. One bad thing is enough to cope with.'

'I guess you're right. Keep your chin up, sis, I'm sure Rachel will come around soon. She's lucky she didn't break her neck instantly, it honestly could have been much worse.'

'I know. I just wish I knew a bit more about how she's doing,' I tell her. 'Suzy isn't replying to my messages.'

'Well, there's a report about it online. I was going to call you about it later actually, but you beat me to it. It says that Rachel fell on her left side and has bruises on her face, arms and legs, and a broken left wrist, and that the doctors have no idea if she will wake up from the coma. The next few days will be crucial, it seems.'

'What site is that?' I ask. I hadn't thought of looking online for news.

'The local newspaper. Look, Ness, it might not be a good idea for you to go online right now... There's a few upsetting comments about the boys. Better you hear it from me. You know what these trolls can be like...'

A cold grip tightens around my chest. 'What are they saying?'

After a pause, Hazel says softly, 'That Jacob or Lucas is responsible, that one of them pushed her. Or that they did it together. And...' I hold my breath waiting for her to finish. 'Some are threatening to make them pay.'

26

'Are you okay, sis?' Hazel sounds worried. 'I had to tell you... I didn't want you – or the boys – to come across it by accident.'

Finally I find my voice. 'I'm fine. I've got to go. Speak to you soon.'

As soon as I've ended the call, I search for the local newspaper on my phone. It doesn't take me long to find the article. It says that Rachel is in intensive care, in a coma caused by a suspected brain injury. Seeing those words in print instantly makes me go cold all over, my head throbbing painfully. Once again my thoughts go to Suzy and Carl. They must be going out of their minds with worry.

It's quite a long article, and I should have got it up on my laptop as the ads keep popping up and driving me mad, but I carry on reading. The article details the fall, and the three scenarios the police are considering – pushed, suicide attempt or accidental fall – and that officers are going door to door to question the neighbours and see if they saw anything suspicious. It ends by saying that two local lads are of particular interest.

It doesn't name Jacob and Lucas, as of course it couldn't, but it's pretty damning under the pretence of simply stating facts.

Our neighbours will know exactly who those 'local lads' are.

Then I brace myself and click on the comments. Hazel was right: they're vile. And both boys are named by countless anonymous people. Surely that's illegal? More than a couple are pointing a finger explicitly at Jacob and some of the comments are openly inciting violence, saying that they hope someone does to them what they did to Rachel. I read them, filled with increasing horror:

Jaz235: That poor girl. What's the world coming to? Those animals need locking up.

Beelzebub: Locking up is too good for them. I know what I'd do if I got my hands on them.

Hellbringer: Anyone know who these bastards are? They need a taste of their own medicine.

Slash: My sister lives in the same street. She said the boys are Jacob and Lucas, step-brothers. They live next door.

Mimix: My kids go to the same school. They saw Rachel and Jacob arguing the other day. I bet it's him.

Beelzebub: He needs stringing up, the bastard.

Then another comment catches my eye, as it's longer than the rest:

Rosy246: I live in the same area as this family and they're all a bit odd. The mum's first husband disappeared years ago, and she keeps herself to herself. And the dad nearly ran into

me the other day when he was out running. He looked really
troubled about something.

My stomach heaves. I can't believe that people can be so
cruel, casting suspicion on us all, judging my whole family.

I can't read any more. I close the tab, my heart pounding.
Have Jacob and Lucas seen this article? I hope not, it's sickening
and their heads are in a mess already. Especially Jacob.

I'm scared that this could drive him over the edge.

I need to let Aaron know about this. First though, I type
'how long are people usually in a coma' into the search bar, then
click the top link that comes up. It says that while some people
do gradually recover from a coma, a lot never do. They remain
in a permanent vegetative state or die.

I cling to the words 'some people'. Hopefully Rachel will be
one of the lucky ones. Apparently though, even if people do
recover they may be left with severe injuries or disabilities, the
article continues. They don't always regain their memory
straight away, and sometimes they never do.

It's too much to think of that lovely girl never walking or
talking again. And if she can't remember anything, will Jacob
always be a suspect, with people hating his guts like those trolls
online, people who don't even know him?

It doesn't look like this nightmare is going to end anytime
soon.

I go into the study and Aaron turns his head away from the
screen. 'What's up?'

I take a breath before replying. 'It seems that our boys have
been judged guilty without trial by the general public. There's a
bit of speculation about us too.'

'What do you mean?' Aaron spins around on his chair to
face me and listens intently while I tell him about my call with
Hazel and the newspaper article. Then he turns back to the

computer, keys in the name of the newspaper and gets it up on the screen. I can see his face darken as he reads it.

'What if the boys read this too? It will destroy them,' I say.

'We need to warn them.' His voice is tight. 'Are they awake yet?'

'I don't know. I took Chloe to nursery then went straight to see Glenda.' I pull out a chair and sit down at the table opposite, the one I should be working on, but I'm too upset to work today. I'm surprised that Aaron can concentrate at all.

Aaron runs his hands over his head, and then stands up. 'I think we ought to talk to them straight away. We can't let them come across this by accident.'

I nod. I know he's right, although I wish I could protect them from those horrible online comments completely.

Aaron goes out into the hall and calls up the stairs, 'Lucas! Jacob! Can you come down please? We need to talk to you.'

We hear a bedroom door open and Lucas comes out, still in his pyjamas, hair unkempt. He's clearly only just woken up. I bet he was up late playing computer games, Jacob too. It's their favourite pastime, and even though we tell them to close down their PlayStations when we go to bed, I wouldn't put it past them to switch them on again. Especially now it's the school holidays, and they'd have needed to decompress after the news about Rachel and their chat with the police last night.

'Can you get dressed and come down, please?' Aaron says. 'Give your brother a knock and tell him to come too.'

'Do I have to? He'll only moan at me if I wake him up,' Lucas protests.

'I'll wake Jacob,' I say, already on my way up the stairs. I want a chance to warn him about the article while he's on his own, particularly as he's been singled out more.

I rap on the door, then walk in. Jacob is sitting up in bed, and when he turns to me and I see his red-rimmed eyes, a lump forms in my throat.

He holds up the phone. 'Everyone's saying it's me, Mum. They're saying I lost my temper and pushed Rachel.'

It's too late. He's already read those terrible comments. 'You've read the article?' I ask, sitting down on the edge of his bed.

'What article?' His voice rises in agitation.

I take the phone off him and look at it. It's a group chat – his school friends, I guess – and one after another they're calling him out, accusing him of hurting Rachel.

Thank goodness school is closed for the summer. I dread to think of the bullying he'd have to endure otherwise.

'Oh, Jacob.' I put my arm around his shoulder and pull him close.

'It's not fair, Mum. Everyone thinks it's me. I wouldn't do anything like that. You believe me, don't you?' He sounds so desperate, his eyes begging me.

'Of course I do,' I say firmly. 'Absolutely.' And I do, with all my heart.

He rubs his eyes. 'What were you saying about an article?'

Despair sweeps over his face as he listens. 'I'm sorry, darling, some of the comments are horrible. I'm telling you about it because I don't want you to stumble across the article by accident,' I explain. 'It's best for you not to read them. You know what online trolls are like. They all pile on, feeling brave behind their anonymous names, saying things they wouldn't say to your face because they think they're invisible and invincible.'

'Yeah, well, everyone at school's saying it too,' he says bitterly. 'I wish Rachel would wake up and tell everyone what happened. I'm sick of everyone thinking it's me and not knowing the whole story.'

'I hope so too. Apparently, a lot of people come round from a coma in a few days, although some take a little longer.' I can't bring myself to warn him that she might never come around at all.

He looks at me, tears filling his eyes. 'What if she has brain damage, Mum? What if she can't remember what happened? Then everyone will always blame me.'

'You're innocent, Jacob, so you don't have anything to worry about. I'm sure that will soon be proved beyond any doubt.'

As I hug my boy tightly, I pray that I can keep him safe and I hope he can't tell how afraid I am.

Those threats I read online were truly horrible and I can't simply convince myself not to take them seriously. I've heard terrible stories of people acting like vigilantes in cases like this.

Some of those people might right now be making very real plans to carry out their supposed revenge.

Until Rachel wakes up – if she wakes up – my boys are in danger.

And I have no idea how to keep them safe.

27

Aaron and Lucas are in the kitchen when I finally come down. Lucas is sitting at the table, his head in his hands, but he looks up as I come in and his eyes are glistening with tears.

'Oh, love, I know it's awful.' I put my arms around him. 'But we must keep positive.'

'She could die though. Rachel could die. And people think we did it.' Lucas's voice breaks.

Aaron turns off the saucepan he's stirring and sits down by Lucas. 'Ness is right, we have to keep hoping for the best.'

Lucas nods and chews his fingernail, still fighting back the tears.

Aaron squeezes his shoulder reassuringly then gives me a concerned look. 'How's Jacob?'

'Distraught, like Lucas.' I wrap my hands around my arms. 'I feel so hopeless. I want to do something to help but I can't.'

'All we can do is carry on with life as normally as possible, and support each other.' Aaron's eyes meet mine and I can see the distress there too, despite his calm tone of voice. 'We'll get through this.' He rose to his feet. 'I expect no one feels like eating but I've made us some pasta for lunch. We've got to keep our strength up.'

I glance at the clock on the wall and see to my surprise that it's gone twelve. None of the boys have even had breakfast yet.

Aaron begins to serve us steaming bowls of pasta, I turn back to Lucas. 'Are you getting messages from kids at school about it?'

'A few. Nothing I can't handle,' he says, fidgeting with the neck of his tee shirt, which is exactly what Aaron does when he's nervous. It tells me he's not as confident as he wants to appear. 'Those newspaper comments are worse.'

Aaron puts a bowl of pasta in front of him and pats him comfortingly on the back. 'I know it's hard, son, but hang in there. Everyone who knows you knows you aren't capable of doing such a horrible thing.'

'Yeah, your dad is right. Hopefully Rachel will wake up soon and tell everyone what really happened.' I take the bowl that Aaron holds out for me. 'Thanks.' I'm starving but my stomach is so jittery that I'm not sure I can eat, although the warmth is comforting.

Jacob comes in then, eyes cast down, and shuffles into his seat. We pick at our food, passing each other the grated cheese and the pepper grinder silently, all wrapped up in our own thoughts.

When the doorbell rings, we all jump. Aaron puts down his fork, and I can see his hand is trembling.

I instantly know it's the police. It's something about the ring, urgent, unignorable. 'I'll get it,' I say, standing up unsteadily. 'I think it's the police.'

'Remember, whatever they say, keep calm. You achieve nothing by losing your cool,' I hear Aaron warn the boys as I go out into the hall.

'Hello again,' I say to the two detectives standing on the doorstep. 'How can we help you?'

'Good afternoon, Mrs Dawson,' DS Byron says pleasantly. 'Are Jacob and Lucas in?'

'They are but we're in the middle of lunch. Have you brought their hoodies back?'

'No, I'm afraid we're not finished with them yet. Could we have another word with them, please,' DC Millet says.

'If you must, although the boys have told you everything they know.' I bite down my irritation and remind myself that they're simply doing their job.

'We need additional information to help us with our enquiries,' DS Byron says.

They're like a double act. I wonder if they always work together.

'You'd better come in then. We're in the kitchen.' I open the door wide and let them step through into the hall. 'Has Rachel woken up?' I ask as they follow me into the kitchen.

'I'm afraid not,' says DS Byron, and she looks at the boys, who have pushed their bowls away and are watching her warily. Jacob has his hands clasped in his lap, Lucas is fiddling with the cutlery. 'Afternoon, all. We'd like to ask you a few questions about some messages we've found on Rachel's phone.'

'Is this necessary?' Aaron asks sharply. 'The boys are very traumatised by this, I don't want them to be put under any more stress.'

'I can assure you that all of our questions are necessary,' DS Byron replies calmly before she turns to Jacob and Lucas, her gaze going from one boy to the other. 'There are some messages on Rachel's laptop and phone that suggest someone was harassing her. Someone she was afraid of. Do you have any idea who it could be?'

Jacob is twisting his earlobe and Lucas is playing with the neck of his tee shirt again. They're both looking down at the table, and Aaron clears his throat but neither of them looks up.

'Surely you can trace the person who sent the messages from the phone number,' I say quickly.

'We normally could, but the phone is unregistered,' DC Millet replies. 'Do either of you boys have what's called a "burner" phone?'

They shake their heads simultaneously.

'Do you know anyone who does?'

They shake their heads again.

It's all so surreal, I feel like I'm in a crime drama. Burner phones. Intimidation. Attempted murder?

If Rachel dies, it will be murder.

DC Millet fixes his gaze on Jacob. 'Jacob, you're in Rachel's class, aren't you? Were you aware of anyone bullying her?'

Jacob shakes his head again and mumbles, 'She gets on with most of them.'

'Most of them?' DS Byron jumps on this. 'So there are some students she doesn't get on with? Who are they?'

'There's always going to be some people you don't get on with,' he stammers, looking as if he wishes the ground could swallow him up.

'Jacob's not likely to know, is he?' I cut in. 'He doesn't mix with the girls that much. You'd be better asking Amy.'

'We have phoned her, and she's been very helpful,' says DS Byron briefly. 'Now, we'd like to talk to the boys separately, please. Is there anywhere we can go to talk in private?'

'Sure. We'll go in the lounge, is that okay, Lucas?' Aaron gets up and heads for the lounge with the detectives and Lucas following him.

I look anxiously at Jacob. He swallows, then stares down at his hands.

'All you have to do is tell the truth, Jacob,' I remind him. 'They're just trying to find out what happened to Rachel. You don't have anything to worry about.'

He doesn't reply. He just sits there, his chest visibly rising and falling as if he's about to have a panic attack.

I don't believe my sweet, gentle son is a killer, of course I don't.

He's hiding something though. I know he is. And I'm sure the police can see it too.

28

Suzy

I sit on the cheap plastic chair by the side of the bed and hold Rachel's hand, talk to her, watch desperately for any sign that she can hear my words. There's none. Her eyes are shut, unresponsive. There are various wires attaching her to monitors that are checking her heart rate, blood pressure and other vitals. They bleep continuously and the nurse told us an alarm would sound if anything falls below the level it should be. So I guess Rachel is stable, although sometimes there's a huge spike in the graph on one of the monitors which scares me, but the nurses come in and out regularly to check on her.

Carl has gone off to get some sandwiches. 'We've got to keep our strength up,' he said, so I told him I'd have egg and mayonnaise even though I know I won't be able to eat. I can't face food. Can't face anything. All I want is for my precious daughter to wake up.

I check my watch and wonder if the police are questioning Jacob and Lucas yet. Carl is convinced it was one of them that Ben saw sneaking out of Rachel's bedroom just after that horrible scream. Mum was in such a state when she called yesterday to tell me what Ben had seen.

Carl says it couldn't have been anyone else. I don't want to think it was one of them, they're nice lads, and their mum has become a good friend of mine.

It's true that they were always competing for Rachel's attention, arguing over her. And Rachel had been a bit quiet and withdrawn lately.

Just like before.

Whoever it was must have sneaked in the front door while Carl was preparing lunch, then crept up the stairs to Rachel's room. The brazenness of them; they could have been spotted at any time. I wish I'd been home. I might have seen that scumbag sneaking up the stairs. I might have been able to prevent what happened next.

How long was he up there? I wonder.

Mum said that Ben had been playing in his room with the door shut. He hadn't heard anything until Rachel screamed, and then he thought she might have seen a spider. When he came out of his room to check what was going on he saw the back of that creep running down the stairs. When Carl had gone out the back to see why he'd heard Rachel scream outside, they must have sneaked out the front door.

If it was Jacob or Lucas, they only had to run next door.

Why did they do it? Did they push Rachel on purpose, or was it an accident somehow? Did they regret it and were hoping she would recover? Or were they still hoping that Rachel would die?

'Your mum said the police are next door,' Carl says when he comes back into the hospital room. He's got me a sandwich and a baguette for himself, and another coffee. I feel like I'm drowning in coffee. 'She said it's a couple of detectives this time.'

'You phoned Mum, then? How's Ben?' I take the sandwich and coffee off him with thanks.

'Finally gone down for a nap after being up most of the night. Mum said he's really shaken up. And he's desperate to see Rachel.' Carl sits down on the other chair and continues. 'I don't think we should let him, Suzy. It might traumatise him to see Rachel like this.'

I'm not sure what to do, and I think it over, sipping my coffee. 'I know,' I say finally, 'but at least he'll see that she's alive. And she's not all bandaged up – apart from her arm. It might reassure him a bit.'

Carl takes a bite out of his baguette and chews as I continue. 'Plus, you never know, maybe hearing Ben's voice might bring Rachel around? It's worth a shot. Maybe Ben can come tomorrow?'

I look down at Rachel, willing her to open her eyes.

How could Carl have not known someone had come into the house? How could he have let this happen?

I shouldn't blame him. It wasn't Carl's fault.

Although, to be honest, I have been having a very dark thought about him. A thought I'm trying to bury.

He and Rachel had been at loggerheads over the boys next door for a while. Carl is so quick-tempered, and he really struggles to manage his emotions. So I must say I was a bit relieved when Mum said Ben had seen someone running out of the house, because although that's awful, the thought that Carl might have lost his temper and hurt Rachel is far worse.

I keep trying to tell myself that Carl loves Rachel and Ben with all his heart. He wouldn't hurt either of them. It's true that he has shouted and thrown things sometimes, but he's never lashed out at them directly.

'She'll be okay, she's strong. She'll come round,' Carl says. He gets up and puts his hand on my shoulder. 'You look shattered, love. Why don't you rest for a bit after you've had your food? Leave the coffee, I'll get you another one later. I'll wake you if anything happens.'

We're grateful that Rachel is in a private room in a paediatric ICU ward and there's a pull-down bed that the nurse said we can sleep in, so that one of us can be with her all the time. We took it in turns last night but I didn't get a wink.

How can I sleep until I know that my precious daughter is okay?

How can I sleep, knowing someone out there might have wanted her dead? And maybe they still do?

29

Vanessa

Jacob sits in silence, scrolling on his phone while I clear our lunch things away, trying to keep myself busy. It's a lovely day outside, the sky clear and blue, our flowers looking gorgeous in the sunlight. Normally the kids would be out there together, enjoying the summer holidays. Will anything be normal again?

Finally Aaron and Lucas come back in. Lucas's shoulders are slouched, and he looks utterly dejected. I give him a reassuring smile. It must be so hard to be questioned like that, to be suspected of harming the girl he adored so much. Jacob is clearly a bag of nerves too – and who can blame him?

Now it's our turn to go into the lounge for questioning. Jacob and I sit on the couch at one side of the room and the two detectives sit across from us. I can't help but feel guilty, as if I've done something wrong, even though I know that's ridiculous. It's a bit like the nerves I get when I'm going through airport security, only much worse. And if I'm feeling like this, poor Jacob must be beside himself with anxiety.

DC Millet takes a sheet of paper out of his pocket and

hands it to Jacob. 'These are text messages between Rachel and an unknown person which we find very concerning. It seems someone was threatening her, and we think it was someone at your school.'

Jacob pales. He takes the paper tentatively, as though expecting it will burn him, and slowly scans his eyes across it. I try to look over his shoulder, but it's like he doesn't want me to see.

'Any idea who it is?' the detective asks.

He shakes his head. 'I don't know anything, Rachel never told me.'

'Never told you who it was? Or never told you she was receiving these threatening messages?'

'I don't know anything,' Jacob repeats, his voice wavering slightly.

He's lying. I'm sure he is.

I take it off him gently and read down the page, gasping when I see the last exchange:

Remember. Keep your mouth shut or you'll be sorry.

I haven't told anyone.

Make sure you're at the rec at 7.

I will.

I look up. 'You're sure there's no way to trace the phone number?'

'As we said, this phone is unregistered. That's why we asked if the boys have a burner phone or know anyone who does.' DS Byron pauses. 'We've made a few enquiries at your school, Jacob. We know that you and Lucas argued over Rachel. If one of you was putting pressure on her to choose between you, then now is the time to say.'

Jacob wipes his sleeve across his eyes. 'I would never threaten Rachel.'

I can see the spark of something – is it guilt, panic? – in his eyes.

I imagine the detectives asked Lucas the same questions too, and I'm sure his answers were basically the same. They might be hiding something, but neither of them would threaten or harm Rachel.

The police prod Jacob a bit more over the texts, but he has nothing to say to them, so after a while we go back into the kitchen. Aaron sees the detectives out and the boys go straight upstairs to their rooms.

'Have the boys gone out?' he asks when he returns.

'No, they're upstairs. They're obviously really shaken up.' So am I. 'It's all getting a bit much, Aaron. It's as if the police have decided one of the boys is responsible for Rachel's fall and are trying to find evidence to prove it. Those messages show someone was threatening her, and they seem to think it was Jacob or Lucas.'

'I know, they're very worrying messages, aren't they? They'll be checking her social media accounts too, which might help them find the person who sent them,' Aaron replies. 'I hope Jacob hasn't messaged anything stupid on Facebook or something.'

'What do you mean?' I demand.

'Oh come on, Ness, you know how angry he was when Rachel started getting pally with Lucas. And he and Rachel had a massive argument just before the fall. You've got to admit there's at least a chance he sent her some angry messages recently.'

How dare he? I step back, my arms crossed, and meet his

eyes. 'Aaron, are you seriously trying to insinuate that Jacob had something to do with what happened to Rachel?'

He looks taken aback. 'Of course I'm not. I'm merely pointing out that Jacob has a bit of a temper and the police may pick up on that. It wasn't that long ago that I had to pull him off Lucas.'

'Lucas started that! He isn't Mr Perfect you know. And he fell out with Rachel too,' I snap back.

'Lucas wasn't even at home when Rachel fell. He was at the Games Fayre all day!'

'You don't know that. He could have left early, like Jacob did!'

'So now you're saying Lucas pushed Rachel? That he's some kind of criminal mastermind, making up an alibi? A killer? Bloody hell, Ness!'

'You accused Jacob of it!'

We stand there glaring at each other, then Aaron sighs. 'Come on, Ness, don't let's argue over this. We both know that neither of our boys would hurt Rachel.'

He holds out his arms. 'I'm sorry. I don't want to fight.'

'Neither do I.'

We need to be united over this, so I step into his embrace, relaxing and leaning into him.

Argument avoided for now. We need each other. We need to stick together.

I can't sleep tonight. I toss and turn, the events of the last couple of days buzzing like a swarm of bees in my mind, and it takes me ages just to doze off for a few hours. I wake up at just gone six to find that Aaron's side of the bed is empty.

I'm guessing he can't sleep either. I go down to make a cuppa, stopping to check the lounge, but there's no sign of him. He goes jogging a couple of times a week, mainly at the week-ends though. He likes to keep fit, and I love that about him. He's slim and toned and quite tall but Lucas is already a little taller than him and Jacob is the same height. They grow up so fast.

It's unusual for him to be out jogging on a weekday, I guess it's his way of dealing with the stress. He's putting on a strong front for me and the boys, but I know he's worried about Rachel and our boys being accused, as am I.

It's so quiet and peaceful this early in the morning. I checked in on Chloe before coming down and she was fast asleep, clutching the little rag doll that she loves so much.

I'm opening the lounge curtains as a taxi pulls up next door and Suzy steps out, wearing the same clothes as the day before yesterday. She's home early! Relief surges through me. Has Rachel woken up?

Before I even stop to think, I rush to open the front door and step outside. 'Suzy?'

She turns to look at me, red-rimmed eyes staring out of a paper-white face. My hand flies to my mouth.

Oh God. Is Rachel...?

30

TWO DAYS AFTER THE FALL

'Rachel... How is she?' I stammer the words out.

For a moment I think that Suzy isn't going to reply, but when she does the words are sharp, desperate. 'Still in a coma.'

It's been two days now. Suzy must be going out of her mind. I want to go to her and hug her, we're friends... but the way she is holding herself has 'keep away' written all over her. 'I'm so sorry, Suze,' I whisper. 'You must be beside yourself with worry. If there's anything I can do...'

'Oh, there's something you can do all right,' she snaps, her lips like thin lines. 'You can get your boys to tell the truth.'

'Suzy, you can't seriously believe that Lucas or Jacob would harm Rachel.' It is the grief talking, I am sure of it. 'The boys are worried sick about Rachel. We all are.'

Suzy looks at me, her eyes cold and hard. 'Please don't pretend like we're in the same boat here. Rachel could die. She's in a coma. A bloody coma! And *if* she regains consciousness, she will probably have brain damage.' She swallows. 'She was pushed, Vanessa. Someone came into my home and pushed my daughter out of her own bedroom window.'

I know she's looking for someone to blame, and if I was her

I'd probably react the same, but I need her to understand that it wasn't my boys. There's just no way.

'I know, love.' I take a step closer then realise that I'm still wearing my slippers. 'It's horrendous, I can only imagine what you're going through. But Jacob and Lucas simply aren't capable of doing such a thing. They adore Rachel.'

She walks back a little, putting distance between us. 'I don't want to think it was them, Ness, but who else could it be?' The raw pain in her voice is like a punch to my stomach. 'The police say either Rachel climbed onto the windowsill to get away from someone, or she was pushed. We know someone was threatening her. And Ben saw what he's sure was a boy in a black hoodie run from her room a few seconds after she fell.' Her eyes are narrowed into dark slits, her tone bitter. 'The only boys who ever come to our house are Lucas and Jacob, and I've seen them in hoodies exactly like the one Ben described. It doesn't take a genius to figure it out.'

I don't know what else to say. How can I convince her how wrong she is? She doesn't know Jacob and Lucas like I do. 'If you could only see how distraught they are...' I stammer.

'Really? Well Rachel has been very *distraught* this past week because of your boys fighting over her. And how *distraught* do you think we are, seeing our daughter lying in a coma, close to death, after someone tried to murder her?' She almost spits the words out. 'We don't know if she's going to make it through the next night, if we'll ever hear her voice again, see her grow up.' Her face twists with pain. 'She was in her own home. She should have been safe, but foolishly we allowed your boys free access. We thought we could trust them, and you, as our neighbours. We won't be making that mistake again.'

'Look, Suzy, lots of kids wear hoodies. And your front door must have been unlocked, so anyone could have come in, it could have been someone else from school,' I protest but Suzy raises her hand to stop me.

'I don't want to hear it. I don't even want to look at you. I'm done with you and your family.'

She walks away down the path and disappears through her front door without giving me as much as a backwards glance.

I can barely imagine her grief, the pain that fills that house right now, and I can't blame her for thinking the way she does, but I know she is wrong. Jacob and Lucas are innocent, and I must prove it.

I can't rely on the police, who seem hell-bent on pinning this on my boys. I'm certain neither of the boys were in Rachel's house that day, but I can't shake the feeling though that they know more than they are saying. Why would they hold things back? They're both fond of Rachel and surely would want whoever hurt her to be caught.

Then another thought occurs to me. Are they being bullied too?

Could the same person who pushed Rachel be a danger to my boys?

31

I make myself a cup of instant coffee and sit down at the kitchen table. I'm mulling over the scene with Suzy when the back door opens and Aaron comes in, dressed in his jogging gear.

'You're up early,' he says as he takes off his trainers and leaves them outside the back door.

'I couldn't sleep,' I tell him. 'I guess you couldn't either.'

He shakes his head, padding over in his socked feet to the fridge, and takes out the water filter jug, pouring himself a glass and downing it all before replying. 'Too much going on in my head. Jogging clears my mind.'

I envy his ability to go for a run and switch off. I want to run too, and keep running, leaving all this behind, but I can't.

'Suzy's come home,' I tell him. 'I saw her a few minutes ago.'

'Is Rachel...?'

I shake my head. 'No change. Suzy and Carl blame the boys.'

He frowns. 'Look, Ness, about last night. I didn't mean it to insinuate that I thought Jacob had hurt Rachel, I was merely pointing out that he has a temper.'

'Like his father, you mean?' I retort defensively. 'That's why every time the boys fight you blame Jacob.'

'I'm not saying that, Ness. I'm sorry if it came out that way.'

I'm wondering if this is why Jacob has been asking about his father lately. Sometimes Aaron makes the distinction between him and Lucas so clear: Lucas is his son, and Jacob isn't.

Maybe I do that too, with Lucas, I acknowledge. And Aaron is good with Jacob, they've always been close. Rachel's fall is tearing us apart. I swallow, take a breath to compose myself. 'And I didn't mean to suggest that it was Lucas. Neither of our lads would do this. I know they wouldn't.'

'Of course they wouldn't. I'm sorry, Ness. This is such a horrendous situation; it's got to us all.' He reaches out to me and we briefly hug, but it feels like we're simply going through the motions because neither of us wants to argue.

'I'd better get Chloe up and ready for nursery,' I say.

'Do you want me to take her?' Aaron offers.

'No, it's fine. I want to do a bit of shopping then I'm meeting Hazel for coffee,' I reply. 'I've booked the day off. I can't concentrate with all this going on.'

When I've dropped Chloe off at nursery I go into town and park up by the river. It's a gorgeous day, with the green bushes lining the banks, the sun sparkling on the water and the swans gliding across. This is one of my favourite spots. There aren't many people about now, most of them are at work, and it feels peaceful and soothing despite everything that's been happening. I walk slowly along the riverbank, watching the swans move on the water. They look so graceful as they float by, but I remember reading that underneath the surface their legs are desperately paddling to keep afloat. That's what I'm doing, paddling like mad to stay above it all, only unlike the swans, I'm drowning under the weight of it.

All I can think of is Rachel, wondering if she will be okay, if she will come round, if she has brain damage. I desperately want to help Suzy and Carl, but I can't. I want to protect my family too, but I can't do that either. We're falling apart, increasingly in divided camps. Them and us. Aaron and his son against me and mine, with little Chloe in the middle.

I know that Jacob has a short fuse sometimes. It worries me, knowing what I went through with Ricky. Only Jacob is nothing like his father. Ricky was cruel, spiteful, violent.

I wonder what Ricky was like at fourteen. When did his violent streak emerge? There had been no sign of it when I first met him, or all the months we dated. He was so easy-going. It was only when we lived together that I saw his anger, felt the force of his blows. Had he always been this way? Did it start off with toddler tantrums, then teenage rage, like Jacob?

I shake my head. Jacob is not like Ricky and he didn't harm Rachel. I hate Aaron for putting these awful thoughts in my head. Lucas was the one who was angry, jealous that Jacob and Rachel were getting friendly.

Then I realise that I'm doing the same thing, blaming Lucas. It was neither of the boys, I am sure of that. It's a horrible thing to even think about.

32

Walking along the river helps me relax; it's the first time since Rachel's fall that the grip around my chest has slackened, letting me breathe more freely. I make my way back to the town centre after a while, where I do a bit of shopping before I go to meet Hazel in Costa Coffee. My big sister is so understanding and level-headed; I can always unburden myself to her and get some good advice back. She texts me as I'm at the till in Next, buying a gorgeous dress for Chloe.

I'm here and just about to order, what do you fancy?

I send back a reply:

Iced latte please. I'll be with you in five.

Hazel is sitting outside the café when I arrive, smartly dressed in a black pencil skirt and light blue blouse, her short blonde bob looking sleek and shiny. I feel quite scruffy beside her in my denim crops and white top. Two lattes are on the table in front of her.

'I needed this,' I say, taking a long, refreshing drink of the cold, milky coffee.

'How's it going?' Hazel asks.

I chew my lip and sit back. 'Truth?'

She nods.

'Awful.' I tell her about the row with Glenda and Suzy, and how the boys are at each other's throats. It feels good to be able to get it off my chest. 'It's not just that article you told me about, everyone is pointing their fingers at Jacob and Lucas, they've even got horrible messages from kids at school. Jacob is getting the brunt of it because he and Rachel fell out a few days ago, and he was at home when she fell.'

'How's Aaron being about it all?'

I consider this. 'You know Aaron, he keeps things close to his chest and always portrays this calm, everything-will-be-okay demeanour.'

She takes a sip of her drink then puts her head on one side as she looks quizzically at me. 'But...'

'Well, he's made a couple of digs at Jacob. About him having a temper.'

Hazel raises a perfectly shaped eyebrow. 'Does he?'

I shrug. 'It's nothing new, you know how easy-going Jacob is until he gets frustrated and blows up.' Hazel witnessed many of Jacob's catastrophic toddler tantrums.

'He still does that?'

'Not often, but he and Lucas have been arguing terribly about Rachel, and since her fall it's been even worse. They've even come to blows a couple of times – Aaron's had to separate them.'

'Teenage hormones, especially when there's a love interest involved.'

'I know but it's awful to witness and now we seem to be split into two camps. Me and Jacob against Aaron and Lucas. Aaron and I have been fighting over it too.'

Hazel's eyes narrow. 'Is Aaron picking on Jacob? Is he being aggressive to you?' she asks sharply.

I quickly shake my head. 'No, of course not. Aaron isn't like that. He's always kind and caring but this is really hard for all of us, it's a lot of pressure.'

Hazel is so protective of me, she'd be round like a shot if she thought Aaron was any kind of threat to my wellbeing. She'd never let anyone hurt me. Not after Ricky.

'That's good.' She leans forward and puts her hand on mine. 'Hang in there, Ness. You'll get through this.'

'I want to believe that. I *do* believe it.' I choke up and fight the tears back. I've been trying to keep my chin up but now it is all getting too much. 'It's all so worrying. The police have taken the boys' hoodies, Haze, and they came back to talk to them last night because someone has been sending Rachel threatening messages from a burner phone. It's obvious that Jacob and Lucas are their main suspects. They're just waiting for something concrete to pin on them and then they'll take them in for proper questioning.'

'Do you think they are involved?'

I hate myself for hesitating. I should say no straight away but I can't, and Hazel seizes upon my hesitation. 'Ness?'

'No, I don't. At least I don't want to, but I'm scared, Haze. They know something. I can sense it.'

'If they knew that Rachel was being bullied, they might be frightened to grass on the bully in case that makes them a target,' Hazel suggests. 'Or maybe Rachel has sworn them to secrecy about something, and they don't want to break her confidence.'

'I did think of that. Whoever did this to Rachel is obviously very dangerous. Who knows what they're capable of? If the boys do know something, I need to get them to talk.'

'They might also be scared that whoever did this to Rachel

will say they're involved.' Hazel looks at me as she swirls the ice around her plastic cup and takes a sip through the straw, her dark pencilled eyebrows furrowed. 'They could be wracked with guilt about not speaking up, but they might feel trapped.'

'You're right. I must try again to get Jacob to understand that he can tell me anything and I'll always protect him.'

'I see what you mean by being divided into two camps...'

I stare at Hazel, confused.

'You said you'd talk to Jacob. No mention of Lucas.'

'I will talk to Lucas, of course, or Aaron will, but I want to chat with Jacob on my own. I think he'll open up more if it's just us two,' I reply defensively.

'I can understand that. Ness...' She leans forward. 'Don't let this tear you apart. You don't have to struggle through it on your own. I'm here, don't shut me out.'

'I won't,' I promise.

She changes the subject then and we chat about her daughter, Zara, who is two years older than Chloe. She's on a play date with a friend from school.

'Remember you can talk to me anytime,' Hazel says as I leave to pick Chloe up from nursery.

'Thanks. And back at you,' I say.

We've always been there for each other, Hazel and I. Especially since our parents died. Hazel says we're each other's lifebelt, although to be honest it's invariably been me who's needed the lifebelt. She's so protective of me, being the elder sister, especially after what happened with Ricky. She was really wary when I got together with Aaron, but she's come to see how happy Jacob and I are now, so she has gradually accepted him.

I'd tried to keep what was happening with Ricky from her, how bad it had got, then she came to visit one day when he had trashed the place. She was fuming and warned him that he'd better get his act together, and that if he ever touched me or Jacob, she'd call the police and get him locked up. When I finally left Ricky, she swore that she would never let anyone hurt me again.

But what's happening to my family now is something even Hazel can't protect me from.

33

The boys are in their rooms when I get home, and I leave Chloe playing with her toys so I can go up to speak to them. I knock on Jacob's door first then go in. He's on his computer and turns to look at me, his eyes wide with hope. 'Has Rachel woken up?'

I shake my head. 'Not yet.' I sit down on his bed. 'Look, love, I need to talk to you. Can you please pause your game for a few minutes?'

He obliges, gets up from his desk and sits down beside me. 'What's up? More nasty messages, is it?' he asks, with bitterness colouring his voice.

'No. Well, not that I've seen, but I haven't looked again and I think it's best if you don't either.' I take a breath as he fidgets with his earlobe. 'Jacob, have you any idea who it could be that Ben saw? Please, darling,' I say earnestly. 'We need to make sure they don't do this to anyone else, and we need to clear yours and Lucas's names.'

He shakes his head and avoids my gaze. 'No, I told you. I don't know anything.'

'Look, Jacob, if someone is threatening you, then please

don't be scared. The police will make sure that no one hurts you.'

'I don't know anything!' he yells, standing up, his eyes blazing. 'Stop nagging me.' Then he runs out of the room, slamming the door behind him.

Lucas is coming out of his room as I leave Jacob's, and he casts me a furtive glance as he hurries past.

'Lucas!' I shout.

He looks over his shoulder. 'I don't know anything either,' he says, then dashes down the stairs.

So, he heard me talking to Jacob.

They're covering something up. I know they are.

Neither of the boys comes home for dinner. As it is only cold meat and salad, I make it up for them and keep it in the fridge. When Chloe has had her bath and is tucked up in bed, the boys are still out and I take the opportunity to talk to Aaron. He's sitting in the lounge watching a crime drama, a can of beer in his hand. 'Want one? Or I can crack open a bottle of wine?' he offers.

I shake my head. I can't face drinking alcohol right now. And I am surprised at Aaron as he rarely drinks, and we had wine together just the other day, I guess he's more anxious than he wants to let on. 'I asked the boys if they know who it could be that Ben saw running out of Rachel's bedroom,' I venture as I sit down beside him.

The can pauses in mid-air and a crease appears in the middle of his forehead. 'And what did they say?'

'They denied knowing anything and they rushed out, and neither has been back since.' I look worriedly at him. 'They're not telling us something, Aaron. I know it.'

He raises the can again and takes a swig from it. 'Why would they be hiding anything? They're close to Rachel, so if they know who did this, I'm sure they'd tell us – and the police for that matter.'

'Well, I think they're scared, and that they have a secret. And the police seem to think our boys are the top suspects,' I point out. 'We have to get them to talk, Aaron. Their freedom could depend on it.'

And their lives, I think, remembering those awful online threats.

Through gritted teeth, he says, 'Lucas and Rachel were in a good place, so it's hardly likely to have been him who was out to get her.'

'I'm not insinuating that!'

'Then what are you insinuating, Ness?' Aaron's eyes pierce mine. 'Obviously you believe that Jacob is totally innocent, you've made that very clear. So you must be suggesting that it was Lucas in Rachel's bedroom – and that either he pushed her or she fell while they were having a fight. And then what, that Jacob knows about it and is covering it up?'

'Of course I'm not saying that! I'm merely pointing out that they seem to be hiding something.'

'I know you never think that your precious son does anything wrong' – Aaron is raising his voice now – 'but clearly you're ready to believe anything of Lucas.'

I'm horrified, I can't believe he's being so defensive. This isn't like him. How many beers has he drunk? 'That's not true, Aaron, and you know it! I – we – treat the boys exactly the same. We always have. Anyway, you're the one who keeps going on about what a terrible temper Jacob has. You clearly think that he's responsible!'

'I'm sick of this.' Aaron slams the can down on the coffee table and beer slops over the sides. 'I'm going for a run.'

'Again? At this time of night? You never run in the evening.'

'I'll run whenever I want to, thanks. I want to clear my head. Don't wait up.' His words are clipped and his jaw set as he stalks out. A few minutes later he comes back downstairs in his tracksuit and trainers and goes out the back door without so much as a goodbye.

I sink down on the sofa, shaking. Did I really make it sound as if Lucas is the culprit, just like Aaron has done with Jacob? We've always tried to avoid picking sides and arguing over the boys, but now there's a huge divide between us and it feels like it's growing wider all the time. I feel defeated, and unsure of myself. Aaron is so convinced that Lucas had nothing to do with it but Lucas is coming across as almost *too* confident to me, compared to the anxiety and fear I'm seeing in Jacob, which seems very normal given the circumstances.

Aaron once told me that when his wife died, he vowed that he would do anything to protect Lucas. And he has devoted his life ever since to making sure his son feels loved and cared for.

Little things float into my mind. How Aaron takes no notice when Lucas borrows his clothes and his aftershave. How whenever Lucas has a problem, Aaron jumps in to fix it.

Just how far would he go to protect his son?

34

Aaron

I run until I can't run anymore. Finally, the stitch in my side and the soreness in my throat force me to stop. I hold my side, my breath coming out in rasps, and I sit down on a bench to rest for a while.

Running has always been my way of dealing with stress. *Running away*, Amanda called it, and maybe she was right. It is something I've done since I was a teen – it got me out of the house and gave me a way to vent all the anger I felt towards my parents: my stern, nothing-was-good-enough-for-him father and my obsessed-with-putting-on-a-front mother.

Even now the memory of them stirs up painful emotions. They were always tough on me whereas my younger brother Scott could do no wrong. If only my parents had known what Scott was really like, how he bullied the younger kids at school mercilessly and did his best to make my life a misery. I hated the injustice of their favouritism and vowed I would never treat any of my children like that.

Amanda and I wanted to have a big family, but tragically

she took ill not long after Lucas was born, and we were never blessed with another child. When I met Vanessa, I immediately loved her gentle nature. I was delighted when she got pregnant and over the moon when she had a little girl, our lovely Chloe.

Vanessa has brought so much happiness to my life, and Jacob is a good lad. I'm really fond of him and try hard to treat both boys the same, remembering how much my parents' favouritism of Scott hurt me when I was a kid, but it's hard sometimes. Amanda's death crushed me, and Lucas and I clung together, drowning in our grief. He was only eight, he needed his mother and all he had was me. I've tried my best to step up and provide the love of both parents. I was worried that Lucas would find it difficult to adjust when I first met Ness, but she was wonderful with him, and the boys hit it off right away. We never had any problems, at least not any big ones, until now.

Now, it's clear that Vanessa thinks if either of our boys hurt Rachel, then it must have been Lucas because her precious Jacob wouldn't hurt a fly.

Even though Jacob is the one who flies off the handle, not Lucas.

Jacob was the one on top of Lucas punching him the other day.

I'm so tired. And thirsty. I wish I'd brought a drink with me, but I was in such a hurry to get out that I didn't stop for anything. I was scared of the argument getting even more heated. Scared of what I would say, what I'd let slip. You can't take back words once they're out there.

I lean back on the bench and stare out at the river. The texts the police have found are bad, but they aren't incriminating. They don't reveal anything specific about who sent them, so there doesn't seem to be anything to worry about.

Rachel must have deleted the others.

Thank goodness. The last thing I need is for it to all start up again.

35

Rachel

I feel warm, safe. Peaceful.

Like nothing and no one can hurt me here.

Where am I?

I try to open my eyes, but they remain firmly shut, and my calmness fades as the panic begins to set in. I sense now that something terrible has happened to me.

Somehow I know that I'm in terrible danger. But I can't remember what happened.

I desperately try to plough through the fog in my brain but all I can feel is fear. Raw, terrifying fear.

Am I dreaming?

I try to pinch myself to check if I'm awake but I can't move my hand.

Then I try to move my legs but they won't respond either. Why can't I move?

I must be dreaming.

I hear the soft murmur of voices and am aware of a strong chemical smell and something bleeping. I concentrate on the voices; they seem very far away but one of them is familiar. It's a woman. Do I know her?

'Is there any improvement?' I recognise the voice now. It's Mum.

Another voice floats through the fog. 'Not yet. But we're hopeful.' I don't recognise this voice.

Then there are soft sobs and I know that it's my mum, she's crying. Something that feels as gentle as a feather touches my hand and I'm sure my mum is holding it. Why can't I feel properly? Why can't I move or speak?

'I just wish I knew what happened,' Mum says.

Me too. What am I doing here?

A powerful, urgent instinct inside me is telling me I'm in immediate danger, even though Mum is here. I need to run, to hide, to get away, right now. But I can't move.

What am I so scared of?

36

THREE DAYS AFTER THE FALL

Vanessa

I've just picked Chloe up from nursery and I'm strapping her into her car seat when a message pings in from Aaron.

Fancy a takeaway tonight? A Chinese for four? xx

I feel my shoulders relax. We've barely spoken after our argument last night. Aaron has been working in the study all day while I opted for my laptop in the lounge, not wanting to share the same space. He's obviously trying to build bridges now, and I love him for that. We do need to stick together; things are bad enough without us quarrelling. A Chinese would be great, it's a favourite with both boys too. And I've had such a hard day trying to concentrate on my edits and resisting the urge to read more of the online comments about the boys. Suzy's silence has been deafening, and my stress has been building constantly, so I feel totally shattered and it will be great not to have to cook. I reply:

Perfect xx

We'll get through this.

I drive home feeling a lot lighter, while Chloe chatters away happily in the back. I'm looking forward to us all having a family meal together, it feels like it's been ages since we did that. Yesterday the boys didn't come home until later and ate their salad for lunch today.

I was intending to talk to Jacob again tonight and gently probe him about anything that is on his mind, but I decide to leave it until tomorrow. We desperately need an evening free of all the worry and distress. We need a chance to reconnect and be a family again.

Aaron greets me with a hug when I get back, then pulls Chloe up into his arms. 'How's my best girl?' He tickles under her arm and she giggles then squirms to get down. We both smile as she dashes into the lounge to play with her toys, and I know she'll be calling for her favourite cartoon to go on in a few minutes. This time of the afternoon is Chloe's TV time; our time is when she's gone to bed.

'Are the boys still out?' I ask. They went out separately after lunch and hadn't come back when I left to get Chloe. It is the holidays, they are probably hanging around with their friends, I tell myself, but I can't help worrying that they might be in some kind of danger.

'Yes, but I've texted and told them I'm ordering a Chinese for later and they've promised to be back.'

I'm pleased that Aaron is making such an effort to bring the family back together. I smile at him. 'I'll fix Chloe something to eat a little earlier, then you can order the Chinese when she's gone to bed,' I suggest.

'Good idea. Want a cuppa?'

'Thanks.'

'Mummeee, cartoons,' Chloe calls, and Aaron chuckles as I go in to her.

Lucas comes home first, while Chloe is finishing off her dinner. She scrambles down off the chair and runs to him, and he picks her up and swings her round. I love how the boys are with her.

'Have you seen Jacob?' I ask him.

'Nope.' He kisses Chloe on the forehead and puts her down. 'I need a drink,' he says, going over to the fridge. He pours himself an icy glass of green Monster, gulps it down as if he's parched, then wipes his mouth. 'Any news about Rachel?'

'Not yet, I'm afraid.'

I change the subject and chat to him about his day. He's been hanging out with some friends at the park, playing football. He doesn't say if anyone has been picking on him about those horrible rumours about Rachel's fall, and I don't ask. If he wanted to say something, he would, and I don't want to push him and cause any stress. Not now. It's important not to let anything spoil tonight; I have to reconnect my family. We all need this.

Jacob gets home just as Chloe is getting ready for bed, and immediately she says she wants him to read her a bedtime story. He always puts a lot of effort into this, using different voices for the characters and making all the sounds. He's such a good brother and is always protective of her.

Once Chloe is settled in bed, Aaron orders the food, and when it arrives we set it all out on the coffee table in the lounge. Jacob and Lucas tuck in and are actually quite pleasant to each other, passing each other the prawn crackers and spring rolls. Then Aaron puts on the latest show from our favourite comedian and we're all soon chuckling away at it.

It seems like such a long time since we've enjoyed an evening like this, as a family, and it feels good.

I look around at them laughing away and my heart swells

with love. We can't let what's happened to Rachel tear us apart. I won't let it, I vow.

Just before I go to bed, I make the mistake of checking the local newspaper's website. I know I shouldn't, but I can't resist. The comments are still utterly vile, although there's not so many today. I guess Rachel's fall is old news now.

I'm about to close the tab when a new comment pops up.

Regi142: It was definitely Jacob. Seems like history repeating itself to me. Look to the father.

I read the words over and over again, my heart thudding.

I don't know how they found out about Ricky but they're wrong, Jacob is nothing like him.

Is he?

37

FOUR DAYS AFTER THE FALL

Despite the lovely evening we all had last night, I'm feeling very anxious when I drop Chloe off at nursery the next day.

If only Rachel would come out of her coma, I think as I pull into our drive. I wish I could text Suzy and ask her how she is, but how can I after her outburst the other morning? I keep hoping I'll hear from her.

I get out of the car and glance at the house next door, it doesn't look like anyone is there. Suzy and Carl are practically living at the hospital, and Ben is with Glenda. It's all so awful. It was only a few months ago when they'd moved in and we'd all been so happy.

As I turn my key in the lock and open the front door, I hear shouting.

'It's all your fault. I told you to keep out of it!' It's Jacob.

What the hell is going on now?

I race up the stairs, hoping to stop the argument before the boys come to blows again.

'I'm not going to stand by and let you bully her!' Lucas shouts back.

'You take that back!'

I'm almost at the top of the stairs and can tell the argument is coming from Lucas's bedroom, the door is wide open.

'Get your hands off me!' I hear Lucas yell.

Suddenly our bedroom door is flung open and Aaron streaks out – I thought he'd gone to work! He runs into Lucas's bedroom and I follow quickly behind. The boys are a tangled heap on the floor, Jacob is on top and it's clear he has the upper hand. Aaron reaches him, grabs his arm and pulls him off Lucas. 'What the bloody hell do you think you're doing?' he demands, his face contorted with fury. 'How dare you hit your brother?'

'He's not my brother and he asked for it,' Jacob mutters, wiping the sleeve of his sweatshirt across his mouth, where I can see traces of blood.

The words 'he's not my brother' repeat in my head as I hurry over to Jacob. It's only anger talking and he doesn't really mean it, but I know that Aaron and Lucas will be hurt.

Aaron is helping Lucas to his feet. 'Are you okay?'

'Yeah, thanks, Dad.' Lucas glares at Jacob. 'You're a nutter.' He points his finger to his temple and twists it. 'You need locking up.'

'That's enough, Lucas.' I put my arm supportively around Jacob's shoulders and try to speak calmly. 'What are you two fighting about now? What did you mean about Jacob bullying someone?'

'He's got the wrong end of the stick, as usual. Rachel wasn't crying over me!' Jacob retorts.

'Why was she crying, then?' I ask, sweeping my gaze from one to the other as they continue to scowl at each other.

'I dunno.' Jacob shrugs.

Aaron and I are on opposite sides of the bedroom. He has his arm around Lucas's shoulders and I have my arm around Jacob's. We're both standing by our sons, protecting them, but we're miles apart from each other.

Then Aaron says something that pushes us even further apart.

He looks steadily at Jacob. 'You need to control that temper of yours, Jacob, before it gets you into big trouble.'

'Yes, Jacob does need to control his temper,' I say, bristling, 'and Lucas, you also need to stop goading people and calling them names. There were two sides to this fight, and you need to take responsibility as well.'

Aaron's steely gaze rests on me across the room and I can see that he isn't pleased with my remark. 'Let's get you cleaned up, Lucas. Thank goodness you managed to control yourself or Jacob would have been badly hurt,' he says before turning to Jacob. 'I won't have you assaulting *my son* like that. Now please leave Lucas's room.'

I stifle a gasp at Aaron's emphasis on 'my son'. We have never done this. We vowed that we wouldn't ever utter those words, not like that, and frankly I've fought hard to bite them back these last few days. I don't want to retaliate and make the situation any worse, but I'll talk to Aaron later and let him know how much he's upset me.

'Fine. And please tell *your* son to leave me alone and not come into my room,' Jacob replies. 'And don't tell me what to do. You're not my dad.'

I hear Aaron suck in his breath as Jacob walks out of Lucas's bedroom. I follow him, putting my foot against his bedroom door as he's about to close it. 'We need to talk, Jacob.'

He takes a deep breath. 'I'm sorry, Mum, I don't want to talk about it.'

'Why did you kick off like that?' I ask, determinedly. 'What is going on? You can tell me. You can tell me anything.'

For a moment I think he's going to speak, then he stares down at the floor. 'I want to be alone now.'

Jacob can never look me in the eye when he's concealing something. I want to put my arms around him like I used to do when he was little and kiss him on the forehead and tell him that whatever he has to say it will be okay, I will understand. I don't though because his body language is telling me he wants me to leave him alone.

'Jacob, we have to talk about this,' I say gently. 'Was someone bullying Rachel? Are they bullying you too, is that why you're scared to tell me what's going on?'

Finally he raises his eyes, I can see the fear in them.

'Jacob?' I reach out and take his hand but he shakes me off. 'I've told you, Mum. I don't know anything. I wish you'd leave me alone!' He turns away and stalks over to his bed, where he sits looking at his feet.

A wave of helplessness sweeps over me. My son is scared, and I can't reach him, can't do anything to comfort him. I'm scared too, scared that he's in danger. Not only from those vile people who are threatening him online, but from the person who hurt Rachel.

Then another fear snakes into my mind.

Jacob is very sensitive. He feels things deeply, overthinks sometimes.

What if it all gets too much for him?

38

Aaron

I flick the kettle on and stand by the sink, staring out of the kitchen window as I wait for it to boil. I shouldn't have said that. As soon as the words were out of my mouth I wanted to take them back. When we moved in with Vanessa and Jacob four years ago, we promised each other we would treat the boys the same, that they were both our sons, and here I am emphasising that Lucas is my son, not Jacob. I was just so furious when I saw Lucas lying on his bedroom floor with Jacob on top of him, pummelling him, that it was all I could do not to whack Jacob myself.

I'm really fond of Jacob, he's a good kid but he has a bit of a temper and Vanessa always pussyfoots around him so as not to provoke him. I'm guessing it's because of Ricky, Jacob's dad. He was a real nasty piece of work and treated Ness badly for years, until finally, after a particularly violent row, Ness left with Jacob and filed for divorce, getting a restraining order against Ricky. Neither of them has seen him since.

It seems to me that she got used to spending her time

walking on eggshells, trying not to provoke Ricky, and now when Jacob gets angry it's like she reverts back to that. I've tried gently talking to her about it but she gets defensive, which is only natural, we all get defensive about our kids. And we all overcompensate when we're their sole parent. I know I do with Lucas. When Amanda died I couldn't bear to tell him off, I felt like he'd suffered enough. Even now, I hate it when we clash, and I'll defend him to the hilt.

Jacob and Lucas get on great – at least they did – and they adore Chloe. Yes, there have been a few tussles over the years, especially as they got older, but we soon sorted it out.

Everything was fine until Rachel moved next door.

She's a lovely girl but our household has been turned into a battlefield over her the past few months. And now she is lying unconscious in a hospital bed and Lucas and Jacob are suspects.

If only they knew that she had never actually been attracted to either of them.

I make myself a black coffee. I'd prefer a beer but I have to work today, although I'm at home again. Which at least means I can keep an eye on things.

'Jacob is really upset about you talking to him like that.'

I turn around slowly, forcing myself to keep calm. Ness is standing behind me, arms folded across her chest.

'Well, I'm pretty upset about Jacob attacking Lucas,' I say evenly.

'He was provoked.'

'There's no excuse for violence, Ness. I thought you of all people would agree with that.'

I can see that my remark has stung.

'Lucas is the one who hit first.'

This might be true. Lucas is easy-going most of the time, but he won't be pushed around or walked over. 'Maybe he did,' I concede, 'but Jacob completely overreacted.'

I can see that she's angry and she's not letting this go. Well neither am I. It was clear that Jacob was seeing red and was totally out of control. I dread to think what could have happened if neither of us was at home.

She purses her lips. 'I'm going out, I'll pick Chloe up from nursery later so you don't need to worry about it.' She grabs her laptop and her handbag from the table and walks out.

I hate the way our family has been split down the middle. Ness is hoping that things will go back to normal once – *if* – Rachel wakes up.

She doesn't realise this might only make things worse.

39

Suzy

Rachel's been in a coma for four days now. We've been talking to her and playing her favourite music just like the doctors advised, but there's been no change. I'm exhausted from lack of sleep, but how can I sleep knowing she could die any minute? I'm trying to hold on to hope, and I'm terrified to leave her side not only in case the worst happens without me there, but also in case she wakes and doesn't see me. And I feel more desperate every day. I can't lose her. I can't face it.

Carl persuaded me to go home for a quick shower and a rest the other day, promising to call me if there was any news, but I worried all the time I was away and can't do it again. Carl's at home now having a shower and change, and I'm sitting holding Rachel's hand, talking to her about an Olivia Rodrigo concert we went to recently – she's mad on her – and playing some of her songs. She lies there silent and unmoving, and I wipe her brow, tidy her hair, hold her hand.

'Oh, Rachel, darling, come back to us, please,' I murmur, hot tears filling my eyes. I would give anything to have my precious daughter back, to be arguing with her once again about using my foundation and hitching up her skirt too short for school.

I fix my eyes on her face, imprinting it on my mind, her dark hair tumbling around her shoulders. She looks so peaceful, as if she's asleep and any moment she'll wake up. I have to believe that my little girl is still in there somewhere and one day soon she will open her eyes. I can't allow myself to think anything else.

I'd been so hopeful about our move, the chance to have a fresh start. Carl had lost his job and things had been tense in the household, especially between him and Rachel. He can be so short-tempered and Rachel's a teenager, they test your patience. Then she started refusing to go to her previous school, locking herself in her bedroom and not coming out. I was sure she was being bullied but she denied it when I asked her. I was really pleased when Carl found work again, and the fact that Rachel was so happy to leave made me think I'd been right about the bullying. Now, though, it seems she got into an even worse situation and those boys next door, who I previously liked and trusted, are responsible. I wish that Rachel would wake up so she could tell us what happened, and I could reassure her that I'll never let it happen again.

I lick my dry lips and start to speak. 'I don't know if you can hear me, Rachel, darling, but you're in hospital. You had a fall. We found you on the ground underneath your bedroom window and the police think that someone pushed you.' I pause and study my daughter's face for any sign that she can hear me, but she just lies there, frozen in time.

'Ben saw someone wearing a black hoodie run from your room,' I continue. 'We don't know who it was but the police are trying to find out. Whoever did this to you, we will find them.' I stop, my eyes scrutinising Rachel's face again.

Did her eyes twitch?

'If someone has been threatening you, bullying you, you can

tell us. We'll sort it, I promise. We'll keep you safe. Please come back to us, darling, and tell us what happened.' I lean over and kiss her on the forehead, a tear falling from my cheek into her hair.

Then the door opens and Carl walks in. He's finally had a shave and looks a lot fresher but there are dark bags under his eyes. His gaze goes straight to Rachel.

'How's she doing?' he asks.

I shake my head. 'No improvement.'

'I brought her favourite perfume, and that book she was reading. Maybe we can read that to her?' he says.

'Good idea,' I agree.

I glance at my phone as a message pings in. It's from Mum.

I'll be there with Ben in about an hour.

Ben has taken Rachel's fall really badly and has been desperate to see her. Carl still isn't sure if it's a good idea, but we've agreed to allow him to visit.

A while later, Ben arrives clutching Mum's hand. He's dressed in blue shorts and a stripey tee shirt and looks terribly pale and shaky. I go over to him and give him a big hug. 'Are you sure about this, darling? You know Rachel won't be able to talk to you. It will be just like she's asleep.'

He nods emphatically, his brown eyes wide. 'I want to see her.'

'I really don't think this is a good idea, Ben,' Carl says, and I'm taken aback at how intimidating he sounds. I know that Carl is only being protective, but can't he see that this is important to Ben? He and Rachel are so close, he looks up to her, he always has. And even if it's difficult for Ben, the chance that hearing him might help Rachel wake up is something we can't afford to lose.

Ben refuses to meet Carl's eyes and nods again, so I lead him into the hospital room and he clutches my hand so tight his nails dig into my flesh. Rachel is only allowed two visitors at a time, so Carl waits outside with Mum. Mum's been so brilliant; I'm really grateful for her right now, especially as Carl's parents live in France and are too ill to travel. Mum's brought us a change of clothes and a bag of food, and I see her put a comforting hand on Carl's arm while Ben and I go in to see Rachel. She's being a pillar of support to him too, even though she never really got on with him well before.

Ben gasps when he sees Rachel, I was worried that seeing her wired up to the machines would freak him out. He lets go of my hand and runs over to her, kneeling down on the bed and wrapping his arms around her. 'Please wake up, Rachel. Please don't die.' Then he starts sobbing uncontrollably.

It's heartbreaking to see his distress. This clearly is too much for him, Carl was right. And Rachel hasn't stirred at all, so it didn't work anyway. I go over and stroke his hair.

'Come on, darling, I think you should go home with Nanny now. I'll let her know as soon as Rachel wakes up, I promise. Then you can come and talk to her.'

He gets up and throws his arms around me, tears spilling down his face, sniffing them back as he sobs. 'Is Rachel going to die, Mummy?'

'We all hope not, darling,' I say, my voice cracking. 'The nurses and doctors are doing all they can to look after her. She's in really good hands here.'

I take him out and Carl throws me a look of annoyance when he sees Ben's tear-streaked face. 'I told you so!'

'It was worth a try,' I reply, deflated.

Mum and Carl go in to see Rachel then, while I comfort Ben, telling him how happy Rachel will be to see him when she wakes up, how we'll all go on a lovely family holiday together somewhere.

'Come on, Ben, let's get you home,' Mum says gently when she comes back out.

'I think you should go too, get some rest, Ness. I'll sit with Rachel,' Carl tells me. I can see he's still angry with me about Ben, but he's not going to pick fights at a time like this.

'Not yet. I'll go home in a while,' I say. I can't leave her side, not yet.

I give my son a final cuddle then go back into the ward to sit with my daughter, next to Carl. And as I look at her, vulnerable and broken, far away where I can't reach her, I feel as if my entire heart has been ripped out.

Beneath all the pain and all the fear, a powerful wave of utter fury is growing larger and larger inside me.

When the police finally prove that Lucas or Jacob did this to her, I'm going to make sure they pay.

40

Rachel

I'm becoming more aware of what's going on around me now. I hear people talking and equipment being moved about, and there's a powerful smell of antiseptic. I know when Mum and Dad come and go, I can hear their whispers even though I can't always make out their words.

Then I hear Ben. He's crying and I want to hug him and tell him I'm okay but I can't move. My head hurts, and all down my left side feels bruised and sore. I can't open my eyes or move or talk, although I can hear.

I must be in hospital, I realise. How long have I been here?

I pick up whispers about the police, hear Jacob's and Lucas's names, and wonder what has happened. It's something bad, I know it is. I'm sure that the truth is there, in the back of my mind, if only I can find it, but I'm too tired. I drift back off to sleep again. I like sleeping, it's peaceful. Nothing can hurt me there.

I don't know how long has passed but suddenly I'm alert. I still can't open my eyes, but behind them I'm awake and I can *hear my mother talking. She sounds so sad and she's saying that I've had an accident. I wish I could comfort her.*

Then suddenly a memory storms into my head.

I'm falling. I can feel the gut-wrenching fear all over again as the ground zooms closer.

I remember what I'm scared of. Who I'm scared of.

I want to tell my mum that I can hear her, I want to reach out and touch her. She needs to know what happened. I must tell her. But I can't move. I can't speak. I can't tell her how terrified I am.

I remember it all now.

And I know that even here, I am not safe.

41

Vanessa

I don't really know where I'm going, I desperately need to get out of the house. The way things are right now I don't want to be in the same space as Aaron and the boys, so once again I take my laptop, intending to work in a café. Although my mind is whirring so much I won't be able to focus. Luckily, I've told my clients what's happened and they're being very understanding.

I drive into town, park the car and walk to the river again, but this time I sit down on the bench by the quay. My head is aching, the stress a relentless pressure. It's a public place and I'm aware of people passing by, of a couple of them looking over at me, but I keep my gaze on the river, trying to still my racing mind. It's all such a mess. I close my eyes and lean back against the bench. I feel exhausted and scared. How has my life changed so much in just a few days?

Rain starts to fall, just fine at first, and I sit there, feeling the dampness on my hair, my cheeks. I don't want to move. I don't want to go back home and face the awful tension there again.

I don't know how long I've been sitting here when the trill

of an incoming call startles me and I realise that I'm drenched to the skin. I take my phone out of my pocket and glance at the screen. It's the nursery. I answer right away, and they tell me that Chloe has been sick, so I need to collect her and take her home. I wonder if she has a bug or maybe she has sensed the difficult atmosphere at home. She's a sensitive little soul.

'Goodness, you're soaked. Have you been out for a walk?' Paula, the nursery leader, asks when I arrive.

'Yes, and I stupidly forgot to take a brolly,' I say lightly. I bend down to speak to Chloe. 'What's the matter, pet? Is your tummy sore?'

She nods. Her face is pinched, her eyes wide and sad.

'It's a good job she's not in now until Tuesday. We don't want the other children getting it,' Paula says.

'Yes, I'm sure she'll be better by then.' I look at Chloe's pale face, she doesn't look at all well, poor mite. 'Have you had any other cases of sickness?' I ask.

'No, but norovirus is doing the rounds so be warned,' Paula tells me.

Great. I hope Chloe hasn't got that. I remember Jacob having it when he was at primary school, he was throwing up every half an hour and got so distressed, it was horrible to see him looking so helpless and miserable.

'Come on, pet.' I hold her hand, not wanting to pick her up as I'm so wet, and we go out to the car. Strapping her into the back seat and sticking her favourite CD on, I drive home hoping that everyone has cooled down by now.

The house is quiet. I guess Aaron is working in the study, I'll bring him a coffee in a bit, a sort of peace offering after this morning's argument. Things are difficult enough, we need to stick together and not be at each other's throats. It would be good if the boys are out, I desperately need some peace. I settle Chloe on the sofa with her cuddly toy and a favourite blanket and put a bowl by her side in case she feels sick again. Then I dash upstairs to change into dry clothes. As I pass Jacob's room, I see that the door is open and I pop my head around to check that he's okay.

I'm totally unprepared for the shock I get as I look inside, and I gasp, stepping backwards.

There are clothes, bits of papers, stuff scattered everywhere. Drawers pulled open. Wardrobe doors swinging out with clothes falling onto the floor.

It's been completely trashed.

My hand goes to my throat as I stare around in horror.

What the hell has happened?

Then I recall what Hazel said about Rachel being bullied, and the bully having a hold on Jacob and Lucas. Maybe it's him, the evil person who pushed Rachel? Did he sneak in and wreck Jacob's bedroom as a way of warning him to keep quiet? Jacob's is the first bedroom he would have come across upstairs, it would have been the obvious one to target.

What if he's still here? My stomach lurches. Chloe is downstairs on her own! If the person responsible is still in the house, she could be in danger. I dash back downstairs two at a time, almost falling, my heart pounding furiously. I will never, ever forgive myself if something happens to my precious little girl.

Aaron steps out into the hall as I jump off the bottom two steps. 'Ness! What's happened?' he asks, obviously seeing the panic on my face.

'Someone has trashed Jacob's room!' My words are coming out in gasps, and I run past him into the lounge to check on Chloe without waiting for his answer, holding on to the door frame for support and letting out a breath of relief when I see her fast asleep on the sofa.

Oh, thank goodness. Hand on my racing heart, I take a few deep breaths to calm my breathing.

'What's going on, Ness?' Aaron asks, a puzzled frown on his face as he looks around the lounge. 'And why is Chloe back?'

I sit down on the sofa beside Chloe and take some more deep breaths to steady my nerves.

'Chloe's been sent home from nursery, she's sick,' I tell him. 'I went up to get some dry clothes, and Jacob's bedroom, it's totally wrecked – his stuff has been thrown everywhere. I think someone was looking for something or leaving a warning.'

The colour drains from Aaron's face and he heads swiftly for the stairs. Chloe is still sleeping so I follow him up. Aaron is standing in the doorway of Jacob's bedroom, rubbing the back of his neck as he surveys the mess. 'Blimey, it looks like some-one's had a right fit in here,' he agrees, 'I don't think anyone's sneaked in though. I've been here all the time, I would have heard.'

'Carl was home too when Rachel was pushed out of the window,' I remind him.

'True, but this looks like Jacob's had a bit of a tantrum to me.'

I prickle at the assumption that Jacob is so out of control that he's trashed his own room. Then an image of Ricky hurtling a chair across the room, pulling out drawers and emptying the contents on the floor when he was in one of his rages jumps into my mind. I push it away.

'Or maybe Lucas did it to get his own back?' I say defensively.

Aaron raises his eyebrow at me. 'You can't seriously believe that Lucas would be petty enough to trash Jacob's room.'

'Why not? You believe that Jacob has done this in a fit of temper, which frankly is bloody insulting.' I don't swear often, but I am sick of his continual criticism of my son.

He sighs. 'Let's call a truce, Ness. We'll find out what happened when the boys are home. I'm so tired of this sniping.'

'So am I.' I agree. 'And I need to get into some dry clothes. Can you keep an eye on Chloe, please? She might be sick again.'

'Sure.' He turns and heads back downstairs.

I get changed and follow him down just as Jacob comes in the front door.

'Mummee!' Chloe shouts.

'What's up, Chloe?' Jacob pushes the lounge door open, and I follow him in.

'I'm poorly,' Chloe tells him sadly. She's still lying on the sofa, resting her head on Aaron's lap. She hasn't been sick again, thank goodness.

'Poor Chloe.' Jacob crouches down next to them and gently strokes her forehead. My heart swells with love as I watch him. He's such a caring boy. He's nothing like Ricky. Nothing at all.

'What's happened to your room, Jacob? Were you looking for something? It looks like a bomb's hit it,' Aaron says.

'What do you mean?' he demands, looking confused.

'I *mean* that everything has been thrown everywhere, it's in an absolute state and it needs tidying up,' Aaron replies. He obviously still thinks that Jacob trashed his room himself in a fit of pique, but while I know Jacob does have a temper, I just don't think he'd go that far. Lucas, on the other hand, has been furious with Jacob lately. Maybe even angry enough to do something like this.

Part of me hopes it was Lucas. The thought that someone else could have come into our home to terrify my son, right under Aaron's nose, is too unbearable.

Clearly alarmed, Jacob jumps up, runs out of the lounge then hurtles up the stairs two at a time.

It's obvious he knows nothing about it.

'Let me handle this. You've said enough,' I warn Aaron, and I follow my son up to his room. When I get there, I find him sitting on the bed amid the chaos, his head in his hands.

'Have you any idea who did this, darling?' I ask him. 'Was it Lucas?'

'It's nothing, leave it,' he says.

'Jacob, if someone else has sneaked into our house and done

this to your room, we need to know. We need to report this to the police.'

'Look, Mum, fine, I admit it. It was me. I was looking for something this morning in a rush. Sorry, I didn't mean to make such a mess, I just got frustrated and lost my cool. I didn't realise it was so bad until coming back and seeing it now. I'll tidy it up.'

I know he's lying. This doesn't make sense, how could he forget leaving his room in such a state? I stand in the doorway staring at him, wishing he would tell me what's wrong.

'Mum, please just go out. Leave me to tidy up. I'll sort this.'

I step back into the hall slowly and Jacob closes the door behind me.

I walk down the stairs heavily, feeling dazed as I go back into the lounge. There's something so strange about all of this. Aaron is still sitting by Chloe, who's now fallen asleep, and looks questioningly at me.

'Jacob said he did it when he was looking for something, he hadn't realised he'd made such a mess. I don't believe him though, he looked so shocked, Aaron. Anyone could see he had nothing to do with it.'

Aaron shakes his head and shrugs at me in response, clearly holding back a retort.

When Lucas comes home for lunch, he denies all knowledge and dashes up the stairs to talk to Jacob. Like Jacob, he seems to be completely taken aback. Could he really be that good an actor?

'I don't think either of the boys trashed Jacob's room,' I tell Aaron. 'I'm sure someone has sneaked in and done this to scare them. I think we should tell the police.'

'And say what? Jacob's room is in a mess, but nothing's been taken, and he said he did it himself?' Aaron shakes his head again. 'I can't understand why you don't believe him.'

I know Jacob didn't do it. And a terrifying idea is forming in my head as I recall the vile online comments, with people vowing to make Jacob and Lucas pay. Maybe it wasn't the person bullying Rachel but someone out to avenge her. Were they hoping to find one of the boys in? If they had, what would they have done to them?

I shiver, my skin prickling at the horrible realisation that Jacob and Lucas are in even more danger than I thought.

Chloe, too.

I must do whatever it takes to keep my children safe.

42

FIVE DAYS AFTER THE FALL

I hardly sleep all night, as I'm so worried about the intruder coming back, even though I got Aaron to double-check that all the windows and doors were locked. 'I don't feel safe in my own bed,' I told him and he hugged me tight, reassuring me that I had nothing to be scared of, that nobody had come into our home.

I wish I could be as sure of that as he is. When I finally drift off to sleep, I have nightmares of me and Jacob running for our lives. Someone is chasing us, and we're terrified. They're dressed in black and wearing a balaclava so we can't see who they are. We run as fast as we can, our breath coming out in ragged gasps, but we can't get away from them. Then they catch up with us and grab my arm. I scream, trying to shake my arm free but I can't. I can't get away. 'Run!' I scream at Jacob as he turns back to help me. 'Run! Save yourself!'

'Ness! Ness!'

I'm vaguely aware that Aaron is calling and relief swamps over me. He's come to help us, thank goodness.

'Ness! Wake up! You're dreaming!'

I open my eyes and realise that it's Aaron holding my arm

and that I'm in bed. A sliver of light has found its way through a gap in the curtains and is shining on the wall opposite. I blink, still shaking, and try to get myself together. The dream was so vivid.

'Are you okay? It sounded like you were having a nightmare. You were screaming and lashing out.' He puts his arm gently around my shoulder. 'It's all getting to you, isn't it, darling?'

I sink into the comforting warmth of his embrace and take a few deep breaths to steady myself. It was such a vivid dream, I haven't had one like that for a long time. 'It was horrible. I dreamt that someone was chasing me and Jacob, they were trying to kill us.'

'Oh, Ness.' He kisses me on the forehead. 'You really must try not to dwell on that thing about Jacob's room. You've been overthinking everything, it's not good for you. It's going to be okay.'

'How can you say that? Someone came into our house, Aaron, they crept past you and went up the stairs then wrecked our son's bedroom. Our home has been violated. Our children are in danger.'

'Calm down, love, I know it was a shock for you to come home and see his room like that, but you must get this into perspective. Jacob admitted he messed it up himself.'

'I just don't believe that, Aaron. He's covering for someone. They both are. And we need to find out who and why before someone gets seriously hurt. Like Rachel.'

'You're overreacting, sweetheart.'

'Stop it!' I push him away angrily and sit up and hug my knees. How dare he keep fobbing this off as me overreacting? 'You saw Jacob's reaction! You saw the alarm on Lucas's face too and how they both huddled together afterwards, whispering. You know that they're hiding something. Admit it!' I glare at him.

He rubs his chin. 'I agree that they might be keeping a

secret from us, Ness, but I was at home yesterday and I would have heard if someone had come in to cause deliberate destruction – there would have been a lot of noise, things thrown about. I think Jacob is telling the truth, he was looking for something then got frustrated and started pulling out the drawers etc, not realising the total mess he'd made. You're anxious because of Rachel and those online comments, and I understand...'

'Please don't patronise me,' I say sharply, throwing the thin summer duvet back and getting out of bed. Aaron has a habit of playing down any worries or concerns I have, and it makes me mad. I know I'm an anxious person, living with someone like Ricky makes you that way. When you've been through what I have, the anxiety and fear stay with you, they're constant companions. I'm not imagining the look of panic on Jacob's face when he saw the state his bedroom was in though. He was scared. So was Lucas. And Aaron knows it.

I glance at the clock on my bedside cabinet, it's five-thirty. 'I'm going to check on Chloe,' I tell him, taking my lilac dressing gown off the chair, putting it on and going to Chloe's room. She hasn't been sick all night so I'm hoping she's a lot better today.

She's still asleep, her head on the pillow, blonde curls spread around her. She looks so sweet and innocent. A fierce need to protect her, protect all my family, consumes me. I must keep my wits about me, keep them all safe. I leave Chloe to sleep and go downstairs to make a coffee. I don't take one up to Aaron, as I usually would, but sit at the kitchen table, clutching the steaming mug, deep in thought. How can I protect Jacob and Lucas if they still won't open up to me?

Chloe is feeling fine when she wakes so I decide to take her clothes shopping, she's growing so fast and she could do with a few more summer outfits.

I keep my eyes focused in front of me, holding Chloe's hand

tight as we walk around the shops. I feel alert and on edge, hyper-conscious of everyone around me.

Chloe is happy to be out and it does me good too, I start to relax. We have a lovely time at the shops, it feels a bit like life is normal again. I buy Chloe a couple of dresses and a tee shirt for each of the boys, and I pick up the book that Aaron has been wanting to read. I'm hoping that giving them all a present will unite us again.

Hazel is working in town today so we meet for lunch and take Chloe to McDonald's for a Happy Meal. I can't face any food myself, my stomach is in knots, so I settle for a coffee. Hazel has a portion of fries and Chloe chooses chicken nuggets and a strawberry milkshake, her favourite. She tears opens the box and searches for the free toy first, smiling in delight when she sees that it's a character from the latest Disney film – and luckily it's one that she hasn't already got. She hands it to me to unwrap so I rip off the plastic then hand it her back.

'Well, she's recovered quickly, look how she's tucking into that,' Hazel says with a smile. She looks at me, her eyes full of concern. 'Are you okay? Has something else happened?'

I nod, wrapping my hands around my coffee as I tell her about Jacob's trashed room.

'I'm scared – make that terrified – Haze. I think the boys are in serious danger. Maybe we all are. But Aaron refuses to take it seriously.'

Hazel dabs her fries into a pool of tomato sauce and takes a bite, her eyes thoughtful and full of concern. 'Aaron is always laid back, that's his nature, and you're always anxious, which is understandable.' She levels her gaze at me. 'I don't know what to think about this, but you should trust your gut, Ness. And if anything else happens, tell the police.'

We chat for a little longer and I feel much better after talking to Hazel. At least she doesn't dismiss my fears like Aaron.

After lunch I do a bit more shopping then head off home, Chloe drifting off to sleep in the car.

I'm a couple of streets away when I spot Jacob and Lucas walking along the street, talking together, hands in the pockets of their grey sweatshirts, their hoods pulled up.

My heart lifts, it's great to see them talking again. Thank goodness. I was so worried after their latest fight. I didn't see how we could get past it, but the incident in Jacob's bedroom seems to have brought them back together.

I toot my horn as I drive past and they swivel around, then wave when they recognise me.

It's not Jacob and Lucas after all. It's *Aaron* and Lucas.

I can't believe how similar they look from behind. Similar height, similar build.

It would be difficult for anyone to tell them apart from the back, if their hair was covered up like now.

43

SIX DAYS AFTER THE FALL

'Fancy a trip to the garden centre?' Aaron asks the next morning after breakfast. 'We could get a couple more pots to liven the garden up a bit?'

It would be good to get out, but I'm worried about leaving Jacob and Lucas here alone and I know they won't want to come with us. 'What about the boys? What if anyone gets in again?'

'Nobody got in before, Ness, but I understand that you're scared. We'll only be an hour or so and I'll double-check all the doors and windows and tell the boys not to answer the door to anyone,' Aaron promises. 'And we're only a few minutes' drive away, we can be back here in no time.'

I nod. 'Okay. Give me a few ticks to get Chloe ready.'

Chloe's excited to be going to the garden centre, it's one of her favourite things to do. She loves looking at all the statues and plants, then having a snack in the café afterwards. The boys are still in bed, so we write a note on the memo board to let them know where we've gone. A sort of truce seems to be restored between them now: they aren't exactly friends but they're leaving each other alone.

We have a lovely morning together, so much so that I forget my fears for a while, or at least I can bury them deep inside me. We get some big pots and a selection of colourful plants to put in them. Then we go to the café for a drink and snack. Aaron reaches for my hand as we sit down, giving it a squeeze, and I turn to smile at him.

Aaron goes to put the plants in the car while Chloe and I finish our drinks. It's been a perfect, relaxing morning, just what I needed. I can feel the tension leaving me as I lean over and wipe a bit of chocolate from Chloe's face.

'Hello, Ness, how are you? Don't tell me this is your little girl?'

I look up. It's Diana and Sven, they used to live over the road a few years ago then moved away. I wouldn't call us friends, although we always stopped for a chat when we saw each other. Diana's bleached blonde hair is cut short now, it suits her, while Sven is balding on the top.

'Hi, yes, this is Chloe. How lovely to see you both, have you moved back to this area?'

'No, we're still over on the other estate, we're managing the post office there.'

'That's great...'

'All done...' Aaron is back and looking at Diana and Sven curiously.

'Diana, this is Aaron, my partner and Chloe's father,' I say. 'Aaron, this is Diana and Sven. They used to live over the road.'

Then I notice that Diana is staring at Aaron as if she knows him from somewhere and Aaron is looking a bit uncomfortable.

'Pleased to meet you both,' he says briefly. He turns away and picks Chloe up. 'Come on, petal, let's get you home.'

'Maybe see you around, Ness,' Diana says as I get to my feet.

'Yes, we must catch up again.' I wave and follow Aaron out.

As I get to the door I look over my shoulder and see Diana staring after us, a frown on her face.

44

When we get home we take the new plants into the garden, placing them down by the wall until we decide where to put them. The back door opens and Jacob comes out, a bowl of cereal in his hand. He looks like he's just got up even though it's gone one now. I don't remark on this and neither does Aaron, who normally would have said something pointed and sarcastic like 'Good afternoon'. I reckon that, like me, he wants a bit of peace and is willing to let little things go.

Jacob scans the array of plants. 'You're going to be busy sorting all those out,' he comments then goes back inside.

Aaron brings in the last two pots from the boot of the car and we begin to discuss where we want them to go, while Chloe trots inside.

'I'm going to get a cold drink, want one?' I ask Aaron a few minutes later. The sun has come out in full force now and I'm baking.

'A beer would be great.'

I go inside and open the fridge, and I'm about to take out a can of beer when I hear Chloe scream from the lounge.

'Chloe?' I race in and stop in my tracks as I see my little daughter lying on the floor sobbing.

Jacob and Lucas are kneeling down beside her. They look up at me when I come in and I can see guilt written across both their faces.

'What's happened?' I ask, running over to Chloe. 'It's okay, darling, Mummy's here.' I pull her into my arms, glaring over her at the boys. 'What happened?' I repeat.

They exchange a quick look, as if they're agreeing what to say. Jacob finally answers. 'It was an accident,' he mumbles.

'Jakey and Lukey were fighting,' Chloe sobs.

I can see a red mark on her forehead.

'How did she get hurt?' I demand.

'She fell off the sofa,' Lucas says. 'Didn't she, Jacob?'

Jacob nods. 'You're okay, aren't you, Chloe? It was only a little fall.'

Chloe nods and clutches on to me, her eyes wide, tears brimming in them.

'*How* did she fall off the sofa?' I ask. She's three years old. She's old enough to sit on the sofa and watch TV without falling.

'It was his fault,' Jacob declares, pointing at Lucas. 'He pushed me and I fell into Chloe and she fell off.'

'Is this true?' I ask Lucas.

'It was an accident. I didn't know Chloe was there. Jacob pushed me first so I pushed him back. I'm really sorry.' Lucas bends down. 'Sorry, Chloe,' he says, holding out his hands, but Chloe shakes her head and snuggles into me.

I look at the coffee table just a short distance from the sofa and shudder as I think what could have happened if Chloe had fallen into that, bumped her head on the corner. She could have damaged an eye. Or been knocked out.

Like Rachel. The words flash across my mind.

Is that what happened to Rachel? I thought Lucas was still out at the Fayre, but had he come home early and were both boys in her bedroom for some reason, arguing over her? Did one of them knock into her, causing her to fall? Maybe they were so scared that they ran out, but Ben only caught sight of one of them?

I shake this terrible thought from my mind and quickly check Chloe over to make sure she has no other damage. Luckily there's only the lump on her forehead although it's a nasty one and is going to leave a bruise.

'I'm sick of you two fighting. Chloe could have been badly hurt!' I say to the boys, my voice raised in anger. 'Jacob, go and wrap a packet of frozen peas in a tea towel quickly, and bring it to me!'

Jacob runs into the kitchen, returning a minute later with the towel-wrapped peas. He passes it to me and I put it straight onto the lump on Chloe's forehead, holding her tightly, while Jacob and Lucas watch me looking worried and ashamed of themselves.

Then I realise that I'm going to have to explain this bruise to the nursery when Chloe goes back on Tuesday. They have to note any cuts and bruises in their 'Incidents' book. What do I say? That our sons were fighting and knocked her over?

What if the nursery think that Chloe is at risk?

What if Chloe *is* at risk? I've been worried about her safety because I still can't shake the idea it was an intruder who trashed Jacob's room.

What if the danger is from inside my own home, my own family?

45

Aaron is furious when he comes in and sees Chloe's bruise. 'What the hell were you two thinking of, fighting around Chloe?' He doesn't shout but his voice is laced with anger. 'You need to stop all this arguing. Haven't you learnt anything from what happened to Rachel? You're both suspects because you fought over her.'

'That was him, not me,' Jacob says, surly. 'He started it this time too.'

'You're the one who knocked Chloe off the sofa. You really need to control that temper of yours, Jacob.'

'Now just hang on a minute,' I cut in. 'Lucas started this argument – and the argument with Rachel, for that matter. He was jealous because she was favouring Jacob,' I point out.

Aaron flicks a despairing look at me. 'You really need to stop being so defensive, Ness. Chloe could have been badly hurt, and Jacob was the one who knocked her off the sofa.'

'Because Lucas pushed me!' Jacob shouted. 'You always stick up for him. You promised to treat us both the same, but you don't.'

'It's not a case of favouritism, Jacob. You need to control your anger. One day it's going to get you into real trouble.'

'You're not my dad, you can't tell me off.' Jacob scowls. 'I hate you! And I hate Lucas! I wish you'd never moved in with us.'

'I wish we hadn't either! I'm sick of living here with you. I wish we still had our own home!' Lucas yells.

Aaron looks horrified. 'Lucas! Apologise for that at once.'

Lucas glares at him defiantly. 'No, I won't! It's true and you know it is. All we ever do is argue. Rachel wouldn't be in hospital if it wasn't for him.' He jabs his finger at Jacob.

Jacob's face goes scarlet with fury. 'You take that back now!' He lunges at Lucas and suddenly they're both on the floor wrestling.

'Stop it!' Chloe sobs.

Aaron quickly pulls Jacob off Lucas, for the second time in less than a week.

'I will not tolerate this kind of behaviour. Do you understand?' His voice is simmering with anger.

'Try correcting your precious son then because I'm sick of his snide remarks,' Jacob snarls.

'Shut your mouth!' Lucas's hands are clenched by his side.

Chloe bursts into tears. 'Stop shouting!' she cries and puts her hands over her ears.

Jacob storms out.

'I think you'd better explain what you mean by blaming Jacob for Rachel falling, Lucas,' I say angrily.

'Forget it!' he shouts and goes out, slamming the lounge door behind him.

'You need to talk to him, it's not right for him to keep accusing Jacob like this,' I say to Aaron.

'Fine, I will, but it's best to leave them both to calm down now. Lucas was only sticking up for himself,' he says, looking exhausted as he presses a hand to his temple. Then he goes back out into the garden.

I wrap my arms around Chloe and hold her tight, once again upset at how Aaron favours Lucas. The happy atmosphere we'd just recaptured has vanished and we are at each other's throats all over again.

And I'm starting to wonder if Jacob is right. Did I make a mistake asking Aaron and Lucas to move in with us?

How much longer can we tolerate this divide before it tears us irreparably apart?

46

A WEEK AFTER THE FALL

The bump on Chloe's head has gone down a bit when she wakes up in the morning, although she still has an angry bruise, and I feel so guilty about it. It's not fair that she's suffered so much because of our family's tension, from the shouting to now getting caught up in a physical fight. She's so small and so innocent, I should be protecting her from all of this. I cuddle her close and let her have breakfast curled up to me on the sofa, watching a cartoon while I stroke her hair. Aaron has gone into work today, thank goodness. I really don't want him around me; we haven't made up after yesterday. Jacob and Lucas are still in bed, and I leave them there, glad for a little bit of peace.

'Mummy's working in the study today, want to come with me?' I ask Chloe.

She nods eagerly. She isn't normally allowed in the study, but I've got a little behind with everything that's been going on, and although I try not to work when Chloe isn't at nursery, I don't have a choice today and I will find it easier to focus sitting at the desk than on my laptop in the kitchen. I also know the boys will be down at some point and frankly I want to shut myself away, block out all the arguments and stress, just like Aaron does when he retreats into there.

'What do you want to play with?' I ask Chloe.

She points to her doll's house, just as I expected. It's her favourite toy lately. I take it into the room and put it on the carpeted floor between the two desks, and she immediately sits down and starts playing with it happily, her little pink legging-clad legs sticking out in front of her. I leave the door open so I can hear her while I go into the kitchen to brew some coffee and get Chloe a drink and some biscuits. Then I carry them in on a tray and set my laptop up on the big table along the wall. Aaron always works on his desktop computer but I like the convenience of being able to work on my laptop in different rooms of the house. When Chloe was a baby I used to sit on the bed, my work spread out around me, and work as she slept.

I place the tray on the floor beside her. 'Here you are, darling. Can you keep playing nicely for a little while, please, while Mummy works?'

She nods, already engrossed in her game, and I fire up my laptop and open up the manuscript I'm editing.

Chloe is absorbed in her own little world, chatting away to the dolls, and I manage to get the final touches of the edit done and sent over to my client with my notes. Only one more to do. I hope the boys don't get up – or at least come downstairs – before then. I need some peace and quiet and Chloe is being so good. I look over at her and frown when I see that she's trying to put a necklace over her head.

Where did she get that from?

As if sensing me watching her, she looks over at me. 'Help me, Mummy.'

I get up and walk over to her, crouching down for a better look at the necklace. It's a big sunflower on a chain and I recognise it straight away as Rachel's. She loves sunflowers. She wore this necklace a lot, and a tee shirt with a sunflower on it. Suzy said Rachel has a bedspread and matching curtains with sunflowers all over them, and I remember thinking how apt that was, as Rachel was always so bright and happy, just like a sunflower. The memory makes me suddenly very sad. That poor girl is now lying in a hospital bed, and no one knows if she will ever wake up and see the sunflowers again.

'Let me see.'

I take the necklace from Chloe and see that the chain is broken, almost as if it's been yanked off. 'Where was this, Chloe?' I ask her, puzzled as to how it got here. Rachel hasn't been around for ages now, so if the necklace had broken one of the times she popped into the study to ask Aaron a question surely she would have noticed it had gone and asked us if we'd seen it? And why didn't I find it when I had a good tidy up and vacuum in here just over a week ago?

'Under Daddy's desk,' Chloe says. 'Put it on me, Mummy.'

'It's broken, darling,' I tell Chloe.

She puckers her mouth as if she's going to cry.

'Let me finish my work then I'll get one of Mummy's necklaces you can wear.' I've got a dolphin on a cord Jacob bought me a few years ago. That's safe for Chloe to wear.

'Kay,' she says, and goes back to playing with her doll's house. She's such a good girl.

I put the sunflower necklace in my pocket, resolving to talk to the boys about it later. Then I sit back down and start work again, and I'm soon caught up in the story I'm now editing. It's a good one, about a family living in Ireland. There's lots of tension and drama sprinkled with humour. I enjoy editing it, adding a few suggestions where the text could be cut a bit or where a character could be fleshed out more. I hope the writer takes my suggestions on board because I honestly think with a bit of work this story could be a bestseller.

I glance down at Chloe after a while and see that she is fast asleep, curled up on the floor. She looks so sweet, her head on the cushion from Aaron's chair, one of the playhouse dolls in her hand.

I move my eyes to the clock on the wall. Goodness, it's almost noon and there hasn't been a sign of either of the boys. I've been so caught up in my work I hadn't noticed the time. I love it when that happens, when I get totally lost in a story I'm editing. And Chloe has played so nicely.

I wonder whether to pick her up, take her into the lounge and lay her on the sofa then decide to leave her where she is. She looks so cosy and peaceful, I don't want to wake her up.

I start to put her toys away when I notice that except for the one in her hands, the doll's house family is missing. I glance around and smile when I spot them all lined up in a row on Aaron's desk, imagining her walking them up the drawers, as if they were mountain climbing. I'd better clear them before Aaron comes home.

Aaron's diary is open on his desk, and I glance at it, wondering what days he's working at home this week. Then I notice that he'd marked last Monday as a day off.

Monday, the day Rachel fell.

Aaron had been at work all day, or so he said.

Where was he if he wasn't at work? And why didn't he tell me that he had a day off?

My mind drifts to Rachel's necklace.

Did she come to see Aaron while I was at the park with Chloe?

47

I sink back down on the chair, my thoughts overwhelming me and my legs feeling weak.

Aaron and Rachel?

I shake my head.

Surely not. She's fourteen for pity's sake! How can I even think that Aaron would...

Thoughts I desperately don't want to have flood through my mind. Aaron has been distant for a while now, preoccupied. He said he was dealing with some blips in the new video game he's working on. I know that just like me, he goes off into a world of his own when he's working on a new project, so I didn't take much notice. Why would he say he was at work when he wasn't? He even told the police that he'd been in work all day.

And he's been going jogging a lot more recently. For longer than usual, too.

I feel sick at what this necklace and Aaron's diary imply, what anyone would think if they knew about them. It's too horrible to even contemplate. There must be another explanation.

Maybe he wasn't meant to go into the office when he wrote

the diary entry, then something came up? If there were issues with the software, he might have had to go in to sort them out? It's plausible. As for going jogging more, well, the atmosphere in the house has been strained so maybe that's just been his way of dealing with it.

What about the necklace...

Leaving the door open so I can keep an eye on Chloe, I go into the kitchen and put the kettle on, my mind spinning. Then, as I look out of the window, I see Carl walking down the path.

I'm so desperate for news of Rachel that I run outside before I even realise what I'm doing.

'Carl!' I shout as I make my way over to the dividing fence.

He ignores me and carries on walking up the garden to the shed.

'Carl!'

He stops and slowly turns to me. He looks totally drained, dark bags under his eyes. I can almost feel his despair.

'How's Rachel?' I ask.

He glares at me, his face like thunder. 'How do you think she is, after being pushed out of the window by one of your bloody lads?'

The angry words are like arrows piercing my skin. 'I'm so sorry, Carl, but it wasn't Lucas and Jacob. They wouldn't—'

He jabs a finger at me. 'Really? I wouldn't put it past them. Rachel was happy until we moved here. Your boys turned her into a shell of herself. Fighting over her all the time, making her miserable. They wouldn't leave her alone.'

'They were friends, they helped her settle into her new school...' I protest.

'Leave us alone, Vanessa. We want nothing to do with you. We wish we'd never moved here. We're moving away as soon as we can. Your family is poison!'

I flinch as if he physically smacked me across the face,

watching wordlessly as Carl turns around and carries on walking to the shed.

I go back inside and check on Chloe again, she's still asleep. Sinking down into the chair, I sit there shaking as the thoughts I've been fighting off finally take over.

Was something going on with Aaron and Rachel?

I know it's sick, evil, but I must face facts.

The truth is Rachel often sought Aaron out, asking him questions about his work. And he always made time for her. I see an image of them both, relaxed, talking, Rachel laughing and pushing a strand of hair behind her ears, Aaron leaning against the doorway.

Aaron could have been in Rachel's room that morning. Maybe she threatened to tell someone what was going on. As for Ben seeing a lad run down the stairs – I remember how I mistook Aaron for Jacob just the other day. Ben could easily have done the same. Aaron has a black hoodie, it could have been him running down the stairs.

I feel like I've been stabbed in the heart. I'm shaking, I don't know what to do. I can't believe that Aaron could be so evil. What other explanation is there though?

I must talk to him about this, demand answers right away. And if those answers don't add up, I have no choice. I need to go to the police and tell them my suspicions. It's awful, unbearable, but I must.

Then the thought sneaks into my mind that by confronting him, I might be putting myself in danger. I never thought Aaron would harm me – even after everything I've been through, I have always felt safe with him.

I hope I'm wrong. Because if Aaron is capable of this, then he is capable of anything.

48

Rachel

I keep drifting in and out of the fog. Sometimes I can hear voices. Mum's and Dad's I pick out easily, but there are others too.

How long have I been here? I can't move, can't open my eyes, can't do anything. Am I paralysed? What sort of life will I have if I can't walk? Or talk?

Perhaps I'll die. I'd rather die than be like this.

I can hear Mum crying and I feel guilty at the upset I've caused.

*Does Mum know about **him** yet? Does she know what happened?*

Maybe I should give up. Let the fog take over.

Then I hear another voice. It's Ben. He's come back to see me.

He must be so distraught.

I love my little brother. I love my family. I want to go back to them, to have my life back.

*I'm not going to let **him** destroy me.*

I try again to open my eyes but I can't, so I focus on my hands, imagine myself moving my fingers.

Did I do it?

'Mum! Mum! Rachel moved her fingers!' Ben is shouting.

I did it, I'm coming back. But I'm absolutely petrified.

Dare I tell the truth even though it will rip my family apart? And put me in even more danger?

49

Aaron

'We need to talk,' Vanessa says as soon as Chloe is in bed. I can see by the look on her face that she's annoyed about something. I'm guessing that Jacob and Lucas have been arguing again, and probably it's all Jacob's fault although Ness won't see it that way. I'm sick of the continual tension sparking in the house. I really tried to restore peace this weekend and for a while I managed it but that boy is impossible. He's got such a short fuse.

From what Vanessa has said about her ex, I'm worried that Jacob's got the same temperament as his father. I realise that Lucas hit back but Vanessa can't seriously expect him to stand there and take it. And Chloe got hurt too. I'm furious over that. Jacob needs to calm it down. We all had a bit of peace when Jacob stormed out yesterday afternoon and stayed out until late. Vanessa was stressing and phoning him but he wouldn't pick up. When he did come home, he went straight up to his room.

There's still four weeks of the school holidays left and, honestly, I'm dreading it.

'At least let me pour us both a glass of wine,' I tell her, hoping it might help us unwind a little.

We both turn as the doorbell rings. *What now?*

'I'll go.' I stride down the hall and open the front door. Those two detectives from before are standing on the doorstep.

'Evening, Mr Paige. We'd like to ask you a few more questions,' DC Millet says.

I could really do without this right now. More questioning. I wonder, with a sickening feeling in my stomach, if Rachel has come around and told the detectives what happened. I open the door wider. 'You'd better come in then,' I say grimly.

Vanessa comes out of the kitchen and her eyes shoot from me to the police. 'Have there been any developments?' she asks apprehensively.

'We're still conducting our investigations and need to question Mr Paige about a couple of things,' DS Byron replies. 'It won't take long.'

'Let's go into the lounge,' Vanessa says, leading the way.

I can see that she's curious about why they want to talk to me. Great. I'd prefer to do this without her, but if I ask her to leave, it will make it look as if I've got something to hide. So I paste a polite smile on my face and follow the officers in.

'Do take a seat,' Ness says, so the detectives sit on the sofa, as if this is just a casual visit.

'What can I do for you, Detectives?' I ask pleasantly.

DC Millet looks from me to Vanessa. 'You might prefer us to question you alone. It's a bit delicate.'

Panic flutters in my stomach like moths around a flame. *Yes,* I want to reply. Whatever they're going to ask me, I don't want Vanessa to hear it. I need her on my side, though, and sending her out of the room will only rouse her suspicions.

'I prefer to stay, unless Aaron wants me to leave?' There is something in the way Vanessa looks at me that makes the moths in my stomach flutter their wings even faster.

'No, I've got nothing to hide.' I'm amazed that my voice comes out so firm and strong.

'We saw that some WhatsApp messages have been deleted on Rachel's phone, so we did a check and discovered that it is your number,' DC Millet says.

Vanessa gasps audibly.

I nod, trying to act casual. 'Yes, she was working on a project for school and messaged me for information a couple of times. I'm a video games developer.'

'So a young teenage girl asked you for your phone number and you gave it to her?' This is from DS Byron. 'Do you think that was appropriate?'

I can feel Vanessa's eyes boring into me. I shake my head. 'It didn't happen like that. Lucas, my son, gave Rachel my number. He thought I could help her with her project, as she's taking a GCSE in computing. I didn't mind, I know how important their coursework is.'

'And you didn't mention to your wife that this young girl messaged you?' she adds.

I glance at Vanessa, whose eyes are narrowed as she stares at me. I wish I could read her thoughts. 'Sorry, Ness, it didn't seem important. It was only a couple of questions.'

'And did Rachel ever come to see you to,' the DS pauses and I can hear the unspoken quote marks, 'to talk about her project?'

I've been a fool. I shouldn't have let this happen, not again.

'She came to see Lucas but he was out. Then she got talking about her project and naturally I answered her questions.'

'And were you in the house alone with her?'

I daren't look at Ness.

How do I answer this without incriminating myself? 'Well, yes, I was working from home and everyone else was out. But she was only here for a few minutes.' I look the detective straight in the eye. 'I don't like what you're insinuating here. Would you please tell me what this is all about?'

'We've spoken to Rachel's friend Amy again, and she has given us some very interesting and important information.' The detective pauses, his gaze inscrutable. 'She informed us that Rachel was involved with someone older who was pressuring her to have a relationship with them. Apparently last time she spoke to Rachel, Rachel was very upset. She said that she couldn't cope with the pressure any longer.'

'Just what the hell are you accusing me of?' I demand.

'We're exploring all options,' the detective says calmly. 'We found a couple of entries in Rachel's diary mentioning someone she referred to as A. Someone she was obviously involved with. So, it's interesting that your phone number is under the initial A in her contacts. And that she deleted some messages between you both.'

I draw in a deep breath before I reply, keeping my voice steady. 'I was not involved with Rachel. I can assure you that my dealings with her were completely proper. She is our neighbour and a friend of our sons, so yes, if she asked me for help with her homework, I obliged. What's wrong with that?'

DC Millet looks at me steadily. 'Nothing at all. As long as that's all you did, Mr Paige.'

'If it's all totally innocent maybe you could show us the WhatsApp messages between you and Rachel, so we can see what's been deleted?' DS Byron asks.

'I'm sorry but my WhatsApp messages are set up to disappear after seven days, so that my phone memory doesn't get clogged up.' I can hear how suspicious this sounds and the two detectives exchange a knowing look. I stifle down the panic that is threatening to overwhelm me, continuing to avoid Ness's gaze.

It's all happening again.

50

Vanessa

'Why didn't you tell me about Rachel?' I demand as soon as the police leave. My voice is brimming over with fury and strain.

'Because there's nothing to tell. She asked me a few questions and I answered them. Like any normal adult would have done.'

'Okay. But it's the fact that you didn't mention it that bothers me.'

I can't get my head round it. Rachel had Aaron's phone number. She had been texting him. She had come round to see him when nobody else was in, and he hadn't mentioned it. He had pretended he was working when he wasn't. And then there's the necklace.

I take a deep breath. 'Aaron, I found Rachel's sunflower necklace in the study today. The chain was broken...' I can feel anger rising in me, hot tears threatening to spill from my eyes. I swallow and look at him squarely. 'And according to your diary, you weren't working on Monday. So that means you told me, and the police, a lie. What exactly are you covering up?'

Aaron's eyes darken and he clenches his jaw. 'How dare you? What the hell are you suggesting, Ness?'

I lick my lips. What am I suggesting? Do I really suspect Aaron of something so terrible, so unspeakable? Rachel is only fourteen.

'I wasn't expecting to go into work, but I was called in at the last minute,' Aaron says evenly. 'As for the necklace, you know the boys are always going into the study to borrow things, even though they're not supposed to. Has it occurred to you that Rachel might have gone in with one of them, that the necklace could have broken without her noticing it and rolled under my desk? Or even that it fell off when I was showing her something on the computer? It could have been lying there for ages.'

He looks distraught, and guilt stabs through me. I guess I could have missed the necklace when I was cleaning up. And it is perfectly feasible that Aaron's work plans changed after he wrote in his diary.

'What about the text messages from Rachel? And her coming around to speak to you alone?'

'I've explained all this!' He runs his hands over his hair and starts to pace around the lounge. 'I can't believe you think this of me, Ness! That you honestly believe I could do such a disgusting thing. Do you think I pushed Rachel out of the window too?'

He turns around and looks at me then, his face one of utter despair.

Do I? Do I really think that of Aaron?

'Of course not! It's just... Look, I don't know what I think. It would have helped if you'd kept me in the loop.'

'So I have to report to you every time I talk to a neighbour's daughter, or one of our sons' friends?' He sinks down onto the sofa, defeated. 'What chance do I get to talk to you about anything, anyway? You're always busy with your editing, and with Chloe.'

'What! You're actually criticising me for working to bring in extra income and for looking after our daughter?' I'm incredulous. 'How about me? I hardly have time to talk to you because you're working all day and sometimes half the evening! Or you're out *jogging*.'

'No shouting!' Chloe calls from the top of the stairs. We must have woken her up.

I start to go to her but Aaron is up the stairs before me, scooping Chloe into his arms and hugging her. 'Sorry, petal, Mummy and I didn't mean to shout. We were just talking loudly.' He kisses her on her cheek and gently smooths her hair as I reach the top step.

I feel guilty as our little girl snuggles into his shoulder. She's right, everyone does keep shouting. Ever since Rachel fell – no, before that, when Jacob and Lucas started vying for her attention. Our family has been falling apart since the new neighbours moved in. And Aaron and I are arguing because a teenage girl asked his advice over a project, something I was aware of, if even I didn't know that she had his phone number and was messaging him. 'I'm sorry, Aaron,' I say. 'It was the way the police were questioning you. If I'd have known, I wouldn't have been so shocked.'

He's still angry, I can tell, but he nods. 'It's okay. We're all on edge. Hopefully Rachel will come around soon and then all this mess can be cleared up and we can go back to a normal life.'

He holds out his free arm and I slip into his embrace, a group hug with Chloe. Chloe chuckles. She loves it when we all hug together. My sweet little girl wants everyone to be happy, but the carefree, loving household we all once had seems eons away.

I pray that Rachel comes out of the coma soon so she can tell everyone what happened. Although part of me can't shake the thought that Rachel might say something I desperately don't want to hear.

51

Rachel

'She's coming round!'

My mum's voice seems to be floating in the air. I want to open my eyes and look at her, but I'm scared. While I'm lying here, not talking to anyone, it's more likely nobody will hurt me, and I want to stay hidden inside my body forever. I don't want to answer their questions. And most of all I don't want to know how badly injured I am. What if I can't walk or live a normal life again? I wish I could go back in time and make a different choice. What had I been thinking?

I can feel Mum squeezing my hand. 'Rachel, darling, can you hear me?' she says. 'Squeeze my hand back if you can.'

I can hear the tremor in her voice. I want to squeeze her hand, I don't want to cause her all this upset. She must be so worried. I don't know how long I've been lying here, how long they've been waiting and praying I will be okay. I can't put them through it any longer. So I slowly open my eyes and there's Mum, looking down at me with red-rimmed eyes, her long dark hair scraped into a ponytail, her face washed out, completely makeup-free. Mum and Nan wear makeup just to go to the corner shop, I'm not used to seeing her like this. She looks older, weary. Her eyes light up as I gaze at her.

'Oh, darling, you've been in a coma for a week. We thought we'd lost you.'

A week! I can't believe that I've been lying here that long.

'Carl!' Mum is saying now. 'She's awake! She's awake!'

I didn't know Dad was here.

I don't want to see him.

Dad kneels down beside me and holds my other hand. 'Rachel, darling, you're okay. Can you remember what happened? Who did this to you?'

I look at his face, which seems to have aged a thousand years since I last saw him. His eyes are piercing mine, fixing them so that I can't look away. I know what I have to do. I have to stop the police investigating further.

'I fell,' I tell them. 'I fell out of my window.'

Dad nods and Mum holds my hand in hers. 'Are you sure, darling? Ben said that he saw someone in a black hoodie running down the stairs.' She swallows, her eyes misting over. 'You're not covering for anyone, are you?'

I shake my head. 'I fell,' I repeat. 'There was no one in my bedroom.'

'How did you fall, darling?' Mum asks softly. 'Were you sitting on the ledge?'

'Yes. I'm sorry, I know you kept warning me about doing that.' Talking is making me feel weak so I pause for a moment before continuing. 'It was such a nice day, I was enjoying the sunshine then I slipped.'

A doctor comes rushing in, clipboard in hand, followed by some nurses. His eyes crinkle at the corner when they rest on me. 'Rachel! You've come round, this is wonderful.' He turns to my parents. 'I need to run some tests on Rachel, it's just routine to check everything is functioning as it should be.'

Mum gets up. 'Of course. We'll go and have a coffee while you do that,' she says.

I don't think I've ever seen her look so happy, or so tired.

I'm relieved when they go out. I know the police will come soon to ask more questions but I'm sticking to my story. There's too much to lose if I don't.

52

Suzy

I'm over the moon, I feel like I'm floating, there's a lightness in me that I've never experienced before. Our precious daughter has opened her eyes and is speaking, she's herself, she's okay. It's the best news ever, I would have given anything for this to happen. I've been praying so hard for this day to come.

There's just one thing that's diluting my happiness. I'm puzzled that Rachel said she fell, and there hadn't been anyone in her room. Ben was so adamant, and so upset that he couldn't identify them.

Something isn't right.

'Do you think Rachel is lying about falling?' I ask Carl. 'I can't believe that Ben imagined it, or made it up.'

'Well, he's only a little kid, he could have said the first thing that came into his head to try and explain what happened to Rachel.' Carl leans across the table, his fingers steepled. 'I always thought it was strange that someone managed to sneak in and out when I was there. I couldn't believe that I didn't see them.'

I shake my head. 'The police found blood on the windowsill, remember?'

'Rachel probably tried to grab it to stop her fall, and scratched herself.'

'What about all those threatening texts?'

'They might sound worse than they are, you know how kids talk to each other. They're probably not even connected to the fall.' Carl pushes his coffee away. 'Don't worry about all of that now. The most important thing is that she's awake, she's talking, she's going to be okay. Let's go and see if the doctors have finished their tests, see what they have to say.'

My relief when the doctor tells us that they're expecting Rachel to make a full recovery is immense; it's like taking a breath of air after being submerged under water for minutes.

'She can move her feet and her hands, and there doesn't seem to be any spinal damage. We'll try to help her stand later, when she's stronger, but all the signs are good.'

'She should be home soon and then things can get back to normal,' Carl says when the doctor leaves, with a smile I haven't seen in a week. 'And we should phone the police, tell them that it was an accident, she slipped and fell. Then they can call off the investigation, we can get back to normal.'

'I'm not sure, Carl. What if she's only saying that because she's scared?'

'Honestly, Suzy, can't you just accept that this was an accident? Can't you be pleased that our daughter has recovered and will be coming home soon?' Carl's smile has vanished, his exasperation causing his voice to rise suddenly. That temper of his, he really does struggle with it.

'No, I can't just be pleased. Because if someone did push Rachel, then she's not safe when she comes home. They could come for her again,' I say, holding my ground.

It's not just me. The police soon arrive to question Rachel, and they tell us that they suspect she is covering for someone too, even though Carl got quite angry with them, trying to convince them to close the case. We can all see Rachel must be hiding something, so why can't Carl?

It's like he doesn't want to. He is so desperate to return to normality that he's willing to just brush it all under the carpet.

Well, I can't. I need to keep Rachel safe.

And a little nagging voice in me wonders why Carl is refusing to see reason. Why isn't he feeling more protective of Rachel, why isn't he more worried about the danger that could still be out there?

Why is he trying so hard to persuade the police to stop their investigation?

53

EIGHT DAYS AFTER THE FALL

Vanessa

Aaron has been restless all night and was up at the crack of dawn to go jogging again. I know he's still upset about our row yesterday, and the awful things I accused him of, but surely he can understand how bad it looked. If the police knew about Rachel's broken necklace and the diary entry, they'd be even more suspicious. I didn't tell them though. I believe him, that he was simply being kind to Rachel – as he always is – because she was our neighbour and a friend of our boys.

I get out of bed and creep across the landing to peep at Chloe. She's still fast asleep so I have a quick shower and get dressed before I wake her. Aaron is working at the office today and said he'd take Chloe to nursery on his way to work so that I can get on with editing. I can't believe it's only been just over a week since Rachel's fall. So much has happened since then, it feels like a lifetime ago.

'Let me know if you hear any news,' Aaron says a little later as he leaves with Chloe.

'I will,' I promise. I texted Suzy last night, saying I was

thinking of her with it being over a week since Rachel fell. She's still not been talking to me, but I'm hopeful she'll at least let me know if Rachel comes round.

The boys stay in their rooms all day, only coming down for something to eat or drink. They seem to have called a truce, thank goodness. I manage to get through all my work and am feeling more relaxed when Aaron comes home with Chloe.

I pop a couple of pizzas in the oven while he prepares a salad, and soon we sit down to eat, managing to make small talk that has nothing to do with the girl next door or the recent division in our family. Just as we've finished, the detectives call again and want to speak to Aaron and Lucas.

I show them into the kitchen while Jacob takes Chloe to the lounge. I want to hear this.

'I'm not sure why you want to talk to us again?' Aaron says as I clear the table and the two detectives sit down.

'We wanted to check your movements last Monday.' DC Millet looks at his notes. 'I understand that you were at work, Mr Paige?'

'That's right, I usually work in the office three days a week and at home two days,' he says.

I press my nails into my palms, feeling a cold shiver run through me.

Is he lying?

'And you, Lucas, you were out all day?'

Lucas nods.

'The thing is' – the detective looks from Lucas to Aaron – 'we did a door-to-door call on all your neighbours, to see if anyone saw anything, or if their CCTVs and doorbell cameras had recorded anything.'

Aaron nods. 'Yes, I know. You said that there was nothing.'

'At the time.' The policeman pauses. 'However, Mr Taylor, who lives two doors away, has since returned from his holiday, and his security camera distinctly shows you returning home at eleven-thirty last Monday morning, Mr Paige, and then you returning half an hour later, Lucas. You both went in through the front door. There is no record of either of you leaving, so I presume you both left through the back door.'

I stagger backwards, leaning against the kitchen door. They've both been lying to me.

What is going on?

Aaron looks confused for a moment then he nods. 'Of course, I forgot to mention that I left my iPad at home and had to come back for it. I was in and out.'

'The doorbell camera shows you arriving not long before Rachel fell, sir,' the detective says. 'Are you sure you didn't hear anything?'

Aaron shakes his head adamantly. 'Nothing at all. I grabbed my iPad, had a quick drink and left,' he replies. He sounds cool but I can see the panic in his eyes and am sure that the detective can too. They leave it there, though, and start questioning Lucas. I wonder why they are questioning them both in front of me. Is it to cast doubt in my mind?

'You came home just after your father. Did you see him at all?' the detective asks.

'No. I guess he must have been in the study. I came back because I forgot my money. I went up to get my wallet then left straight away.'

The two detectives exchange glances.

'And neither of you saw each other? Or realised that Jacob was home?'

'No,' Aaron and Lucas answer in unison.

Even I can see how far-fetched this seems. When Rachel fell, everyone in my family was home, except for me and Chloe. Yet none of them heard anything, apart from Jacob, who heard her scream.

Even I don't know what to believe anymore.

The detectives make a couple of notes. 'That's all for now. We may be back to question you further,' they say as they leave.

'I can't believe you two didn't mention this to the police earlier,' I say when they've gone. 'Surely you realised how important it was?'

Lucas shrugs. 'It's no big deal, we both popped home for a few minutes. We didn't see Rachel or hear anything.'

Aaron stands up. 'Please don't make this more than it is, Ness.' His voice is thick with emotion.

I want to believe that it is all true, and perfectly innocent. But why didn't Aaron say that he'd popped home that day? And that it was just before Rachel fell.

54

NINE DAYS AFTER THE FALL

The boys are still in bed when I get back from taking Chloe to nursery the next morning. I make myself a strong coffee and take it into the study, ready to try to catch up with some work, but Hazel rings just as I'm booting up my laptop.

'How's things? Any news?' she asks.

'Not yet. The waiting is killing me,' I admit. Then I can't help myself, I blurt it all out. The police questioning Aaron, Rachel's broken necklace, the diary, the text messages. Everything.

Hazel gives a low whistle. 'Wow, Ness, that's massive. Do you believe him?'

'I think so. I want to. I can't believe that he would... Rachel is only fourteen!'

'I know.'

There's a pause and I can feel that Hazel is wondering whether to tell me something. 'What is it?' I ask.

'Well, from what you've told me he's really pally with Rachel, isn't he? It sounds a bit suspicious to me.'

'Are you saying you think there might be something in it?'

'I don't know. Just keep your eyes peeled, Ness. And let me know as soon as you hear anything.'

'Okay, of course I will— oh, Haze, I've got to go, I've another call coming in. It might be the police.' I end the call quickly and take the incoming one.

I listen in relief, my heart racing, as the DC tells me Rachel has come out of the coma and insists that she accidentally fell out of the window. The boys are in the clear. So is Aaron. It was simply an accident. This is incredible. I want to whoop with joy but his next statement brings me crashing back to earth.

'However, in view of the blood on the windowsill, the threatening messages and Ben's statement that he saw someone running from the room, we'll still be continuing the investigation,' he says.

Not in the clear then.

The police suspect that Rachel is covering for someone.

Is she?

Maybe she is, but at least she's come out of the coma. She's going to be fine. No one will face a murder charge.

I'm in a whirlwind of emotions as I text Hazel to tell her the news, promising to phone her with an update later, then go upstairs to tell the boys, but when I knock on Jacob's door, there's no answer.

Maybe he's still asleep. I open the door and step inside. The bed is empty and the duvet pulled over. He must have gone out when I working in the study.

Lucas comes out of his room then, sleepy-eyed and still in his pjs.

'Have you seen Jacob?' I ask. 'The police just phoned. Rachel has come out of the coma.'

His eyes light up. 'That's amazing! How is she?'

'They're expecting her to make a full recovery.'

He grins. 'That's fantastic!' Then he frowns. 'Did she say what happened?' he asks anxiously.

I watch his face carefully as I reply. 'She said she fell.'

'Fell?' He looks taken aback. 'But Ben said he saw someone...'

I nod. 'The police are still investigating but the good news is that Rachel is alive, and has no serious damage. I'll phone Jacob and tell him.'

I take my phone out of my pocket and give him a ring, but his phone rings out. I try again.

No answer.

55

Aaron

I sit at my desk at work mulling over Vanessa's call. Rachel has regained consciousness and is expected to make a full recovery, which is incredible. And she insists she accidentally fell, which is a big relief. I wasn't expecting that.

However, Ness said that the police are still investigating the case because of Ben's statement and the threatening messages on her phone, so it seems that they don't believe her. If she sticks to her story, though, they will surely have to drop the case.

The main thing is that Rachel is okay, I remind myself. It could have all been so much worse. Hopefully peace will be restored to our household now and all this will become a distant memory. Ness is worried because the boys' names haven't been cleared yet, but all this will be forgotten in a month or two.

I don't know where all this leaves me and Ness though. That awful row the other evening, the accusations. She believes me now, I think, but the scars are still there.

. . .

Ness is preparing dinner when I get home with Chloe. She looks up and gives me a warm smile.

'I thought we'd eat a bit earlier today, it's only quiche and salad,' she says. 'Nothing heavy.'

'That's great. I'm hungry, I skipped lunch,' I tell her. 'Isn't it amazing news about Rachel? Where are the boys? How have they taken the news?'

She kneels down to greet Chloe, focusing on our daughter. 'Hello, darling. Have you had a nice day at nursery?'

Chloe nods and shows her the painting she did. Vanessa coos over it and sticks it on the fridge before turning her attention back to me and finally answering my question.

'They're both out,' she tells me. 'I've told Lucas about Rachel and he was so relieved, but he looked surprised when he heard that Rachel said she fell. I've texted Jacob but he hasn't replied yet.'

'It is fantastic news that Rachel is okay, isn't it? I've been so worried. We all have.' I pause and gaze at Ness. I can still see anxiety in her eyes.

'Ness, this is good news. Maybe now we can start building our family back together?'

'I hope so. It's what I want.'

'Me too. Let's draw a line under everything. We've all been under a lot of strain, said things we didn't mean.'

Chloe tugs on my trouser leg. 'Can I play in the garden?' she says.

I open the back door to let her outside, looking over at the gate to make sure it's locked, then go back into the kitchen and take the jug of chilled water out of the fridge, pouring myself a glass. Ness is rinsing lettuce. 'I'll go and get changed then give you a hand with dinner.'

'Thanks, but it's all in hand.'

This has all taken a terrible toll on Ness, and she's also been upset over losing Suzy's friendship, I think as I go upstairs. I wonder how things will be when Rachel gets home. It can't be how it was, that's for sure. I certainly won't encourage Rachel to pop in and out of our house again, or for the boys to go around there. It's probably best if we all stay away from each other.

When I go back downstairs Vanessa has laid the table in the kitchen: a quiche, a big bowl of salad and hummus and carrot sticks are all in the centre of the table. Five places are set. Chloe is already tucking into some carrot sticks and hummus – she loves this.

'I wish the boys would come home for their meals, this is becoming a habit,' Vanessa says as she cuts the quiche into portions.

I pick up the serving spoons and dish some salad onto my plate. 'They'll be back when they're hungry. At least this won't go cold.'

We're halfway through dinner when the back door opens and Lucas comes in. 'Have you heard anything else? When will Rachel be well enough to come home?' he asks as he washes his hands at the kitchen sink then joins us at the table.

'I don't know, love. I haven't seen any signs of anyone next door,' Ness tells him.

'I would think they'll keep her in a little while to run more tests on her,' I tell him.

'Did you see Jacob while you were out, Lucas? I'm really annoyed with him, he hasn't answered my calls all day,' Vanessa says. 'I thought he'd be so happy to hear that Rachel has recovered that he'd call me right away.'

Lucas shakes his head and starts piling food onto his plate. 'This looks good.'

'He's probably lost track of time,' I console Vanessa.

Ness tries to phone Jacob again when we've finished dinner. 'His phone just keeps ringing out. I wonder if he's left it in his bedroom,' she says.

'You must be kidding, that phone is welded to him,' I reply, clearing the plates off the table. I'm getting annoyed with Jacob now. He must have got his mum's messages, he could at least reply to her. He knows how she frets. I'm fed up with Jacob's moods, frankly, but know better than to say anything right now. Vanessa defends him like a lioness defends her cub.

'I'll go and check that he hasn't left his phone in his room.'

I glance over at Lucas as Vanessa goes out of the room. 'You sure you don't know where he is?'

'How would I? We don't hang around together,' he replies.

They used to. They used to go everywhere together. Now they barely speak to each other, and if they do, it's usually only to argue.

'Here you go, Daddy,' Chloe says, handing me a dirty spoon.

I look down at her and smile. 'Thank you, petal.'

This last week has just been a blip. We'll work it out. We have to. I don't want to lose Vanessa or, heaven forbid, Chloe.

And I could. If the police are still investigating, it will only be a matter of time before the past comes out. What will Vanessa do then?

It was years ago. It's in the past, I've moved on. We all did.

Will Ness accept that?

Vanessa

I dial Jacob's number as I open his bedroom door, but the phone rings and rings on the line. It isn't here.

He's never been great at answering the phone, but usually he at least sends me a text. This isn't like him.

What if something bad has happened? I can't get those awful online messages out of my head, along with images of Jacob being beaten up in some dark alleyway.

Then I see a folded sheet of paper resting on the pillow. *Mum* is written on the front in big blue letters. That note wasn't there this morning. As I stare at it, a worm of fear wriggles its way into my stomach. Jacob must have sneaked back home when I was working and left it on the bed for me to find. I sink down on the bed and open it with shaking fingers.

I'm sorry, Mum. I can't take any more so I've gone away for a bit

The worm of fear is now a snake and it's around my throat,

choking me as I dash over to the wardrobe and fling open the doors. Some of Jacob's clothes are missing. So are his charger and backpack.

He's gone. My son has run away.

Where? Why?

Panic consumes me.

How long has he been gone?

'Aaron!' I run out of the room and down the stairs, leaping them a couple at a time, crashing into Aaron at the bottom.

'Vanessa! What is it?' He takes me in his arms. 'Calm down, please, it'll be okay, just tell me what's happened.'

'Jacob...' I gasp as I sink into his embrace.

'Jacob? What's happened?' Aaron pulls away, his eyes raking my face, his own pallid.

I feel like my legs are going to collapse underneath me, so I sink down onto the bottom step and try to pull myself together. It takes me a few seconds to catch my breath. 'Jacob's run away,' I gasp, tears flooding down my cheeks.

'What?' Aaron's eyes are wide with horror. 'Are you sure?'

'He left me this. I've just found it.' I hand him the note, trying to calm my breathing. Panicking won't help Jacob, I need to think clearly. I hope I haven't scared Chloe by screaming. 'Where's Chloe?'

'Lucas has taken her out in the garden to play,' Aaron says, his eyes fixed on the note. 'When did you last talk to Jacob?'

'Last night when he went to bed. He was out early this morning. I sent him a message telling him that Rachel's come round, but he didn't reply, and he hasn't been picking up my calls since then.' My breath catches in my throat. 'He must have sneaked back to get his clothes while I was working in the study because that note wasn't on his pillow this morning.' I swallow. 'He ran away after I told him Rachel has come round. Why would he do that?'

'Did you tell him that she's expected to make a full recovery?' Aaron asks.

'I told him that she was okay and said that the fall was an accident, she fell.'

Aaron sits down on the step beside me. 'He might be worried she's got brain damage. Perhaps the stress of thinking about how she might be has really got to him.'

Maybe he's right. I should have told Jacob that Rachel was going to be fine.

'Look, he's probably just staying with a friend, so let's ring around. Don't worry, darling, I'm sure we'll find out where he is soon enough,' Aaron suggests. 'I'll ask Lucas who Jacob's friends are and contact them all.'

He goes outside to see Lucas while I go into the downstairs bathroom and splash my face with water. I don't want Chloe to see me like this.

Aaron comes back in, a frown darkening his face. 'Lucas is adamant that he knows nothing. I've asked him to contact Jacob's friends to see if he is staying with any of them,' he says. 'Damn, I wish he hadn't run away, Ness. It doesn't look good.'

'Look good?! Is that all you care about, what people think?' I snap, furious with him. Jacob could be anywhere. He could be in danger. I close my eyes and take a few deep breaths. I need to calm down and think. Where would Jacob go? Who might know where he is?

'Any luck?' I ask when Lucas comes in with Chloe a few minutes later.

He shakes his head, his eyes clouded with anxiety. 'I've messaged everyone. No one has seen Jacob.'

'Are you sure you don't know where he is?'

'No, I swear I don't. I'd tell you if I did.' He fidgets with the neck of his tee shirt. 'I'm worried about him too.'

I believe him. I think.

'We've got to call the police. We need to find Jacob before it gets dark.'

I break into a cold sweat at the thought of Jacob being out there when night falls. Alone. Anything could happen to him.

Aaron wraps his arms around me. 'We'll find him,' he reassures me. 'I'll call the police, you're too shaken up.'

'Thank you.' My whole body is shaking as the enormity of the situation hits me again and again, in waves of shock.

Where is my son?

Lucas bites his bottom lip, his eyes darting from me to Aaron. 'I'll take Chloe to watch TV for a bit,' he offers, and he takes her hand. 'Come on, Chloe, let's watch some cartoons.'

We go into the kitchen and Aaron calls the police, putting his phone on speaker.

'Have you contacted his friends?' the woman on the other end of the phone asks.

'Yes, and none of them have seen him.'

'Look, try not to worry. The reality of running away is a lot worse than the idea. As it gets dark Jacob could think twice about it and come back home. One-fifth of runaways return home within twenty-four hours, and three-quarters return home within a week.' Her voice is gentle and reassuring and I want to believe that she's right, that Jacob will walk back in as soon as it gets dark. She promises to send some officers around as soon as they can.

'She's right, Jacob could change his mind and come back. It would be scary for him out there once night falls,' Aaron says after he's ended the call.

I wish he hadn't said that. I'm trying so hard not to think of Jacob wandering around in the dark.

I long to ring Hazel, tell her what's happened, but she's away overnight at a conference and I don't want to worry her. She's back tomorrow so I'll talk to her then.

I'm on autopilot as I bathe Chloe and settle her in bed,

giving her an extra big cuddle. It only seems like yesterday when Jacob was this age and I was tucking him into bed at night with a story and a hug. Did he run away because he was worried about Rachel, or because he can't stand it here anymore? Have I failed him so badly? His heart-wrenching words saying he wished Aaron and Lucas had never moved in with us echo in my mind. Could I have prevented this?

It's dangerous out there on the streets at the best of times for a young lad. But Jacob has hordes of people hating him online, calling for vengeance, thinking he tried to kill Rachel. I think someone even came into his room and trashed it to threaten him. Someone is clearly hell-bent on harming my son, and now he's out there alone.

57

Rachel

I can't believe that I've been in hospital over a week. Part of me longs to go home, and another part of me is afraid to. Mum told me that the police have questioned Jacob and Lucas, taken their hoodies away for forensics. And questioned all the kids in my class. I don't want to face everyone.

Especially *him*. Will *he* leave me alone now?

I glance over as the door opens and Mum comes in. She smiles at me. 'I've brought you some snacks, and a couple of magazines.' She puts a carrier bag down then sits in the chair beside my bed and reaches out for my hand. 'How are you, darling?'

'I'm all right, just a bit achy,' I tell her. Then I ask her the question that I've been worrying over all morning. 'Mum, are the police calling off the investigation now?'

She squeezes my hand. 'I'm not sure. They're bothered about Ben saying he saw someone running from your room. And the threatening texts you've received.'

'Ben's wrong!' I blurt out.

Mum nods. 'I know, love. Dad's been talking to him, and he's admitted that he didn't really see anyone. He must have been so confused and upset, poor kid, and was desperately trying to think of what could have happened to you. There's such a blur between truth and imagination at that age.' I can see the pain and worry etched on her face, the dark circles under her eyes. Her skin has lost its lustre and she's thinner, her leggings are loose on her legs. This is all my fault.

'The police want to talk to you about the messages when you're feeling a bit stronger.' Mum squeezes my hand. 'No one is bullying you, are they, darling? You would tell me, wouldn't you, if you didn't really fall?'

'I leant out too far, that's all. It was stupid of me. You're always warning me about it.' I fix a smile on my face. 'I won't be doing that again. And nobody is bullying me, it's just normal school stuff, nothing I can't handle.'

'That's good. You will tell me if anything's worrying you, won't you? You can talk to me about anything. Remember that.'

'I know, Mum.' I wish I could. I wish she could make it all go away. But how can I after what *he* threatened?

'The doctor said you should be able to go home in a few days,' Mum is saying now. She looks so pleased, but fear surges through me. I don't want to go home. I can't.

'I still feel weak, Mum. I don't think I'm ready yet.'

She places the back of her hand on my forehead. 'You do seem to still have a bit of a temperature. I'll ask the doctor to check you over.'

Then Dad comes into the room. He whispers something to Mum, and I can tell by the looks on their faces that it's serious.

'What's the matter?' I ask.

They exchange a look.

'Please tell me otherwise I'll think it's something really bad,' I beg, my stomach churning.

'Well...' Mum begins. They are watching me carefully,

clearly wondering how I'll take the news. What are they about to tell me? What have they found out?

'It's Jacob. He's run away. No one knows where he is.'

It all gets too much for me then. I start crying, big heaving sobs pulsing through my body, and Mum pulls me in for a hug.

Little does she know these are not only tears of worry and pain.

They're also tears of relief.

58

Vanessa

DC Millet and DS Byron arrive within the hour, and we sit with them in the lounge. Lucas makes us all cups of tea and Aaron has his arm around me, trying to keep me calm. My foot is jiggling impatiently as they talk to us about Jacob's mental state, if there have been many rows, if he had shown any sign of being unhappy. Why aren't they out there looking for him right now?

When they ask if Jacob knew Rachel had woken up, I know what they're insinuating. That my son is responsible for putting Rachel into a coma, and is scared that she will blame him. Aaron hinted the same. Well, they're way off track.

'I think he's in danger.' I tell them about the ransacked room and the online threats. 'He's scared of someone. Whoever was threatening Rachel might be after him, too.'

DC Millet writes a few notes down in his notebook and also questions Lucas, who has nothing further to say. I feel like I'm bursting at the seams, like they're all acting in slow motion, and all I want to do is run out of the door, find my son, have every police officer in the town out there looking for him too. Why aren't they taking this more seriously?

'We've contacted all Jacob's friends, and they haven't seen him,' Aaron is saying. His arm is squeezing around me, it feels like he's holding me together. If it weren't for his obvious suspicions about my son, I'd be so grateful for him right now. But he's made it clear that he suspects Jacob of doing something terrible, and if it was accusations like that which caused my son to run away, I don't think I can ever forgive Aaron. I pull away from him, putting distance between us on the sofa. The detectives exchange looks and I know they've noted my action.

'I'm guessing that you don't have a tracking app on Jacob's phone?' DS Byron asks me.

'No, he's fourteen. It seems an infringement of his privacy to keep track of him like that,' Aaron says, while I shake my head wordlessly. We used to have tracking apps on the boys' phones, to be fair, but they objected as they got older and Aaron agreed with them. So we took them off.

Why did I listen to Aaron? If I hadn't, I could find out where Jacob is right now.

Finally, DC Millet puts away his notebook. 'We've sent out an alert to all our patrol cars and will be conducting a search for Jacob. I'll be in touch with any further developments. Meanwhile, if you hear from him or can think of anywhere he could have run away to, please let us know.'

As soon as they leave, I grab my handbag and car keys. 'I can't just sit here doing nothing. I'm going to drive around and see if I can find Jacob.'

'It will be dark soon, Ness. And you're in no fit state to go out, you've been so upset. Let me go,' Aaron says.

I shake my head. 'He's my son. *I'll* find him.'

Aaron jerks as if he's been slapped across the face, but I don't care. Anyway, I doubt he'd be able to convince Jacob to come home even if he did find him. Not after how he's treated him lately. If Jacob sees me on my own though, he won't run away, I'm sure of it.

I'm going to find my son. And nothing or no one is going to stop me.

59

I've been driving and walking around for over an hour, desperately hoping to see Jacob huddled in a shop doorway somewhere, hanging about the park, walking along the streets. There's no sign of him, and now it's almost dark. I park the car and walk around the town, searching for Jacob's familiar face and calling his name. He's taken his grey hoodie – the police still haven't returned the black ones – but I'll still recognise him even with the hood up. I'd know my son anywhere.

I'm shocked at the number of homeless people I see, lying on benches, sitting in shop doorways with a grubby duvet wrapped around them. My heart goes out to them. It's bad enough to have no shelter now, in the summer, but it must be unbearable on the cold, winter nights.

Where will Jacob sleep tonight if I don't find him? Has a friend we don't know put him up or is he planning on huddling in a shop doorway? I can't bear to think of him out here alone. He must have been so terrified to run away. Why didn't he feel like he could come to me for help? I'm his mother, I'm meant to protect him.

I phone him again. I've phoned him countless times, left him dozens of messages. Surely he knows that I'm worried sick.

Maybe he can't reply. Maybe he's been attacked and is lying injured somewhere.

My head is aching from all the crying, but I can't give up. I need to find him, fast.

After a while I decide to drive further out and park the car near the canal, wondering if Jacob's hiding down there. It's isolated and frightening, with dark shadows dancing on the murky water and on the walls of the locked industrial buildings. I feel vulnerable, exposed. Goodness knows how poor Jacob must be feeling.

My phone rings and I don't have to look at the screen to know that it's Aaron. He's been phoning me every half an hour, checking that I'm safe and begging me to come home, but I can't come home without Jacob. I wish I'd brought a torch with me – the darkness is coming down so fast I'll soon barely be able to see. I can use my phone torch but the battery is only half charged and I don't want to run it down. I need it to phone Jacob. I decide to check the doorways of the buildings, which are all locked up for the night.

Suddenly I'm aware that someone is behind me, and a shard of fear pierces me. I resist the urge to turn around, instead turning sideways, pretending I'm looking at the canal. Out of the corner of my eye I can see a man with a dog walking towards me. Can I trust him because he has a dog? I think of all the horror stories I've read in the newspapers about women being attacked. Will I be a statistic soon, too? How will I help Jacob then?

I take slow, steady breaths, trying to block out my panicked thoughts.

The man with the dog is coming closer now so I walk into the centre of the path. I don't want to be near the canal, where I could be pushed in, or near the buildings, where I could be pulled into a doorway. My senses are on full alert and my breathing is fast, ragged. Then I hear loud shouts and spin around to see a gang of youths approaching, they're swearing and kicking cans.

A shudder runs through me. They don't look a friendly lot. I need to get out of here. I walk swiftly past the man and head back to my car. Once safely inside I lock the doors and drive away, my heart pounding so hard I feel like it might burst out of my chest.

I desperately want to carry on looking but I'm so shaken up and exhausted, and I know that I'm putting myself in danger if I walk around in the night by myself. I have to keep myself safe for Chloe and Jacob's sake.

I see that the local pub is still open so I pull into the car park, text Aaron to let him know I'm safe and will be home soon, then go inside and order a lemonade. I'd love a stiff drink right now, but there's no way I'd risk drinking and driving, even if we do only live five minutes away.

I feel like everyone knows who I am, that they're staring and pointing at me, whispering: *there's the woman whose son pushed the girl next door out of the window.* I keep my eyes averted as I sit down at a table near the window.

How did my life come to this? I long to turn back the clock to three months ago before Rachel moved in, when we were all one happy family. Jacob is innocent, I know he is, and all I want is for him to come home.

'Hello again, Ness.' I glance up and see Diana standing by me, clad in jeans and a short-sleeved blouse, a half pint of lager in her hand. 'Mind if I join you?' She pulls out a chair and sits down opposite me without waiting for my reply. I'm really not in the mood for chit-chat, but it doesn't feel like I have a choice.

'Are you okay? Word has it that your lad has run away,' she says sympathetically, her green eyes wide and curious.

It doesn't take long for the gossip to get around, does it? I bet the neighbours have all been watching the police come and go from our house.

Then I remember that Lucas called Jacob's friends, and the police have put the word out too, so of course everyone will know that Jacob has run away. And they'll all have their own theories as to why. I dread to think what the comments are like online, but I haven't got the stomach to check.

I stare into my glass and nod. 'I've been out looking for him but...'

'Look, I'll be straight with you, Ness, everyone's blaming your lad for what happened to Rachel but I reckon he's run away because he's scared. And I think that girl isn't talking because she's protecting someone else.' She takes a sip of her lager.

'Who?' I ask.

She fixes her gaze on me. 'I thought I recognised your chap, Aaron, but I couldn't remember where I'd seen him. Now I do. My sister used to live in the same street as him.' She chews her lip anxiously. 'Look, I have to tell you something, but you're not going to like it.'

I press my hands into my knees, digging in my fingertips until it hurts. 'What is it?'

'My sister's neighbour's daughter used to babysit for him. The girl had a crush on him and, the truth is, he should have acted more professionally. He said that there was nothing in it, that he was helping her with a project, but she was heartbroken and she took an overdose. Luckily her mum found her in time. Aaron wasn't charged but he was given a slap on the wrist, and lots of us thought more should have happened to him. The family moved away soon after though, and all the gossip died down.'

'He said he was helping her with a project?' I feel a shiver of apprehension. Then I recall one of the online comments. *Seems like history repeating itself to me. Look to the father.*

I thought they had meant Ricky. Had they been talking about Aaron?

Then a horrible feeling sinks into my chest.

What if Jacob found out about this? Is that why he ran away?

Aaron has lied to me, kept so much from me for years. What is he capable of? And is it possible that he knows where my son is?

60

'I'm so sorry, Vanessa. I don't like to meddle but I thought you had a right to know, after what happened to Rachel and now your son going missing. I'm sure the police must already be aware and they must have looked into it, but I couldn't keep quiet about it to you, not if there was a chance you didn't know. It wouldn't be right,' Diana says. 'Are you okay?'

I nod. 'Thanks for telling me,' I stammer.

Of course I'm not okay. I'm shaken to the core. I need to think. I don't know how to react. I have absolutely no idea how to deal with this, everything is crashing down on me at once and I feel so fragile, as if I could break any second. Part of me wants to call Hazel, but I don't want her to go Full Hazel, all guns blazing, I can't handle the drama right now. I need to focus on Jacob.

Diana gets up and rests her hand on my shoulder in a silent display of sympathy. 'I'd better go, leave you to it. I hope you find your son soon.'

I nod again and watch her as she walks back over to the bar, then I stare down into my glass, thoughts tumbling around in my head.

I remember how Aaron couldn't wait to get away when we met Diana at the garden centre. And how she'd stared after him, with a frown on her face.

What the hell do I do now?

My phone rings again, and it's Aaron. I reject the call. Then I finish my drink and walk out of the pub, my mind still in a whirl.

I've done it again. I've brought a monster into my home.

Aaron comes into the hall as soon as I open the front door. 'Thank goodness, I've been so worried about you.' He goes to embrace me, but I step back. There is no way I can hug him after what I've learnt tonight, but I also don't think I can physically cope with the confrontation right now. I can barely stand up, I'm so exhausted from all the emotion, all I can think about is Jacob.

'I didn't find him.'

'You look so tired. Let me get you a drink before we go to bed.'

I shake my head, not looking at him. 'No, I can't go to bed. I won't be able to sleep. You go up, I'll come up later.'

'Don't push me away, Ness.' I can hear the hurt in his voice, well if he could see the anger burning in my heart, he would keep away from me.

'Please. Just leave me alone,' I snap.

'Okay, Ness. If that's what you want.' He turns away slowly and goes up the stairs.

I go into the kitchen, pour myself a brandy and take it into the lounge, where I lie on the sofa and phone Jacob again and again. There is no answer.

I thought my tears had run dry, then suddenly they pour out of my eyes, streaming like rivers down my cheeks. Loud, noisy sobs wrack my body and I bury my head in a cushion to muffle the sound.

Finally I fall into an exhausted sleep, and when I wake up it's just starting to get light. I grab my phone immediately and check it for messages. The battery is flat. What if Jacob has been trying to get hold of me?

I scramble up and hurry to the kitchen, where I plug it into the spare charger – I don't want to go into our bedroom to get mine and risk waking Aaron. I don't want to talk to him right now. After a couple of long, unbearable minutes the screen springs to life. And there, across the top of the screen, is a message from Jacob.

He's alive.

My hand trembling, I open the message.

I'm okay but I can't come home until Rachel tells the truth, I'm sorry. Please believe me that I had nothing to do with Rachel's fall. Whatever anyone says, you have to believe me. Please. Jacob x

61

TEN DAYS AFTER THE FALL

Aaron

I hear Chloe cry out, her voice frightened and urgent, and I glance at the clock. Quarter past five. I rub my eyes, slipping out of bed. Chloe usually sleeps for longer than this unless she has a nightmare. I'll go to her, I don't want to wake Ness, she needs her sleep. Then I notice that her side of the bed is empty. Either she's fallen asleep on the sofa or she's gone out to look for Jacob again.

'What's up, sweetheart?' I whisper as I go into Chloe's bedroom and sit down on the side of the bed.

She sits up, pushing away her duvet, and rubs her eyes sleepily. 'Bad dream,' she mumbles.

'Daddy will hug it away.' I wrap my arms around her and kiss her on the cheek. She nestles against me and is soon fast asleep again. I hold her for a few minutes, thinking that before I know it she will be grown and will no longer want cuddles. Then my mind goes to Rachel and I feel a pang of guilt.

I lower Chloe back down on the bed, pull the duvet over her

and go down to make myself a coffee, as I know I won't be able to go back to sleep now.

Ness wouldn't even let me hug her last night. I understand that she's terrified about Jacob, but I'm sure he's fine and will come home soon. Frankly, right now it's hard not to blame him for the tension. And things will get even worse if the truth comes out.

The kettle finishes boiling and I'm pouring water into the cafetière when Lucas walks into the kitchen. His hair's messy and he's in his pjs. He holds up his phone. 'Dad, Jacob's messaged me.'

I splash boiling water over the kitchen surface. 'What did he say?'

'He said he's not coming back until Rachel tells the truth.' Lucas sounds anxious, his eyes small and pinched from lack of sleep.

I lean back against the work surface and take a deep breath. 'Okay. Let's just keep calm, Lucas. Have you tried phoning and talking to him?'

'Yes, but he won't pick up,' Lucas replies. 'What shall we do? Shall we tell Vanessa?'

'Yes, I'll go tell her now in case he didn't text her too, although I'm sure he did. She was so exhausted she fell asleep on the sofa last night.'

My movements deliberate and almost robotic, I pour a cup of coffee for Ness and take it to her while Lucas heads back upstairs. She's awake. She's sitting up on the sofa, staring at her phone. She turns to me then, and there's something about her expression, something cold and fierce, that makes me even more anxious than I already am.

'Jacob's messaged. He's okay, but he's not coming home until Rachel tells the truth,' she says, her words toneless and clipped.

I carefully place the mug down on the coffee table in front

of her, trying to read her eyes. 'Yes, I was just coming to tell you. He's messaged Lucas too.'

She is out of the lounge and up the stairs like a shot, clearly off to question Lucas for more details.

I sink down into the chair, nursing my mug of coffee.

I honestly didn't think Rachel would get away with saying she fell. Not for long, anyway. Secrets never stay buried for long, no matter how hard you try.

I should have known that. I should have learnt from the past.

Whatever I do next, I need to be very careful.

62

Vanessa

I read the message from Jacob again, sitting on Lucas's bed amid the piles of clothes he hasn't bothered to put away.

'Do you know what the truth is, what Jacob is talking about?' I ask him.

He doesn't meet my eye. 'I keep telling you, I don't know what happened. I wasn't here that day except for when I dropped back home briefly.'

'Well, but do you know what – or who – Rachel is scared of? Please, Lucas, it might help us to understand why Jacob ran away, and how we can help him.'

'I'm sure that if Lucas knew anything, he would say.' I look up to see Aaron standing in the doorway.

Is Aaron the person they are all protecting – Lucas, Jacob and Rachel?

I can't believe where my thoughts are taking me.

I stand up, fury pulsing through me, my fists clenched. 'Someone was in Rachel's bedroom that day, I'm sure of it, no matter what she's saying now. It's someone she's still scared of.

And this same person has threatened Jacob, and that's why he's run away.'

'If she is so scared of him, surely she would tell the police, then they can arrest him,' Aaron replies evenly.

Unless she's protecting someone. Did Rachel jump because Aaron rejected her or, even worse, got involved with her? Perhaps he told her he was finishing it, and she couldn't take it? And now he's standing by and letting Jacob take the blame?

Bile rises up in my throat as I look at my partner, the love of my life, wondering if I know him at all. I don't know how to play this, I don't know what my next move could be. I don't want to jump to conclusions I'll regret. What if I'm wrong about everything?

'We need to tell the police about Jacob's messages this morning,' I say finally. 'They might even be able to use them to track his location.'

I want Jacob home so desperately.

After calling the police I take Chloe to nursery, and on the way back, I resolve that now Chloe is safely out of the way I'm going to have it out with Aaron, no matter how exhausted, weak and frightened I feel.

This conversation can't wait another minute.

'We need to talk,' I say grimly as I enter the house. 'Where's Lucas?'

'Gone out.' Aaron looks at me apprehensively. 'What's this about, Ness?'

'I know, Aaron,' I tell him. 'I know everything. I know all about that poor girl who tried to kill herself because of you.'

Aaron's jaw drops. 'What the hell do you mean?'

'Don't play the innocent! I met Diana last night and she told me all about it. Apparently you got off with a caution?'

'Because I didn't do anything. Bloody hell, Ness. Surely you don't really believe I would molest a child. It's vile, unspeakable. You can't possibly think I'm capable of this?'

'I think it's too much of a coincidence that the same thing has happened to Rachel. There's no smoke without a fire, Aaron. Did Rachel jump out of the window because of your sick relationship with her? Or did you push her?' My voice is raised now, I'm standing on one side of the kitchen table with him on the other, and in that moment I'm grateful for the furniture between us and that I'm close to the door. I could get out in seconds.

A muscle in Aaron's jaw twitches and I notice, with my stomach lurching, that he clenches his fist by side. His eyes have darkened, his stance threatening.

Fear roars through me. I've seen this before, with Ricky. Well, this time I am not hanging around to be beaten. I swivel on my heels, yank the back door open and run as fast as I can.

63

Suzy

The doctors have said that Rachel can come home in a few days and I'm terrified. Whilst I'm happy she's recovering so well I'm convinced that she's still in danger, and I have no idea how to keep her safe in her own home. While she's in hospital, with all the staff and the alarms and me by her side almost round the clock, I feel reassured that she's safe. At home though, in her room, where it all happened... How can I ever let her out of my sight? How can I protect her?

'What if that boy comes back and tries to hurt her again?' I say to Carl as we sit in Mum's lounge drinking coffee. We've left Rachel sleeping peacefully and Ben is playing out in Mum's small, secure garden.

'Like I keep saying, Suzy, nothing happened. Rachel told us she fell, and Ben has admitted he didn't see a boy that day. We need to let this go, and hopefully the police will too, soon enough. We all need to move on with our lives. Look, if it makes you feel better, one of us will stay with her all the time, for the foreseeable future anyway,' he says.

'What about work?' I ask him. Both our employers have been very understanding and given us compassionate leave with pay, but we can't expect that forever.

'Stay with me,' Mum suggests. 'I know it's a bit of a squeeze but we can manage until you find another house to rent. I wouldn't want to go back to that home either if I were you, not with those two lads next door.'

Her offer is tempting, but it's not practical, her home is too small for all of us. I explain this to her gently, and she nods.

'Okay, well, maybe Rachel can stay with me for the rest of the holidays, and I can keep an eye on her while you're at work?'

I sigh and shake my head. 'It's really kind of you, Mum, and I'm very grateful but I want Rachel with us, especially after we almost lost her. I can't be separated from her.' I don't want to add that if someone did try to hurt Rachel and they come after her again, Mum isn't strong enough to protect her. Carl is, though. Carl would win in a fight against most people. He can be intimidating without even having to use force.

'Look, Suzy, I really don't think we have anything to worry about now. It was an awful accident. Rachel won't be daft enough to sit on the windowsill again. She's learnt her lesson,' Carl says.

I find it really frustrating that Carl won't even entertain the idea that Rachel is lying because she is scared, that she could have been pushed. That someone could have tried to kill her. He even talked Ben into retracting his statement to the police, and I'm honestly not convinced Ben would have changed his mind if Carl hadn't persuaded him to do so. Carl is so one-track-minded, so blinkered sometimes. All he wants to do is move on, he's in total denial that this can't all just be brushed under the mat.

'I'm not convinced. I think we should look for another property to rent, we need to move out as soon as we can. I don't want to stay in that house after what happened, for any longer than we have to.' We've only got two months left on our six-month contract, and we'd been planning on renewing it for another year. Moving house will probably mean the kids moving schools again, and maybe me being transferred to another branch of the store, but I don't care. I'll do anything to keep Rachel safe.

I can tell by the look on Carl's face that he doesn't think this is a very good idea. 'We can't keep uprooting the kids, Suzy. And it will mean travelling further to work, or new jobs for us.'

Why is Carl so certain that Rachel is safe? Why isn't he taking this more seriously?

Even if he is right, Ben was mistaken and there was nobody else involved, what if Rachel didn't fall by accident? What if she jumped?

I think back to that awful moment when I saw Rachel lying on the ground beneath her open bedroom window. My immediate fear was that Carl had finally completely lost his rag at her and upset her so much that she'd jumped. He had such a short fuse lately and always seemed to be shouting, especially about Rachel hanging about with Jacob and Lucas. I'd tried speaking to him about it but he'd said that she was still a child and had to learn to toe the line. I do understand him wanting to be protective, to give her boundaries, but teenagers can be so vulnerable, they really take things to heart, and I know my girl. I know how sensitive she is.

I will never forgive him if I find out he drove her to do that. I don't think he would forgive himself either. He adores the kids, and they adore him, but he can be scary.

I need to talk to him, let him know that there must be changes in his behaviour. I don't want to leave him, especially after what we've all been through, but Rachel's safety comes first. I can't risk this happening again.

If I'm honest, though, part of me is scared of how Carl will react.

64

Vanessa

'Ness, what's happened?' Hazel pulls the door open, her eyes widening as she takes in my clearly terrible appearance. 'You've just caught me, I've not been back long.'

I was so desperate to speak to Hazel that I drove straight over, taking a chance that she'd be home from her work conference now.

'It's Jacob, he's run away,' I gasp. 'He messaged a few hours ago. He's safe but I don't know where, and he won't come home.' I'm shaking from head to foot. Even on the fifteen-minute drive to Hazel's home, I was so panicked, paranoid that Aaron might be following, my whole nervous system was pushed past the point of functioning normally.

Hazel puts her hand on my elbow and guides me inside, closing the door behind her. She keeps hold of my elbow as we turn to the right into the lounge then through to the dining room. As usual, everywhere is neat and tidy, Hazel hates mess. She pulls out a chair. 'Sit down and take a few breaths, then let's talk. It'll be okay, Ness. The main thing is you've heard from Jacob and he's all right.'

She steps into the small kitchen and I watch her through the open doorway as she switches on the coffee machine, pops in a pod and takes a mug off the rack. By the time she's put the mug of steaming coffee on a coaster on the dining table in front of me, I've managed to pull myself together. Hazel makes a coffee for herself and sits down across from me. 'I understand that you're worried about Jacob, but you know he's safe so what's shaken you up so much?'

'It's Aaron.' My hands are still shaking as I pick up my mug and take a slow sip to calm myself down.

Then I tell Hazel what Diana said to me last night.

Hazel sucks in her breath then releases it. 'I can't believe this. Have you had it out with him?'

'Yes, and he said it was all completely innocent. He was investigated and the charges were dropped. Same as now.' I raise my eyes to meet Hazel's. 'I mean, what are the chances, Haze? I told him I didn't believe him and he was furious. I've never seen him like that before. It was like... I ran out of there as quickly as I could.' I'm crying now, again, as if I haven't spilled enough tears over the last few days, but telling Hazel what's happened, seeing the concern and anger in her eyes, it's unlocking all the emotion I'm carrying in me.

'What?' Hazel's face is thunderous. 'Ness, did he threaten you? Hurt you?'

'Not exactly, but he was so angry, I ran out of there before anything could happen. It reminded me of Ricky and I was scared. Chloe is at nursery, so she's okay,' I add quickly.

'If he ever touches you, he'll regret it,' Hazel says grimly, her voice simmering with rage. 'I promised you that no one would ever hurt you again, and I meant it.'

'Do you think I should tell the police about this other girl?' I ask, sinking my head into my hands. 'Aaron says that he wasn't charged so I wonder if it's even on record, maybe they don't know?'

'Yes, I absolutely do. You can't hide things like this, Ness. If he had anything to do with Rachel... She could have died. Just like that girl from before. It's way too much of a coincidence.' She reaches across, taking one of my hands in hers. 'Don't go back home, Ness. Don't go back to him. You and Chloe should stay here. Liam is working in Manchester for a couple of weeks so there's plenty of room. Zara stayed over at a friend's last night while I was away, but I'm going to collect her later – she will love to have the company.'

I lick my lips, unsure what to do. 'It's my house...'

'I know it is, and Aaron should be the one to go, but please put your safety first, we can get the house back for you later.'

I feel like I'm drowning, I'm so exhausted and over-whelmed, and I don't know what to do. Surely Aaron wouldn't hurt me? Not Aaron. I just overreacted because his anger had triggered me. He's nothing like Ricky. This thing about the girl in the past, it doesn't look good but shouldn't I give him the benefit of the doubt? Maybe he really is just the victim of a very unfortunate series of events?

Anyway, if I leave home now, won't Jacob feel even more lost and disorientated? He might even blame himself for breaking up our family. It might make him more likely to stay away. And what about Lucas?

'I need to go back for now, Hazel. I'll be safe, I promise. I can take care of myself.' I stand up slowly and grab my bag. 'Please don't worry, I'm okay, and if there's any trouble, I'll phone you. I promise.'

'Okay, but will you at least bring Chloe here to stay overnight while you think about what to do?' Hazel begs. 'You don't want to be fighting with her around.'

'Yes, that makes sense, thank you. I'll grab some of her things and bring her after nursery,' I promise.

I leave feeling determined, with a strength inside me that's more powerful than ever before. I can face Aaron. I'm going to find out the truth, and get my son back.

65

Aaron

Vanessa has been gone all morning. I've phoned her countless times and messaged to ask if we can talk calmly, begging her to come home. Eventually she replies to say she's at Hazel's and will be back later. My nerves are so frayed. All the black coffees I'm drinking won't be helping that, but I'm so exhausted, I feel like I barely have any energy left in me.

I knew Hazel would be Ness's first port of call, those two are thick as thieves and always have been. I'm betting she's told Hazel everything and Hazel has been telling her to leave me. Hazel is so overprotective over Ness, and I get why, but I'm not like Ricky. The way Ness ran off, you'd think I was going to hurt her. I would never do that, but yes, I was angry, and I had a right to be. She wouldn't listen to a word I said. She just thought the worst of me, jumped to conclusions without knowing the whole story. She's supposed to trust me more than anyone else.

The doorbell rings, breaking into my thoughts, and I go to the window to check who it is. It's the two detectives. Great. I'm guessing Vanessa has told them about Jacob's message. Let's hope they've come with good news.

'Have you found Jacob?' I ask immediately as I open the door, skipping over the usual exchange of greetings. I step aside to let them in.

'No, but we're working on it. It's great that he's been in touch and confirmed that he's safe,' DS Byron says as they follow me into the kitchen.

'I'm sorry but neither Vanessa nor Lucas is in right now, so I can't show you the messages he sent. He didn't message me,' I add.

'And why do you think that is, Mr Paige?' DC Millet asks.

'Well, I guess since he'd told his mother and brother, he didn't feel the need to tell me too,' I say, sitting down at the kitchen table and gesturing to them to take a seat too. I don't offer them a drink, I don't want them to get too comfortable, I want them to leave as soon as they've told me what they've come for.

'Or maybe it's because he doesn't feel like he can talk to you?' The DS tilts her head to one side as if she's assessing my reaction.

I frown. I don't like how this is going. 'What do you mean?'

'Jacob's messages to Vanessa and Lucas said he wouldn't come home until Rachel told the truth. We assume this is to do with the fall, which she's now saying was an accident. Have you any idea what this "truth" is that he's referring to?'

They're both watching me intently, their faces impassive, and panic rises in me. I feel sick, my stomach churning. 'No, I do not.'

'Maybe she's scared to say what really happened that day? Maybe she's scared that it will get someone in trouble? And maybe Jacob is scared, too.'

I know where they're going with this. I've been here before.

'We've been through this,' I say. 'I've explained everything that happened that day.'

'Yes, but we've now received information that this isn't the first time you've been questioned over your relationship with a young girl. And both young girls almost died. I'd call that a bit of a coincidence, wouldn't you?' The DC leans in.

I stare at him, at a loss for words. What can I say? What can I do?

'We'd like you to come down to the police station for questioning,' the DC says.

I can't believe this is happening. Vanessa must have told them. How could she do this to me?

'Mr Paige?'

'If I must.' I grab my phone, slip it in my pocket and follow them out, my legs so shaky I worry they'll collapse underneath me.

As I get into the police car, I look around hoping no neighbours are watching, and see Vanessa driving up the road. The policeman drives off, and I stare straight ahead as we pass her. I can't cope with seeing the accusation in her eyes. And I don't want her to see the fury in mine.

66

As I sit in the back of the police car on my way to the station, my mind is thrust back to that awful time eight years ago. We'd just got back from a wonderful week away – me, Amanda and Lucas in Portugal with Amanda's parents. We visited Amanda's parents a couple of times every year and they came over to the UK to visit us when they could – they doted on Lucas. I feel guilty that we've drifted apart now and they hardly see Lucas apart from a FaceTime call now and again.

It had been so good to spend some time together as Amanda and I were always both so busy, like ships that pass in the night, but at Amanda's parents' villa we could relax, sunbathe, sit out on the terrace soaking in the sun with a glass of wine and chat. We had even had the occasional meal out because Amanda's parents were delighted to babysit so they could spend some quality time with Lucas.

Amanda and I had been happy and relaxed as we flew home, determined to make time together in the future for days out and regular date nights. But we hadn't been in more than five minutes when the police showed up at the door.

It all happened so quickly. They took me into the station for questioning, like something out of a nightmare. Heidi, the teenage girl who babysat for us, had tried to take her own life. She lived over the road and adored Lucas, popping in to see how he was when she came home from school. She was a pretty, intelligent girl and often used to talk to me, asking me questions or bringing her homework over for me to help her with. Moira, her mother, was single and trying hard to bring up Heidi and her twin brothers while holding down a full-time job. I guessed Heidi was looking for a father figure and, yes, it's true that we had got quite close.

The police grilled me for hours. They told me that they'd found Heidi's diary, and there was an entry in which she said she couldn't go on anymore because she couldn't fight her feelings for me.

I was under suspicion for days, until Heidi told everyone that she'd had a crush on me and confirmed that I hadn't done anything wrong. I was so grateful to her for that. I think she could see that the suspicion was ruining my life and marriage. Heidi adored Lucas, she wouldn't want to be the cause of him losing his dad. Heidi and her family moved away not long after that, then Amanda became ill and died within a year, and I moved away too. I wanted a fresh start, away from the gossip. I bought a modern apartment just for the two of us.

I recognised Diana right away when we were at the garden centre the other day, and I knew she had recognised me. I was dreading her telling Vanessa and had been trying to find the words to tell her myself. How could I though when she was already suspicious of me, after she found the necklace in the study?

I'd been so careful with Rachel. How could it all have gone so terribly wrong?

And now how do I prevent it from getting even worse?

67

Rachel

I'm feeling so much better today. I've been moved out of intensive care and have even managed to walk to the bathroom by myself and eat some breakfast. Apart from the bruises and broken left wrist, I feel fine. It's such a relief to know that I'm getting better, that I won't be damaged and broken for the rest of my life.

Except part of me wishes I could have stayed in that coma. Blissfully unaware of who started all of this. Of what they could still do to me.

I'm sitting up in bed reading one of the magazines Mum brought me when the doctor comes in. It's a different one today, and he's quite old, balding and looks exhausted, like he's been up all night. Maybe he has, the staff seem to work long hours here.

'I think you're ready to go home soon.' He peers through his glasses at me. 'How do you feel about that?'

Of course part of me longs to go home, back with my mum, to have my own bed and my things around me, but I feel safer here in hospital. Not completely safe though. Hopefully I'll be okay, as long as I keep my mouth shut. Anyway, I can't tell the doctor the truth. I can't tell anyone.

'That would be good,' I reply, giving him my widest smile.

Mum and Dad come to visit me later, with Ben and Nan. We're only allowed two visitors at a time on the ward so Mum and Ben come in first. He runs over to me and gives me a big hug. 'I missed you. I thought you were dead,' he says, as I squeeze him into me.

'Nah, you don't get rid of me that easily,' I say, grinning.

He frowns then, his eyes worried. 'Are you sure that you are okay, though? Does your head hurt?'

'A bit. I'm achy all over but I'm good,' I reassure him. I muss his hair with my good hand. 'Stop worrying about me, honestly. I'm fine.'

We chat for a while and Ben tells me about the adventure book he's reading, it's part of a series I used to love too when I was his age. I feel suddenly so full of love for him, and a fierce protectiveness of my little brother. I'll get through this for him, and I'll keep him safe too.

Mum sends Ben back out after I give him one last big hug, promising to take him to the cinema soon when I'm home. 'Tell Nan to come in in five minutes,' Mum says to him. 'I want to talk to Rachel alone for a bit.'

I can see by the expression on Mum's face that something bad has happened.

'What is it?' I ask as soon as Ben leaves.

She leans forward. 'Aaron from next door, he's been arrested. I saw them taking him off in the police car.'

My heart is racing. 'What? Why?'

Mum looks as if she wants to say more then decides against it. 'I don't know.'

I can't meet her eyes, so I look down and fiddle with the sheet covering me. This is the last thing I wanted to happen.

Then Nan joins us and Mum gently asks me if I'd like to live with Nan for a bit, where I might feel safer after everything that happened. It would only be for a little while until Mum and Dad find a new place for us to live.

The thing is, as much as I love Nan, I'm not sure I could cope with her fussing around me right now. It would just make me even more anxious. And she has a way of getting me to tell her things and open up, and I can't afford to do that. I need to be very careful about what I say.

'Thanks, Nan, that's so kind, but I'm fine to go back home, honestly. All my things are there.'

When Nan goes out, Dad comes in – he kisses me on the cheek but I notice he's avoiding my gaze. Mum is chatting about the upcoming move. 'We're leaving as soon as our contract is up in two months. We could all do with a fresh start. I realise it means you and Ben starting a new school again, but I think it's for the best,' she says.

My mind drifts back to Ben, how happy he was just now to think of life going back to normal. He'd been struggling to settle in but he's just starting to find his feet, and now he'll have to start all over again in a new school, and it's all my fault. I realise my parents are scared for me, and I am too. Terrified. *But this isn't the answer.*

'I know I said I was happy to move, but I've thought about it some more and I don't want Ben to have to adjust and make new friends all over again,' I say. 'Don't be worried about me. It was all a silly accident. I'll make sure I keep away from the window in future.'

'Ben wants to change schools, he's not happy where he is,' Mum tells me.

'I don't want the upheaval of moving again either, but your mum's right, it's best if we do,' Dad says in his 'no argument' voice. 'We want you away from those lads next door. They've caused you nothing but trouble.'

'Is Jacob back home?' I ask.

'No, the police are still looking for him,' Mum replies.

This is all such a mess. Aaron has been arrested, Jacob has run away. I can't run away from this though, even if we move, I still won't be safe.

68

Vanessa

I'm shaking as I let myself into the house after seeing Aaron being driven away in the police car. Have the police found out about the incident with the other girl?

I feel like my whole life is imploding. Jacob has gone, Aaron has been arrested. I have no idea what to do, what to think. I phone the police station but they won't give me any information apart from saying that Aaron is helping with their enquires. Nausea swills around in the pit of my stomach, and I phone Hazel to tell her what has happened. She once again tries to persuade me to move in with her, she thinks I'm not safe with Aaron. I realise how bad it looks, I've had my doubts too but I can't bring myself to believe this of him, I really can't. In all the years I've known him, he's proved himself to be a caring, decent man.

It could be an act, a small voice says inside me. *Once again, you've trusted the wrong man. He's not who you thought he was.*

And then there's Lucas. I've come to look on him as my own son, I can't walk out on him. What if Aaron isn't released?

Lucas can't stay here on his own and we can't all stay with Hazel, she doesn't have room. No, I have to stay put. This is my home. If the police do charge Aaron, then I don't think he'd be allowed back here anyway. Not while Rachel is next door.

The next few hours crawl by. There's no sign of Lucas – which isn't unusual as he's barely in now – and Jacob still isn't returning my calls. I have a pile of work to do but can't concentrate on it. Finally, I grab my handbag and decide to go for a walk.

When I return, Aaron is sitting in the kitchen nursing a mug of tea, his hand shaking. The police have obviously let him go.

He puts the mug down and looks at me, his expression wounded, strained. 'I've been released without charge, you'll be disappointed to know,' he says bitterly. 'I can't believe that you reported me to the police without even giving me a chance to put my side of the story.'

He's acting the victim and I'm not going to let him play that game. He might have been released but he has some serious questions to answer. I take a deep breath before I speak.

'I didn't report you, actually, someone else must have done that,' I retort as I sit down opposite him. 'I want the truth, Aaron. You need to tell me everything, now.'

He shakes his head slowly and stares down at the table. When he finally speaks his voice is thick with emotion.

'A teenage girl, Heidi, used to babysit Lucas when Amanda and I went out. She was doing her GCSEs and sometimes asked my advice or for help with a project.'

'Like Rachel,' I butt in.

'Yes, like Rachel.' His eyes are still fixed firmly on the table. 'And like lots of other mates of Lucas's, or neighbours' kids,' he adds, his tone flat, defeated. 'I work in video game development, Ness, kids are interested in what I do.'

'Fair enough,' I acknowledge. 'Go on.'

'Heidi spent a lot of time at our house and Amanda was glad of the help with Lucas. I had no idea she had a crush on me. Why would I? I was years older than her.'

He looks and sounds genuine. I say nothing and leave him to continue. He picks up his mug and takes a sip then puts it down, staring into it.

'Then one night as I dropped Heidi off home after she'd been babysitting for us, she leant over and tried to kiss me in the car. I was horrified.' He finally raises his eyes to meet mine. 'I pulled away, of course, and Heidi... she opened the door and ran out. The next day she took an overdose of her mum's sleeping pills but luckily was found in time.' He sits back and closes his eyes as if the memory is too much for him. It all sounds completely genuine, and I want to offer him some comfort, but I don't.

'Then the police found Heidi's diary, where she confessed that she was in love with me. They questioned me for hours. I thought they were going to keep me in overnight. Amanda was going frantic at home. Finally Heidi told them that nothing improper had happened between us. That she'd taken the overdose because of how I'd reacted when she'd tried to kiss me – she felt rejected and mortified with shame.'

'Is that what happened with Rachel too?' I ask slowly. 'Did she have a crush on you and make a move on you too?' I remember the broken sunflower necklace. He runs his hand over his chin. He's such a handsome man, it's no wonder so many young girls develop crushes on him. That's hardly his fault, is it?

'What do you take me for, Ness? Do you really think that I'm so wicked? That I'd... with a young girl? Is that really what you think of me?'

I hesitate. 'I don't want to, but for it to happen twice...' I stammer.

'So what is it you're saying? That Rachel wanted to end it

all because of me? Like Heidi?' He stands up suddenly, pushing the chair back so quickly it falls over. 'Or do you think that I pushed her to keep her quiet? That I was the person Ben thought he saw running out of Rachel's bedroom? And that I'm standing by, letting our sons be questioned, to protect myself?'

I can see the pain and hurt in his eyes. It's so real, so potent. It can't all be lies, can it?

I look at him, this man I love, the father of my little girl, and I truly don't know what to believe.

'Ness, please!' He is distraught by my silence. 'If you don't believe me, how can I expect the police and everyone else to?'

I close my eyes for a long time, running through everything in my mind. The necklace, the diary. The girl from the past, Rachel's fall. Aaron's secrets.

The raw emotion in his voice, and the honesty in his eyes. The happy years we have spent together, his love for Chloe and for both of our boys.

'I believe you,' I say finally, reaching out for him.

Relief floods over his face and he hugs me tight. 'Thank goodness, you had me worried for a bit. This is a nightmare but please don't let it come between us.'

As I rest my head on his shoulder, I can't deny that there is still a trickle of doubt in my mind.

As my mother always said: once is an accident, twice is damn careless.

69

ELEVEN DAYS AFTER THE FALL

This is the third day that Jacob's been missing, and even though he texted to say he's okay, I'm losing my mind with worry. Where is he? Has he got shelter? Food? Is he hurt? I try to take my mind off it by concentrating on the book I'm editing, but how can I? My son could be lying injured somewhere.

I'm working in the kitchen because Aaron is working at home and I don't want to be in the same room as him. I wish he would go to the office so I could have some headspace. You'd think he'd want to get out of the house but it's like he's staying here to keep an eye on things. We've sort of made up, and he believes me that I didn't report him to the police, but I can't hide the fact that I'm feeling uncertain around him, and things are still strained between us.

'All right?' Lucas asks as he wanders barefoot into the kitchen. He's been up in his room all morning, I think he's trying to keep out of the way. We're all tiptoeing around each other, being ultra-polite.

'Anything from Jacob?' I ask him and he shakes his head.

He takes a glass out of the cupboard, opens the freezer and

takes an ice cube out of the tray, pops it into a glass and fills it with apple juice. 'Do you want one?' he asks.

'No, thanks.' I turn to the window and look out. The sky is clear blue and the sun is shining. Chloe is having a picnic in nursery today, and I imagine her sitting on the grass with her friends, munching sandwich triangles and crisps. She'll love that.

After my talk with Aaron yesterday I decided not to take her to Hazel's. Hazel wasn't too happy when I phoned to let her know. She's not convinced about Aaron's innocence and warned me to be careful, trying to persuade me to leave Chloe with her for a few days. 'The atmosphere in the house isn't good for her, Ness,' she pointed out. 'And you need to focus all your efforts on finding Jacob.' I can see her point, but Chloe belongs with me, with her family. I want her home with us. One of my children is missing, I'm not going to be without her too. Besides, Chloe gives us all something to focus on, she binds us together.

'I think Rachel's folks have moved back in, I saw Ben in the garden this morning,' Lucas says.

'I guess they're getting ready for Rachel to come home,' I reply.

'Maybe Jacob will come home then,' Lucas says. 'I keep messaging and asking him to come back.' I see the sadness in his eyes. All this has been hard on him too. I reach out and hug him and for a moment he rests his head on my shoulder, then he pulls away, looking a bit embarrassed. 'Later,' he mumbles and goes back upstairs.

I wonder when Rachel will be home. It will be so awkward for us all then.

I'm not sure how I feel about seeing them. It's terrible what they went through, and my heart goes out to them, but my family has nearly been destroyed too and they've been accusing us all the way through. My son is still missing, goodness knows where, and Suzy hasn't even sent me a single message of support or care.

Aaron comes into the kitchen and puts the toaster on. 'Want some toast?'

I shake my head. I can barely eat, I'm so filled with worry about Jacob. 'No, thanks.'

He's buttering his toast when the doorbell rings and makes us jump.

'I'll get it.' I head for the door before Aaron can. The two detectives are standing on the doorstep, and my breath catches in my throat. I'm praying it's good news.

'Could we have a word with you, Mrs Dawson?' DC Millet asks.

'Is it Jacob?' I say desperately, terrified about what they're going to say.

'Yes, we're pleased to let you know that we've found him and he's absolutely fine,' DC Millet continues as they step into the hall.

'You have!' I'm almost crying with relief. Since he ran away, I've been constantly tormented by images of my son lying in a gutter, mixing with junkies or getting beaten up. I would know if something had happened to him, wouldn't I? I would sense it, he's my flesh and blood. 'Oh, what a relief! Where is he? Are you bringing him home?'

The two detectives exchange a look then DS Byron says softly, 'I'm sorry but he insists that he doesn't want to come home.'

'Where *is* he?'

'He's with his father.'

70

Ricky.

Ricky has Jacob.

I can't believe it. I haven't seen that man for years, not since a particularly bad row which left me with a bruised and bloodied lip. It wasn't the first time that he had hit me, but that day Jacob, only five years old, had been watching and had been so upset I found the strength to call the police.

Ricky was charged with assault and I filed for divorce, determined that Jacob would never witness anything like that again. Ricky received a suspended sentence and was ordered to keep away from me, which, thankfully, he did. I guess he was happy to go back to his single lifestyle with no restrictions, where all his money was his own. He always was a selfish man. Jacob had never asked after his dad until recently – I think he was so frightened that day that he was glad he had gone too. Well, it seems that they had somehow been in touch again and were now friendly enough for Jacob to turn to Ricky for support and somewhere to live. How long has this been going on? Who made the first move?

Aaron has come into the hall now – he heard what the

detectives said. 'Jacob hasn't seen his father for years, how did this happen?'

The detectives look at me sympathetically. I'm clearly shaken up, leaning against the corridor wall as if my legs might collapse underneath me. 'It seems they've been in touch for several months now. We traced Mr Dawson and he admitted that Jacob was with him, said that Jacob had come to him for help. Officers have talked to Jacob to ascertain that he's okay and that he wants to stay with Mr Dawson, and he's confirmed that he does.' DS Byron looks at me. 'Do you have full custody of Jacob?'

'Yes, I do. Look, Ricky was abusive. He received a suspended sentence for attacking me. He was ordered to keep away. Jacob can't stay with him, he isn't safe.' My voice rises in panic.

'How long ago was this abusive history?' asks DC Millet, his tone matter-of-fact, like we're discussing the weather.

'Nine years ago, and he hasn't seen his father since.'

'And did Ricky ever hit Jacob?' he asks.

'No, but Jacob was present when the last assault on me took place. He was only five,' I reply.

The two detectives exchange a look. 'If it was nine years ago, the restraining order will be invalid now,' DS Byron says. 'You have custody of Jacob, but at his age he is old enough to contest this. If he starts proceedings, he can live with his father until the court decides otherwise.'

'You mean I can't make him come home?' I sink down onto the bottom stair. I can't believe this is happening.

Aaron crouches down next to me, a firm hand stroking my back.

'He said that if we make him come home, he will run away again. He's very unhappy at home. He feels that everyone – particularly Mr Paige and Lucas – blames him for what happened to Rachel, but he insists that he had nothing to do with it.'

'We don't blame him,' I protest.

Aaron and Lucas do, though, don't they? They've made that very clear so many times. Even so, how could Jacob turn to Ricky? Ricky, who has had nothing to do with him for so long, and who didn't care one jot about Jacob until now. Did Jacob try to find his father because Aaron and Lucas have made him feel unwanted at home?

I feel so betrayed to think that for months they've secretly been in touch, but Jacob hasn't said a word to me. Has Ricky been poisoning him against me? Is that why Jacob had become so moody and withdrawn lately?

I remember being so hurt and shocked when our friends told me the things Ricky had said about me. How he had made me out to be the controlling, abusive one. What if he is playing with Jacob's mind now, like he played with mine?

Then I think of how Ricky was when I first met him. He was charming, sweet, nothing was too much trouble. Until Jacob came along, and he couldn't cope with being a father, with the sleepless nights, the restrictions on our money and time. He still wanted to live like a single man. We had so many arguments about him going out drinking with his friends then coming back drunk in the early hours, waking up Jacob when I'd just got him to sleep.

The arguments gradually got more physical: a shove, a slap, until that awful punch in the mouth that made me report him. He erased us from his life then, no birthday cards for Jacob, no presents. I didn't even push him for maintenance because I wanted a clean break, I didn't want Jacob to be influenced by him. And now here he is, back in our life at the very worst time possible, and he's trying to take Jacob away from me.

Well, I'm not going to let him. I want Jacob back home with me. Safe.

71

Rachel

'I was so scared, I thought you'd died.' Amy flicks her long blonde hair off her face as she sits on the end of my bed, eating her way through the grapes she brought me. I am glad she is back from Spain, it's so good to see her after everything that's happened, and it gives my parents the chance to go home for a few hours.

'Well, here I am, alive. And I'm going home soon,' I tell her.

Amy pauses in the act of putting a grape into her mouth and studies me. 'Aren't you scared?'

'Terrified,' I admit. 'But what can I do? My folks are moving house soon anyway and I'm going to another school. They think that will make everything better.'

'Except it won't, will it?' Amy quizzes me, head on one side.

'Well, it will a bit, but nothing is really going to make it go away.'

We both tuck into the grapes in silence for a while then Amy says, 'Did you hear about Jacob running away?'

'Yeah. He's back now though, isn't he?'

'No. He's stopping at his dad's. Can you believe that?'

I remember that Jacob had started contacting his dad and didn't want his mum to know.

'His bedroom was trashed before he ran away,' Amy continues. 'I think it was a threat.'

'What!' I stare at her. 'No one told me that.'

'Yeah. You need to be careful,' she warns.

72

Vanessa

The police phone me a little later to confirm that Jacob has again refused to come home and is taking legal advice so that he can stay with Ricky. I'm beyond devastated, I feel like my heart has shattered irreparably. I try ringing Jacob again but no answer, so I leave him a message asking him if he will please meet me and talk to me, and that we all desperately want him home.

Finally, he replies.

I'm okay, Mum. Don't worry about me. I love you but I want to stay here with my dad.

As if it's that simple, not to worry about him, when he's with that man. I reply straight away, asking him for Ricky's number so I can talk to him. Of course, I'm scared of having any contact with Ricky, but my son's safety comes first. I don't know where they are, the police won't give me the address. Jacob doesn't answer.

. . .

'What? This is crazy, I can't believe he's gone to live with that scumbag,' Hazel says, her voice full of horror when I phone to fill her in on the latest development. 'I told you to tell him what his dad is like, Ness. I bet Ricky's fed him a load of lies. He's probably giving him the full charm offensive, and with what's going on in your house it's no wonder Jacob doesn't want to come home.'

She's right. It's my fault. I should have talked to Jacob about Ricky, then none of this would have happened. Or if I'd protected him from Aaron and Lucas's accusations, if they hadn't united against him and pushed him out.

'How are things with you and Aaron now?' Hazel asks as if she has read my mind.

'Okay,' I say cagily. Part of me wants to tell her all about the police discovering that Lucas and Aaron both came home the day Rachel fell, but Aaron would never forgive me for saying that. And I do think he's telling the truth, he's innocent. At least, most of me thinks that.

Later that afternoon I get a message from Ricky.

> Hello Vee. Jacob gave me your number. I just want to let you know that he's safe here with me. I've changed a lot, Vee, and I'm really sorry for how cruel I was to you back then. I was young and stupid. I'd like to meet and talk about things if you're willing to do that.

I am shaking as I read it, words from the man I never thought I'd see or talk to again. I don't want to see him, not now, not ever but I don't have a choice. I agree to meet him the next day outside the café by the river, a public place, and I ask him to bring Jacob too. I doubt my son will come, but it's worth a chance.

When I tell Aaron about Ricky's message he immediately says he will come with me. I don't want him to though.

'I can handle this,' I say. 'Chloe has a play date tomorrow with a friend from nursery so I'll drop her off, meet Ricky then pick her back up and come home.'

I'm nervous about seeing my abusive ex again but I'm determined not to show it. I'm not going to let him have any power over me now. Somehow I'm going to get my son back.

73

TWELVE DAYS AFTER THE FALL

When I arrive at the café I don't recognise Ricky at first. He was always clean-shaven and very slim, now he has a beard and a moustache and is a bit tubby. He obviously recognises me as he waves from the table where he's sitting outside, in the bright sunlight. I look around and I bite down my disappointment when I see that there's no sign of Jacob. Ricky's dark eyes rest on mine as I walk over to him, and he smiles. So, he hasn't come to fight then. He gets up from the table. 'Vee, so lovely to see you again.'

Ricky is the only one who has ever called me Vee. To everyone else, including Aaron, I'm Ness or Vanessa.

'Thanks, but this isn't a social call,' I say shortly, sitting down and clutching my handbag on my lap as if it can protect me. I level my gaze at him. 'Where's Jacob? Why didn't you bring him with you?'

Ricky gives me a wry smile. 'Straight to the point as always.' He sighs, not sitting back down. 'Jacob wouldn't come, I did try to persuade him. Let me get you a drink then we can talk. Is it still cappuccino?'

I shake my head. 'Skinny latte, please.' I do actually like

cappuccinos still, but I want him to realise that I've changed, I'm not the same woman anymore. I take a deep breath as he walks into the café, keeping my eyes on his back. It's so strange to see him again. Ricky was the first man I ever loved, and I fell for him hook, line and sinker – until I found out what he was really like.

I wait, my foot jiggling nervously under the table, until Ricky returns with the coffees. His is black, no change there then.

'Where's Jacob?' I demand again as soon as he sits back down.

'At home – my place,' he quickly corrects, but doesn't elaborate. 'How are you, Vee? You look well.'

I don't want to do this. I don't want to chat as if we're old friends, as if he didn't hit me, abuse me and force me to call the police for my own protection. 'Let's cut to the chase, Ricky,' I say. 'How did Jacob find you? Or did you find him?'

He takes a sip of his coffee before replying, taking his time, keeping me waiting. 'I found him. I've been wanting to find him for a while, Vee. I feel bad, really bad, about how I treated you. And it cost me my son.'

Is that resentment I can hear in his voice? Is he actually trying to blame me for this?

'It wasn't exactly easy for me,' I say slowly, 'having to start a new life and bring up a child on my own, but you weren't safe to be around.'

He winces. 'I know. I regret it so much and I can't apologise enough. I had anger issues, I admit it, but I've dealt with them. I would never harm Jacob. Or you. Not again.' Then he reaches out to put his hand on mine but I snatch it away.

'I don't want to hear it,' I snap. 'How did you find Jacob? And where are you living, is it around here?'

'No, I'm in Birmingham, but I've got a friend who lives the other side of the river,' he replies. 'I was at his flat when I saw the local newspaper report about Jacob winning the art prize. He's the spitting image of me when I was his age.' I'd noticed that too. Jacob has some of Ricky's mannerisms as well, like twisting his earlobe, which Ricky is doing right now. Blood will out, as my gran always used to say.

Ricky looks at me over the rim of his cup, his eyes calm and steady, as if he's done nothing wrong. 'I went to the school the article said he attended and waited for him to come out. He was with a blond-haired lad and a young girl with dark, curly hair.'

Lucas and Rachel.

So it's only been a couple of months at the most since Jacob met his father. Yet here he is, living with him instead of me. How has this happened?

'I didn't approach him at first, I just watched them for a couple of days. I wasn't sure how to go about it.'

'Through me.' I say this through gritted teeth. 'You should have approached him through me not gone behind my back, creeping on a child, watching him like that.' I am utterly furious, I feel like throwing my coffee over him, shoving him into the river. I need to stay calm though and play this carefully, think about my next move, if I'm going to get Jacob back.

'Please understand, Vee. I was scared to contact you. You took a restraining order against me. You had me banned from seeing my own son.'

'And why was that?' I hiss.

'I know it was my fault, Vee. I'm just stating facts. I was scared to approach you in case I got myself in trouble. Jacob is almost fifteen, not a child anymore, so I thought it best to contact him.' He hesitates. 'I saw him coming out of school one day by himself so I walked over to him and told him who I was, showed him photos of me and you with him as a baby, and said I'd like to have contact if he did too. I left him my phone number. A week or so later he messaged me.'

Jacob has been so angry and resentful lately, and I thought it was because he was jealous of Lucas and Rachel. Was it really because he'd met Ricky, and Ricky had made out that I was the one to blame for him not having his dad in his life?

'I bet you asked him to come and live with you,' I accuse him. 'You couldn't wait to turn him against me, could you? As soon as things got a bit tough because of Rachel's accident you encouraged Jacob to run away and come and live with you.'

Ricky shakes his head, putting his coffee down as he leans back and looks at me squarely. 'No, that's not what happened. You've got it wrong, Vee. I didn't encourage Jacob to run away. He messaged me and asked if he could stay for a bit, and when I met him, he looked awful and he had a bruise on his cheek – he said he'd tripped up but I'm not sure he was telling the truth. Anyway, he said he'd run away, that he wasn't going home and had nowhere else to go, so of course I let him stay. Would you prefer me to have sent him packing to sleep on the streets?'

'No, of course not but you should have known I'd be worried and at least let me know he was okay.'

'How? I didn't have your number. I did tell Jacob to let you know he was safe though, and he said he texted you. Did he?'

I nod, but I feel sick to the stomach. Jacob had a bruise on his face. What happened to him? Did he trip up as he said, or did someone attack him? Why didn't he think he could come to me to protect him?

'I want the same as you, Vee. I want our son to be safe,' Ricky says softy.

I want to tell him that Jacob isn't his son, that he gave up the right to be a father to him years ago, but I can't.

Jacob will always be his son, and it was Ricky he turned to when he needed help. Not me.

74

I let Ricky leave first, watching him walk away. He's promised to ask Jacob again to make contact with me, to arrange for him to meet me soon. I don't know what else to do, I feel completely helpless.

I gaze out over the river for a few minutes, then I check my phone and see that I have several missed calls from Aaron. I send a quick text saying that I'm fine and that I'll be home soon. I can't face him yet, I'm feeling so angry with him after what Ricky said about Jacob not wanting to come home because of Aaron and Lucas. They've driven my son away.

We can't keep living like this. I need to have it out with Aaron, so I decide that it's best if I take up Hazel's suggestion of letting Chloe stay with her for a couple of days.

I text Hazel to let her know and check it's okay, then pick Chloe up from her friend's. She's so happy, I can see that she's had a lovely time, and she grins in delight when I tell her that she's going to stay with Auntie Hazel and Zara for a while.

'How did it go?' Hazel asks when the two girls are busy playing.

'All right, actually. I mean it was obviously weird to see Ricky again but it was okay, I managed, and he was friendly enough.'

'Turned on the charm, did he?'

'Sort of. He apologised for everything, said he regretted it all.' I change the subject. Hazel will never forgive Ricky, no matter how much he says he's changed. 'Anyway, as I said, I really need to thrash things out with Aaron. I want Jacob to come back home where he belongs. Are you sure it's okay to leave Chloe with you over the weekend?'

'Of course! She can stay as long as you want. You all can. I've told you that.'

'Thanks, I really appreciate that. I'll go back and talk to Aaron. I'll call you later and pop over with some more things for Chloe.'

'Oh, don't worry about that, there's plenty of toys for her to play with here, and I've got some clothes that Zara has grown out of – I'd put them aside for her anyway.'

I'm so relieved as I set off home. Hazel has always been here for me, my rock. I know that whatever happens with Aaron, she'll be here to help me pick up the pieces.

Aaron and Lucas are both in the kitchen when I get home, tucking into a plate of chips at the kitchen table. They stop talking as I walk in.

'Where's Chloe?' Aaron asks, looking puzzled. 'I thought you were going to pick her up after you met Ricky?'

'She's staying at Hazel's over the weekend.'

He looks annoyed. 'Why? I want her home with us. You can't just do that without asking me, Ness, I'm her dad.'

'Well, I think she's better staying with Hazel and playing with Zara. I don't like her being in this atmosphere, it's not good for her,' I reply curtly.

I can see that Aaron isn't happy at all, but he drops it and asks how I got on with Ricky. 'I've been worried sick,' he adds, clearly a bit annoyed that I didn't call him back.

'It was fine,' I say briefly. 'He said that Jacob had a bruise on his cheek when he got to Ricky's, said he'd tripped over but I'm worried that someone attacked him.' My voice breaks at the thought of someone hurting my son. I can't handle this, not being able to be there for him, not knowing what is happening or even when I'll see him again.

'That's not good. Sit down, love.' Aaron gets up and eases me into a chair, seeing my pain.

I take a deep breath to calm myself, and grab a couple of chips from the plate with shaking hands. I haven't eaten all day. Aaron sits back down at the table and Lucas makes us all a cup of tea, and suddenly something is twisting inside me, something bitter and poisonous. I'm so angry with them both. This is my home. They're both here, in my kitchen. They're here, and Jacob, my son, has been driven away.

Finally I explode; it all comes out in a rush. 'Jacob ran away because he's sick of the way you two unite against him, and how you've been accusing him of what happened to Rachel. It's all your fault that this happened, that I've lost my son!'

'That's not fair, Ness.' Aaron looks wounded. 'And doesn't Jacob realise that by running away he's making himself look even more suspicious?'

A shadow falls over Lucas's face and he looks nervously from one to the other of us.

'Suspicious? Jacob is the only one who has told the truth right from the beginning. He has always admitted that he was in his bedroom when Rachel fell, that he heard the scream, saw her on the ground. Whereas you two... you pretended that you were out all day when actually you both returned just before it happened, then went back out again. Why did you do that if you had nothing to hide? Why did you lie?'

'I was in and out, it was nothing. I told you that,' Lucas stammers. 'I'm not hiding anything.'

'Don't make this out to be more than it is, Ness,' Aaron says quietly. 'Naturally you're upset about Jacob hunting out Ricky after all you've gone through, but I guess it's only natural that he's drawn to his father. He's a lot like him.'

'What the hell do you mean by that?' I'm up on my feet now, absolutely furious at Aaron's insinuation, and at how neither of them seems at all concerned or bothered about all of this. I've just told them Jacob was hurt. Why don't they care? 'You're always trying to point the finger at Jacob. Yes, he flared up a couple of times. That doesn't make him a criminal, he's just a normal kid, and he has his limits, everyone does.' I glare at Lucas. 'You've provoked him, you know you have. That's how Chloe got hurt, too.'

Lucas flushes and I know I've hit a nerve. 'That was an accident, I said I'm really sorry about it. I would never deliberately hurt Chloe.'

I take a breath to calm myself. That was too far. Lucas adores Chloe, he always has.

I soften my voice. 'I know you're sorry, Lucas, but this is exactly why Jacob won't come home, he's sick of the arguments and accusations. He doesn't feel welcome here. And he knows something about what happened to Rachel, that's why he said he needed Rachel to tell the truth.' I sweep my gaze from Lucas to Aaron. 'I think one of you knows something too. I'm fed up of being kept in the dark. You need to tell the truth.'

Aaron groans, pushing his mug away. 'Look, Ness, if you don't believe us and trust us, then I don't know what else we can say. We're never going to convince you.'

That's it. I can't stand to be here anymore. Jacob isn't here, Chloe is at Hazel's, and honestly, this doesn't feel like my home anymore.

'Then I'm going away for a while too,' I say, angry tears

spilling from my eyes. 'I need a break from all of this, I'm going to stay with Hazel, and I'm keeping Chloe with me there.'

'Ness, please don't go. Don't do this. You're making a mistake. This has nothing to do with me or Lucas. We wouldn't hurt Rachel, and what happened to Jacob isn't our fault.' Aaron sounds emotional, tears brimming in his eyes.

'I want to believe you but there have been too many lies.' I shake my head sadly. 'I can't think straight anymore. Like Jacob, I'm not coming back until you two start telling the truth.'

75

'They're both lying to me, I can sense it,' I tell Hazel as we both settle down on the sofa that night with a glass of wine each when Chloe and Zara are tucked up in bed. They're so excited to be having a sleepover together again. 'And why would they be, if they have nothing to hide?'

She shakes her head. 'It all sounds very suspicious to me, Ness. I think you've done the right thing coming here, giving yourself a bit of space and Aaron and Lucas time to think. They need to be straight with you.'

I take a long gulp of my wine. I know that drinking isn't really a good idea, tempted as I am to drown my sorrows and block everything out. I have Chloe to think about, but a couple of glasses might relax me and help me sleep. 'I wish Jacob would come home,' I say. 'I'm scared I've lost him. I feel like I've lost everything, my family, my home. And Aaron.' A sob breaks out. 'It's like it's all happening again.'

Hazel puts her glass down and moves nearer to give me a hug. 'You still have Chloe, and Jacob will be back. And that house is yours, we will get it back for you. I'll help you.'

I'm so tired. I don't want to have to deal with all this. I

want to rewind to a few months ago before Suzy and her family moved in next door. I want my life back. I have to do it, though. I have to fight for Jacob and Chloe's sake. And I will. 'Thanks, sis,' I say. I really don't know what I'd do without Hazel.

We sit up talking until late, and by the time I go to bed I'm so exhausted I fall asleep almost as soon as my head hits the pillow.

When I wake up the sun is streaming in through a gap in the curtains. Glancing at the clock on the bedside table I can see that it's ten-thirty. I check my phone, hoping to see a message from Jacob, but there's nothing from him, although there are several messages and missed calls from Aaron. I jump out of bed quickly, pulling on my dressing gown and going downstairs to check on Chloe. It's all quiet downstairs but I can hear squeals from the garden. Chloe and Zara are playing in the paddling pool, Hazel is sitting at the little mosaic table watching them, a carton of orange juice and two glasses on the table in front of her.

'Gosh, sorry, I didn't mean to sleep so long,' I say as I go out to join them.

'No worries, I'm glad you got a chance to rest,' Hazel says as I pull out a chair and sit down by her.

'Thanks. I do feel much better this morning. How has Chloe been? Have you been up long?'

'A couple of hours, and Chloe has been just fine. Want some juice or do you prefer tea or coffee?'

'Juice will be fine.' I pour myself a glass and take a long drink. I'm thirsty. 'It's so peaceful here,' I say wistfully as I watch Chloe and Zara play.

Hazel lives in a spacious detached house and her garden is very private – their neighbours aren't close like ours, no chatting over the garden fence or sitting on the windowsill to talk to each other.

My phone pings again, bursting through my thoughts. Hazel watches me as I glance at the screen, her eyebrows raised questioningly. 'Aaron?'

I nod. 'Again.' I open the message. It says the same as all the others. How sorry he is and begging me to come home. I only read them in case he has news of Jacob. I bite my lip as I think about what to do. 'I need to go home. I can't just run away from this,' I blurt out.

'Stay here, where you're safe and away from the drama.' Hazel turns to me, she seems uneasy. 'I read on one of those local news pages that Rachel is being discharged tomorrow. You're better off not being there.'

'Really? She must have completely recovered then. That's great news. And even more reason for me to go home. I might get a chance to talk to her, encourage her to speak up.'

Hazel frowns. 'I really think you should stay, and if you let Jacob know you're here, he might come too.'

I know she cares about Jacob's safety, and I also think she's scared that Ricky will tell Jacob what she did all those years ago. Hazel was only trying to protect me, but I bet Ricky won't tell it that way.

I shake my head firmly. 'No, I need to go back. That's my house, Hazel. My children's home.'

'At least stay here for today, tonight,' she says. 'Take a bit more time to relax and get your head straight. If you must go home tomorrow, why not leave Chloe with me for a bit longer? She isn't at nursery until Tuesday, and Zara will love having her to play with, plus it will give you a chance to sort things out without having to worry about Chloe being upset.'

She's right. 'Thanks so much. You're the best, Haze. I don't know what I'd do without you.'

'You'd do the same for me. We're sisters, we'll always have each other's backs,' she says, the emotion heavy in her voice.

Hazel put her neck on the line for me all those years ago, and I know she would do it again in an instant. I would do it for her too, but Hazel has never needed my help. She's so calm and her life is always under control – she and her husband, Liam, are great together. Whereas my life with Ricky was one disaster after another – it settled down once I left him and then met Aaron, but now it is a mess all over again.

I message Jacob to tell him that Rachel is going to be discharged, and that I'm staying over at Hazel's tonight. I don't want him returning home when I'm not there. I end by asking him if he will come to Hazel's too, but he doesn't reply.

I'm not going to let Ricky take my son away, I vow. I'm going to fight for him. I'll go back and hear Aaron out but I'm going to be firm. I put my son first when I left Ricky all those years ago, and I'm going to put him and Chloe first now.

76

TWO WEEKS AFTER THE FALL

'Remember you're welcome to come back if you want to,' Hazel tells me as I set off the next morning, after giving Chloe a big hug goodbye.

'Thanks so much. I'll call you later,' I promise.

As I drive down my street, I see Suzy's car parked in front of her house. She gets out of the driver's seat then goes around to the other side and opens the passenger door. I pull up and watch as she helps someone out of the car. It's Rachel.

I'm so pleased that she's well enough to come home. I swallow a lump in my throat as I see that her left arm is in plaster and she looks pale, vulnerable. Frightened. I want to get out and hug her, tell her how sorry I am this has happened to her, ask if she's all right, offer Suzy support. I don't do any of those things because Suzy turns and darts a warning look at me. She doesn't want me to talk to them. So I stay right there, in the driver's seat, my heart aching for how things used to be.

Then I see our front door open. Jacob is standing in the doorway, dressed in a grey tee shirt, black trackie shorts and trainers.

He's come home! My son's back! Now my heart is soaring and I open the car door as Jacob walks down the path.

He's not looking at me though, he's looking at Rachel. 'Rachel. Are you okay?' he calls.

She turns her head to him then and I catch my breath when I see the fear in her eyes. 'Leave me alone. I don't want to talk to you.' Her voice carries to me in the still summer air and I can hear the fear in it. She clutches Suzy's arm tight.

'Don't worry, love, no one is going to come near you,' Suzy assures her, then she faces Jacob. 'You stay away from my daughter, you and your brother,' she spits. 'Do you understand?'

'Please, Rachel, please talk to me,' Jacob begs, looking beseechingly at Rachel, but she refuses to meet his eye.

She bows her head and scuttles up the path, darting inside as soon as Suzy opens the door without even a backwards glance.

Nausea churns in my stomach.

The way she responded to Jacob was with fear, pure fear. I recognise that expression all too well, I used to see it on my own face every time I looked in the mirror, back in those awful days with Ricky.

Surely she isn't terrified of my son?

77

Rachel

I'm shaking as I go inside. I didn't know that Jacob had come back home – I would have tried to stay in hospital a little longer or gone to Nan's if I had. I don't want to see him or talk to him. I want him to leave me alone but I know he won't.

Mum fusses over me, making me comfortable on the sofa. 'Are you sure you don't want to come and get some fresh air, love? You could sit in the garden or we can go for a drive to the river and sit and watch the ducks, like we used to when you were little? You've been stuck in that hospital so long, you must be going stir-crazy.'

I tell her that I just want to be here, in the house, with my family, but Mum has that worried look on her face.

Later, I hear her and Dad talking in the kitchen, when they think I'm asleep in the lounge. Mum thinks I'm still in danger. They are both constantly checking on me, and the back and front doors are double-bolted so no one can get in, which is annoying Ben as he can't let himself out to play in the garden. Mum's been trying to get me to tell her who sent those messages, but I won't. I can't. Hopefully she'll eventually give up.

I haven't heard from him since I've been in hospital. I hope he'll keep away now, I doubt it though. He's got a hold over me and he knows it. And now I'm weak, bruised and with a broken wrist. If I couldn't escape him before, how can I now?

The truth is I can never escape him. I was stupid to think he cared about me. Stupid to trust him.

And to think that it was me who made the first move, the one who set all this in motion.

78

Vanessa

I'm so pleased to see Jacob and I want to hug him, hold him close, but he seems so distant. He doesn't even look at me, just turns away. I reach out and touch his arm to stop him leaving. I need to talk to him, try to get him to open up.

'It's so good to see you, Jacob. I've been worried about you,' I say softly.

He keeps his back to me and murmurs, 'I'm fine, Mum.'

I hate this distance between us, but this isn't the time to push him. He is on the verge of walking away again, back to Ricky's. I guess. I must persuade him to stay, this is my opportunity and I need to be careful, sensitive. 'I've missed you so much, darling. Please will you at least come in and have a drink so we can chat for a bit?'

He hesitates then shrugs and follows me into our house.

'What do you want to drink?' I ask as we walk into the kitchen.

'Do you have milkshake?' he asks hopefully.

'Of course.' I stop myself from getting a glass out of the

cupboard and pouring the milkshake into it. I'm not treating him like a guest, this is Jacob's home and I want him to remember that. 'Help yourself.' I switch on the coffee machine and put in an espresso pod – I need my coffee strong today.

The coffee machine whirrs into action, and when I turn around I see Jacob has filled the glass with chocolate milkshake, his hand is shaking and he's staring down into his glass. He looks so distressed that my heart lurches in a painful jolt.

I rest my back against the worktop and try to keep my voice steady. 'What is it, Jacob? What's troubling you?'

He is still staring at the glass, and I bite my lip as I watch him. Somehow I have to get him to speak. And whatever he says, I must make sure that I stay calm and supportive. 'You can tell me anything. You know that, don't you? I will always try to help you. You're my son. I love you and nothing you can tell me will change that.'

He looks up at me, his eyes shining with tears. 'Everything's such a mess, Mum, and I don't know what to do.'

'Oh, darling.' I wrap my arms around him and hug him tight as he sobs into my shoulder, releasing deep, guttural sobs that shake his whole body. Finally he stops crying so heavily and he pulls away, wiping his eyes with the hem of his tee shirt.

'I saw you talking to Rachel just now, and she seemed scared. What's going on?' I ask gently.

'I didn't hurt her, Mum. I would never hurt Rachel. I wouldn't hurt anyone. I'm not like my dad, even though Aaron thinks I am.' He takes a deep, shuddering breath. 'I know what Dad did to you, he told me. I don't remember any of it. He also told me he is really sorry, that he was a different person back then and has changed,' Jacob says.

'I guess he said I provoked him,' I say bitterly, because that's what Ricky always said. It was never his fault.

'No, he didn't. He said it was all his fault. If he had said it was your fault, I'd never have had anything to do with him. I hate that he hurt you like that, and that you had to leave him to protect yourself and me.' He swallows, his watery eyes meeting mine. 'He's changed, Mum, and he's sorry and he wants to get to know me, if I want that too. And I do. He's my dad.'

'Well, that's your choice to make but you don't have to live with him. You could live here and visit him. I won't stop you,' I say. I want my son back and if it's on those terms, then so be it. At least if he's living with me I can protect him.

At least, I think I can.

'No, I can't come home, Mum. There's too much stuff I can't handle here. I'd prefer to live with my dad. I'd like to come and visit though, to see you and Chloe now and again. If that's okay?'

'I'd love that.' I wrap my arms around him again, crying myself now, and he hugs me back, just like when he was a little boy. Only he's not a little boy any longer, he's almost grown up, and although his decision is breaking my heart I have to accept it.

'Can I go and get some of my stuff?' he asks after a while.

'Of course, take whatever you want, they're your things,' I say.

He goes upstairs and I can hear him and Lucas talking in low voices.

I look around the kitchen then and notice that it's clean and tidy. I don't know what Aaron and Lucas had to eat over the weekend but at least they cleared up after themselves. I open the back door and go out into the garden.

Suzy is hanging out some washing, and I remember how we always used to chat over the fence, how nice it was to have a friend next door. She turns to look at me now, and she seems so angry that I involuntarily take a step back.

'You tell your son to keep away from my daughter. He couldn't even give her a chance to get in, could he, before he had a go at her.'

I try to keep my voice calm. 'Jacob didn't threaten her, Suzy. He simply asked how she was.'

'She's afraid of him, anyone can see that.' Suzy's voice is shaking and I long to reach out and hug her, tell her that Jacob would never harm her daughter, but the words won't come out because I saw Rachel's face too. She was terrified.

'Just so you know, we're moving away as soon as we can,' Suzy continues. 'Until then, keep Jacob and Lucas away from Rachel. If you don't, we'll get a restraining order against them.' She turns away and continues pegging out her washing, her back a rigid barrier between us.

I stand motionless, her words sending a chill through me. A restraining order against Jacob. Just like the one I got against Ricky all those years ago.

I want to protect Jacob. But do others need protecting from him?

79

Aaron

My heart lifts as I read the text from Lucas. Ness is home, and Jacob came back too. No Chloe though. I miss our little girl and am not happy that Ness didn't discuss this with me, but I know she is right. Home isn't a good place for Chloe to be right now.

Lucas said that Jacob came by for a few hours but he's gone back to stay with Ricky now. I'm so glad he came to see Ness, she misses him so much. I think she should put her foot down, she has custody of Jacob after all, but he's threatened to run away again if he can't stay with his dad so I guess she feels she's got no option.

I know that a lot of this is my fault, I never meant this to happen. Sometimes you make one decision, take one action, and it's like a domino effect. Before you know it, your life is out of control.

There aren't many people at the office today, it's quiet and empty. It used to be such a buzzing place to be before people started working from home when Covid struck a few years ago and a lot of them never came back, preferring to avoid the travel.

I guess that's when it all started, lots of businesses went under because of lockdown and although it managed to keep going, the company started struggling, there just wasn't enough work coming in. One by one people were let go, last in first out as there wouldn't be so much redundancy pay to shell out. Then we were put on a three-day week.

I didn't tell Ness, as I didn't want to worry her, so I've been pretending to work from home on those days off. It isn't a total lie though – I've been working in a way, trying to get another job. I've lost count of the CVs I've sent out and the job interviews I've been to in the last few months, but no luck. Money has been getting tighter and tighter so in the end I took out a loan, telling myself things would get better. Only they haven't. Everything keeps spiralling and I can't control it no matter how hard I try. I should have told Ness as soon as it all started but I was so scared of losing her. I know how hard it was for her to trust and let a man in her life again after Ricky. And I was embarrassed, ashamed. I didn't want her to think that I'd let her down.

Now the company is finally closing and I've lost my job. I collect my things, say goodbye to the few people who are here, and head to the car, carrying the few items that were on my desk. I start up the car and drive away slowly, taking a last look at the place where I've worked for ten years.

Anyone's life can change in a moment. I learnt that when Amanda received her diagnosis and then died less than a year later. It was hard but I pulled myself together and tried to make a new life for me and Lucas, to give him everything he needed. When I met Ness I was blown away by her straight away. She was so beautiful and fiery, and full of a determination not to be hurt again. I soon came to love Jacob too, he was such a quiet, sensitive boy, so protective of his mother. Gradually they both came to trust me, and Jacob and Lucas bonded.

I always knew that Hazel didn't trust me, but I understood

that she was looking out for her sister, and that Ness needed her, so I vowed to never come between them no matter how much Hazel annoyed me. We built our family unit and were so good together until Suzy and Carl moved in and the boys started arguing over Rachel.

The house is so empty without Chloe and Jacob. I have to try and make everything better, make it right. I know I should talk to Vanessa and confess what I've done. But I can't.

80

THE FOLLOWING TUESDAY

Vanessa

It's been such a difficult week, my emotions are all over the place. Jacob is still at Ricky's but at least he messages me every day and has been home twice. He and Lucas seem to have come to some kind of understanding, and while they aren't as pally as they were, they're not arguing. Like me and Aaron. He's been going to the office to work every day this week and he's trying hard to make things right, I can see that, but I'm battered by it all.

I go into the study to get some work done while Chloe is at nursery, but I can't concentrate so I surf the net a bit, idly checking out the news. I pause when something jumps out at me. Gamestec, the firm Aaron works for, went into liquidation last week, but have apparently been struggling and laying people off for months. I read the paragraph again and again. Then I go to the company website and see that it's down. I lean back in my chair, stunned.

If Aaron's company is closed, where has he been going every day?

I get up and pace around, adrenaline coursing through me. He's lying. Again.

I try to call him, but the line rings out. A few minutes later a message pings in.

Sorry, love, in a meeting. Is everything okay?

I'm furious. He's still lying through his teeth.
I shoot a text back.

Oh, is that right? Tell me, then, how can you be at work when your bloody company has gone into liquidation?

A few minutes later he calls me. 'Ness, it's not what you think. I can explain,' he blurts down the phone.

'Fine, go ahead. But please don't insult me by telling me more lies,' I say icily.

He pauses before he begins speaking slowly, his voice heavy. 'The company has been struggling for ages. I was on a three-day week for months, I was applying for jobs when you thought I was working at home. I've been to lots of interviews and finally got a new job just before the company closed last week. Just in time, as there were no funds so we didn't even get redundancy pay.'

'And your reason for not telling me all this is…?' I demand.

'I know I should have done, I didn't want to worry you. I thought things would pick up, or that I'd get another job soon. Then with everything that's been happening, I worried it would be the straw that broke the camel's back. I've finally got a new job, that's where I am now. I was going to tell you, Ness, really, I was trying to find the right time.'

Something inside me snaps. 'You know what, Aaron, I've had enough. I've given you chance after chance and it's just one lie after another. I'm leaving. I'm taking Chloe and going back to stay with Hazel. I don't want to be with you anymore. I don't trust you, not at all.'

'Ness, please! Just wait until I come home and I'll explain everything.'

I cut off the call.

'Are you really leaving us? For good?'

I spin around to see Lucas standing behind me, in the open doorway of the study. He looks like he's about to cry. Poor kid. I go and wrap my arms around him.

'I'm sorry you heard that. I don't want to, love, but your dad hasn't been telling me the truth. I don't trust him. We simply can't live like this anymore.'

'He didn't want to worry you, about the job. That's all.'

I pull my head back and meet his gaze. 'So you knew all about it?'

He nods. 'Dad asked me not to say.'

And, of course, his first loyalty is going to be to his dad.

'I don't want you to go, Dad doesn't want you to go. I like living with you, you're the nearest I've got to a mum. I know me and Jacob argue a bit but we're good now. Please don't go,' Lucas pleads with me.

'I'm sorry, love, I have to. I need time to think. This is all too much for me.'

Lucas chokes back tears and runs out. This is horrible. I hate Aaron for doing this to us. Hazel is at work so I leave her a message, telling her that I'll be round with Chloe later when I've picked her up from nursery, and this time we'll be staying. I phone Jacob but he doesn't answer either so I text him. Then I go upstairs to pack my bags.

Hazel phones just as I finish packing, getting ready to leave. 'I'm so glad you've seen sense at last,' she says. 'You can't believe a word that man says. That's why I reported him to the police.'

I'm speechless as Hazel's words register slowly.

'You... you reported Aaron? You were the one who told the police about the other girl?'

'I had to, Ness. I was worried about your safety, and Chloe and Jacob, too. You know I'll never let anything happen to you. I'll do anything it takes to keep you safe. I'll always protect you, against anyone. You know that.'

I'm too astounded to reply.

'Are you okay, Ness? I must go back to work now, I've only got a short break,' Hazel says.

'Yes, I'm fine. See you later,' I reply numbly.

She ends the call and I sit down on the nearest chair as a memory floods into my mind, as vivid and detailed as if it were happening all over again.

It was a couple of weeks after I left Ricky. He'd been charged with assault, and I'd got a restraining order against him. Hazel came to take me shopping one day when Jacob was at school, and we were going to a big shopping centre on the outskirts of town. We were about to park when I saw Ricky walking towards us, two carrier bags in his hand. I gasped and immediately started shaking, hyperventilating. 'It's Ricky! Turn around quick, I don't want him to see me.'

'That bastard. I'll make sure that he never hurts you again.'

Before I knew what was happening, Hazel hit the pedal and accelerated towards him.

'Hazel, stop!' I shouted but she carried on, her expression fixed, focused, full of sheer determination. Then Ricky spotted us, and I saw the terror on his face.

'Who's scared now?' Hazel said, a little smile playing around her mouth.

Ricky started walking backwards, the shopping spilling out of his bag. I was frozen in my seat, my mouth open.

Finally I came to my senses. 'Stop!' I yelled, reaching over and pulling the handbrake. Only our seatbelts prevented us from going through the windscreen. Ricky was so close that we could see the whites of his eyes.

I was trembling like a leaf, but Hazel was triumphant. She looked like she'd enjoyed every second of it, as if it were a fun rollercoaster ride. 'That shook him.'

'You were going to kill him!' I gasped.

She turned to me, her eyes innocent, wide. 'Of course I wasn't. I just wanted to scare him.'

But I didn't believe her.

I think she would have killed Ricky that day, if I hadn't stopped her in time.

81

Rachel

'Now remember, don't answer the door to anyone,' Mum repeats. She's standing by the lounge door, looking anxiously over at the sofa, where I'm lying. I know that she doesn't want to go to work, but she has to, she needs the money. And I want her to go. I'm sick of them all fussing over me. I want to be alone. I'm okay, I can manage. I'm stronger than everyone thinks I am.

'I won't,' I promise, trying to smile as reassuringly at her as I can.

'Especially those lads next door. I want you to keep well away from them. I can't wait until we can move away from here.'

We've had this conversation every day since I came out of hospital.

'Nan will be here later, as soon as Ben has finished at the dentist,' Mum tells me for the umpteenth time.

'I know, Mum. I'm just going to listen to some music, and maybe watch a film. I'll be totally fine,' I tell her.

'I might be able to leave early...'

'Mum, go! I promise I'll call you if I need you.'

Finally, after another long, worried look at me, she leaves and I breathe a sigh of relief. Now I have an hour or so alone before Nan and Ben return. I can relax, unwind a bit. Get my thoughts together.

I haven't heard from *him* since I fell from my bedroom window. Perhaps he will leave me alone now. I've kept my mouth shut. Now I just have to hope he keeps his end of the bargain.

Then a text pings in, and I almost drop my phone when I see the message.

I'm coming over.

I squeeze my eyes shut, trying to stem the onset of tears.

I was wrong. He won't leave me alone.

This nightmare will never end.

82

Vanessa

I can't stop thinking about Hazel's words, my mind is in chaos as I sit on one of the garden chairs, gazing towards the house next door.

Hazel. Hazel would protect me from being hurt, she'd do anything for me.

If she found out Rachel was doing something that could put my marriage, my home, my wellbeing at risk... would she go and have it out with her?

Would she lose her cool? Would she threaten her, tell her to stop?

Hazel? Do I seriously think that my beloved older sister, my rock, the person who has always looked out for me, would harm a young girl?

Of course she wouldn't. It's ridiculous.

Slowly I get to my feet and finish packing my cases, then I go out into the corridor. Lucas's bedroom is firmly closed. I can't just go and leave him like this, so I knock on the door.

'Go away!' he shouts.

I knock again and open the door. He's sitting on his bed, his back against the wall, hands wrapped around his bent knees. He glares defiantly at me as I walk in.

'Lucas, I'm so sorry about this,' I tell him softly. 'I really am. I want you to know that I'm still there for you, you know I think of you as my own son, and I always will. You can come and see me and Chloe and Jacob anytime.'

I can see that he's trying really hard not to cry. 'Are you definitely not coming back?'

'I don't know, but I promise this doesn't change anything between us.' I sit down on the bed and wrap my arms around him. I've been his mother for five years, nobody can take that away from me. 'I'll miss you so much. Keep in touch with me. Promise?'

'I will,' he whispers, and we hug for a long time.

Finally, I take the cases downstairs and go back out into the garden. I need to pause, get some fresh air, gather my thoughts. I sit down on the bench underneath the kitchen window, surrounded by the new plants we bought at the garden centre a couple of weeks ago, back when it looked like Aaron and I might still be okay.

Am I doing the right thing?

I look once more at the fence separating us from next door's garden, remembering that first day when Suzy, Carl and their family moved in, and how happy we'd been to have neighbours at last. I'm feeling overwhelmed with sadness and emotion, lost in reminiscing about a past I'll never be able to go back to.

Then I gasp as I see a figure wearing a grey hoodie running down the path next door.

He's opening the back door.

He's going in.

What the hell?

I'm already on my feet, running up the path, out the gate

and into next door's garden. I'm hurtling through their garden when screams and shouts ring out from the house.

Rachel!

I can't let him hurt her again. I yank open the back door just as an enormous crash comes from the kitchen. I dash in then stop in the doorway, my hand flying to my mouth.

Oh crap!

Rachel is crouched on the floor, terrified, and there are two boys rolling around, fighting as if they want to kill each other, their punches vicious, unrestrained. They are both wearing hoodies, one black and one grey. Then the boy wearing the grey hoodie is flung over and is now on the bottom, and I can see his face.

It's Jacob.

I have no idea who the other boy is, I don't recognise him at all. He's gaining the upper hand and is clearly intending to win. He raises his fist and punches Jacob hard in the face.

Fury rages through me. 'Get your bloody hands off my son!' I yell, running over to him and dragging him off Jacob. He snarls, twists around and lunges for me, grabbing hold of my shoulders and pushing me to the ground. 'Do you really want to take me on?' he growls, swearing at me and spitting into my face.

'Gerrof my mum!' Jacob is up on his feet now and yanks the lad off me.

'Call the police!' I yell to Rachel, struggling to get to my feet, but she's rooted to the spot, cowering on the floor with her back against the kitchen counter, trembling with fear.

I pull out my phone from my jeans pocket and take a quick snap of the lad who is now thrashing about on the floor as he and Jacob roll over, so we can identify him if he gets away. Then I begin dialling 999 but the lad kicks Jacob off him, sending him crashing back into a cupboard. He leaps over to me, snatches my phone and hurls it against the wall. It hits it with a crash and falls to the floor.

His face twists into a snarl. 'You're not phoning anyone, lady.'

He pulls out a knife, the blade glistening in the ray of sunlight coming from the window. 'Stay where you are, all of you!' he orders.

I look at his eyes, they look blank, dead. I know with absolute certainty that he means to use that knife.

83

I back against the kitchen cupboards as the thug comes closer towards me, the knife gleaming in front of him. His lips are curled slightly, his expression hard and set, and I can see his hand trembling around the handle of the knife.

He's just a kid. He can't be much older than Jacob. Will he really kill us?

'Stop it!' Rachel screams. 'Stop it!'

I can see Jacob lying motionless on the floor. I think he's unconscious.

'Please, just let me see if my son is okay. I won't call the police.' I make a step towards Jacob but the lad snarls and grabs me by the shoulder.

'Do you think I won't use this? I've got nothing to lose now, thanks to you and your fucking interfering son.'

His face is red, his eyes spitting with anger and desperation. He might only be a lad but he's dangerous and that knife blade is only inches from my neck. I have to act fast. I reach behind me for the ground pepper pot which Suzy always keeps on the worktop under the top cupboards, my hand curling around it. I have only one chance. I have to aim right.

I slip the top off the pepper pot with my thumb then I bring my arm forward and throw the pepper in his face. He screams, bringing his free hand up to his eyes. Suddenly Jacob springs up from the floor and grabs the knife from his hands. He must have been playing at being unconscious, waiting for his chance to pounce.

The thug buckles over, screaming as the pepper burns his eyes, and Jacob jumps on his back, knocking him to the floor. I pick up my phone from the floor, my hands shaking. The screen is cracked but it's still usable.

'No. Please don't!' Rachel screams. 'You can't call the police. You can't.'

'She has to. He could have killed us,' Jacob says. He is now sitting on the lad, pinning him down.

Rachel is shaking, begging me not to call the police, her eyes wide and petrified.

'Is this the lad who hurt you before, Rachel?' I ask softly, taking slow steps towards the terrified girl. 'Did he push you out of the window, love? I have to call the police but it's going to be okay now, I promise. It's all going to be okay.'

The lad on the floor is groaning and twisting under Jacob, and finally he breaks free, pushes Jacob off his back and scrambles to his feet.

'You'll be effing sorry for this, you just wait,' he growls, as he legs it towards the kitchen door.

Just at that moment, Carl charges in and they both collide.

'Who the hell are you?' Carl grabs the lad in an armlock. 'And what the fuck are you all doing in my house?' he demands when he spots me and Jacob in the kitchen.

'Saving your daughter. And I'm calling the police now,' I tell him.

84

'You'd better start talking, and fast!' Carl growls, bending the lad's arm further. He's just a kid, I want to protest, but he would have killed us, I remind myself. And I'm pretty sure he's the one who hurt Rachel.

'Gerrof! You'll break my arm!' the lad yells.

'I'll break your fucking neck if you don't start talking,' Carl snarls.

'Dad, no! Let him go! It's all been a big misunderstanding!' Rachel cries out, and she's on her feet now, trying to pull Carl off the lad, but she slips and falls back to the ground.

Jacob dashes over to help her back up.

'Are you okay, love?' Carl calls to Rachel, still hanging on to the lad.

'Yes. I'm okay. You've got to let him go, Dad,' she whimpers as Jacob puts his arms around her.

'Like hell I'll let him go!' Carl looks like he'd kill the lad given half a chance. 'And you get the fuck away from my daughter!' he yells at Jacob.

'You need to calm down, Jacob saved your daughter!' I shout. I go over to the two kids huddled together on the floor and wrap my arms around them both. I understand Carl's anger, this thug could have killed his daughter, but I'm worried how far Carl will go to restrain him.

Then with huge relief, I hear people come clattering in through the back door and yelling as they burst into the kitchen. 'Police! Put your hands in the air! Now!' Some burly policemen are here, and I've never been more grateful to see police in my life.

'We'll take over now, sir,' one of them says, and within minutes they've handcuffed the lad and bundled him outside.

I help Jacob and Rachel up off the floor and tell them to sit down at the table. I'm shaking but looking after them is my priority.

Carl takes a deep breath and walks over to Rachel, who is crying bitterly. 'Are you sure you're all right, love? Has that scumbag hurt you?' he demands, pulling her into his arms.

She rests her head on his shoulder. 'Jacob and Ness stopped him,' she says, her voice trembling.

I boil the kettle, put teabags into mugs and spoon in some sugar to calm all our nerves, feeling safer now that the police are here. One of them stays behind with us. 'We were on patrol nearby, so your call was put through to us,' says the police officer, accepting a cup of tea from me with thanks. 'Other officers are on their way to take statements from you all.'

I text Aaron, telling him to come home ASAP, and Carl phones Suzy. After fifteen minutes or so, Jacob and I go back next door. Suzy is on the way home and the police officer is staying there, with Rachel and Carl.

I'm still so shaken up that when Aaron comes in and holds out his arms, I walk unsteadily into them and sink into his hug, clinging to him as if I haven't seen him in years.

I could have died today. We all could have.

Even scarier is the knowledge that if I hadn't seen and heard what was happening next door, if I hadn't been in the right place at the right time, my son could have been killed. And Rachel too. I can't bear to think how close I came to losing Jacob.

The police come around about half an hour later, wanting a statement. They tell us that Rachel is clearly absolutely terrified of the lad and she refuses to talk. She won't say a single word to them, neither will the boy they arrested and there is nothing on him to identify him. 'Can you tell us anything about him? His name, anything at all?' they ask Jacob as we all sit down in the lounge.

Jacob chews his lip, and he looks at me as if for reassurance. 'Jacob, it's time you tell the truth. You could have died today, and Rachel. We all could have.'

So slowly, haltingly, Jacob tells us everything.

The lad is called Dale. He attended Rachel's previous school, before she moved next door. He is a couple of years older than her and she was flattered when he asked her out.

Then he pressured her into sharing some explicit photos with him on Snapchat, promising to delete them. Only he saved them and used them to blackmail her.

He wouldn't leave Rachel alone. She'd thought she was safe when they moved, but he found out her new address and her school. He kept demanding she give him more and more money or he would upload the photos to the internet.

'Rachel made me promise not to tell anyone,' Jacob says, and he looks at Lucas, who is listening, astonished.

'That must have been hard.' I put my hand over his. 'Why did she confide in you?' I ask him.

He chews his fingernail. 'I caught her stealing some money from the office at school. She broke down and told me every-thing, but begged me not to tell on her. She was so scared, Mum.' He looks at Lucas again. 'That's why she was crying and yelling at me to leave her alone. Not because I was bullying her! I tried to persuade her to talk to her folks, but she wouldn't, she was too ashamed and scared about what they would say, especially her dad. She thought he'd lose it at her completely. He's got a temper, he frightens her sometimes, and she really hates disappointing and upsetting him, and her mum too.'

Lucas leans over and squeezes his arm. 'I got it badly wrong. Sorry, bro.'

Aaron and I look at each other and I see that there are tears in his eyes too.

'So, do you think this Dale pushed Rachel out of the window?' the police ask.

'I... I don't know.' Jacob swallows and his eyes fill up. 'I think maybe she leant out and called over to me to let me know Dale was coming over, so I could come and help, but she leant too far and fell.' He wipes his hand across his eyes. 'The truth is I heard her calling my name and I ignored her because I was mad at her. I'd tried to help her before but she'd fallen out with me over it.' He twists his hands together, his eyes downcast. 'It was all my fault. If I hadn't ignored her, I could have helped. I don't know if she fell or if he pushed her, but either way, it wouldn't have happened if it wasn't for me.'

I squeeze his hands. 'Jacob, absolutely none of this is your fault. Thank you for telling us.'

'Your mum is right, Jacob, you've done nothing wrong,' Aaron says gently. He places his hand on Jacob's shoulder. 'All you've done is try to help and support Rachel, the best way you knew how.'

Jacob breaks down and sobs, and I wrap my arms around him, holding him tight. He's been carrying this burden alone for the past few weeks, suspected of hurting Rachel when all he was doing was trying to help her.

'You've done the right thing telling us, Jacob, and Rachel doesn't need to worry about those photos at all. We'll confiscate

Dale's phone and laptop and we will delete them. We'll make sure he can't hurt her again,' the policeman assures him.

'Rachel will hate me. I swore I wouldn't tell,' Jacob sobs. 'She's so scared about what her dad will say, what he'll do when he finds out.'

'I would think that Carl is just relieved that his daughter is still alive,' Aaron says.

After the police leave, we sit together nursing strong cups of tea, talking it all through. Jacob has told us everything now, and Lucas and Aaron are being really kind to him, comforting him that he did nothing wrong, that they're sorry they ever doubted him. I'm so relieved to have my family back. I'm glad Chloe is still with Hazel for now, that she didn't hear any of this. But I can't wait to bring her home, too.

'I saw her with a lad just like the one you're describing a couple of times,' Aaron is saying. 'I thought they were together, that she'd got tired of Lucas and Jacob and taken up with someone else.'

'Why didn't you mention this before?' I ask him.

'Well, it didn't look menacing, otherwise I'd have told him to clear off myself. They were huddled up together, like a couple. I didn't think there was anything in it. I should have done, I feel bad about that now.'

'I can't believe that creep went around to threaten her again. And with a knife! Good job you were there, bro,' Lucas says, patting Jacob on the back, clearly proud of his brother. 'What made you go around there though?'

Jacob smiles at him gratefully, but as he speaks his voice is still shaky. He's been through so much. 'Rachel phoned me, she was so scared. She said he was coming over for more money, and she didn't have any, so I said I'd give her some.' Jacob throws me a guilty look. 'I took it out of my savings account. Sorry, Mum. I'd just reached her house when I saw someone go in through the back door. I guessed it was him so I legged it, and when I got in Dale was attacking her, threatening her, even despite her broken wrist and everything. She was in pain, she was so frightened, screaming. I pulled him off her. That's when Mum came in.' He grins at me. 'You were brilliant, like a ninja!'

I grin back. I'm glad he thought I had it all under control, it sure didn't feel like it. I just did what I had to do to protect my son. 'Well, I'm so glad it's all out in the open now,' I say. 'Promise me that you won't keep secrets again, Jacob. This could have turned out such a lot worse. Was it that lad who trashed your room, then? I know you didn't do that yourself. Was he threatening you too, because he knew Rachel had confided in you?'

I spot Lucas looking at Aaron, who licks his lips nervously.

'Tell Ness, Dad,' Lucas says. 'She's going to find out now anyway.'

I look at Aaron's guilty face and brace myself. What else don't I know?

He sits down and rests his head in his hands for a moment. This looks bad. Then he lifts his head. 'I've got something to confess, too. Jacob's room being trashed was a warning to me, not Jacob.'

I listen in total disbelief as he explains. 'I told you I've been having money problems, after my hours were reduced. Well, I borrowed some money. A lot of money, from a loan shark. I was desperate. The bank wouldn't lend me any, I've already maxed out the overdraft and my credit cards, and I'm behind with my car payments.' His voice falters, he can't meet my eyes. 'I tried to get work. I applied for so many jobs before I got this one, Ness, went to countless interviews, but there were always so many other people after the jobs too. I kept hoping things would pick up but they didn't. Then I couldn't pay back the loan.'

'You mean the loan shark sent someone into our home to threaten you and they trashed my son's bedroom because you didn't pay them?' I demand incredulously, my voice rising despite my efforts to keep calm.

'It was a warning. I don't know why they chose Jacob's room but I know it was them because they sent me a text later, saying it would be the whole house next.' I can't believe I'm hearing this. 'I know I should have told you before but I was really hoping I could get another job and put everything right. And now I have finally got a new job, I'll pay it back as quickly as I can, I promise. I've made an arrangement with them and as long as I keep to it they'll back off.'

I feel cold, frozen. Furious.

More lies.

'You brought loan sharks to *my home*? Anything could have happened. Chloe could have got hurt.'

'I know. I'm sorry, I'm so sorry, but I was desperate.' He swallows. 'That morning, the morning of Rachel's accident, it was my day off work but I had a job interview. I was halfway there when I realised that I'd forgotten my iPad, so I came back for it.'

'Didn't the police find out about this when they questioned you?' I ask, puzzled. 'They must have checked whether you were actually at work or not.'

'Yes, they even checked out the job interview to make sure I had an alibi,' he admits. 'I asked them not to tell you. Sorry.'

I stand up and pace around. 'And you wonder why I didn't trust you! Why didn't you tell me the truth right from the start?'

I demand. 'At least then I'd know you weren't involved in anything to do with Rachel.'

Aaron looks ashamed. 'I just couldn't. I was terrified of losing you. All of you. The longer I kept the truth from you, the harder it was to come clean.' He swallows then looks from me to Jacob. 'I love you so much, Ness. You and Jacob, you're as much a part of my family as Lucas and Chloe. I couldn't bear to lose either of you.' His shoulders slump. 'But I have, haven't I? You're going to go to Hazel's. And I know it's my own fault. I'm so, so sorry for all the lies, really I am. Can you ever forgive me?'

I can see the love and pain in his eyes. I don't want to lose my family either.

'Dad wouldn't hurt Rachel!' Lucas looks aghast. 'How could you even think that just because of a diary entry saying he had the day off work?'

'It wasn't just a diary entry.' I go to my handbag, and take out Rachel's sunflower necklace, which I'd placed in the zip compartment for safekeeping. 'I found this under your father's desk. The chain was broken.'

'Rachel lost that a few weeks ago, she was really upset about it,' Jacob says. 'She'll be so pleased you've found it.'

'The question is, how did it get there?' I ask.

Lucas frowns. 'It must have fallen off when you were helping her with her project, Dad. Remember, you were both looking at something on your computer?'

Aaron nods, then his eyes widen as if he's suddenly realised something. 'So that's why she asked me all those questions about tracing information about yourself on the internet and getting photos taken down.' He rubbed his hand over his head. 'I wish I'd known why she really wanted the information.'

It was all making sense now. I think it's time Aaron and I had a long chat and cleared the air. 'I think we need to talk. Boys, could you leave us both alone for a bit please?'

Lucas gets up. 'Yep, shall we leave them to it and play *Kryakdon*, bro?' he asks.

Jacob nods. 'Prepare to be thrashed.'

Aaron and I talk for hours, and as I listen to him I realise that things aren't black and white. Things spiralled out of control for Aaron, and then there was the complication of Rachel's fall, where everything got muddled and stressful, and he found it impossible to think straight. It was all a series of bad mistakes and poor judgement rather than deceit, I can see that now. And I understand why Aaron didn't want to add to the tension in the household, why he withheld all this from me.

That doesn't mean I agree with what he did, but I know he's a good man and he loves me, loves us all. And I'm so glad that my worst fears were unfounded, that no one in my family harmed Rachel. I feel so guilty that I suspected them all at some point over the last few weeks, even my sister, and I'm enormously relieved that I was wrong. Aaron admits that he suspected the boys too, especially Jacob. 'I knew they wouldn't hurt Rachel on purpose,' he confesses, 'but I thought they might have argued and accidentally...'

He says 'the boys' but I knew Jacob had been his prime suspect.

I've withheld things from Aaron too, I remind myself. I haven't told him what Hazel almost did to Ricky. Or that she was the one who reported him to the police. We all have our secrets.

'We'll sort out the debts together, darling. I can take on more editorial work,' I tell him. 'Just please promise that you'll never lie to me again.'

'I promise,' he says, and I believe him.

He wraps his arms around me and we hug and kiss, like we haven't in weeks, and I know it's all going to be okay.

'Please can you bring Chloe back?' he asks after a while, pulling away from me and stroking my hair. 'I want our little girl home.'

So do I. I've got my family back now. And nobody is going to tear us apart again.

EPILOGUE

Rachel

Dale was the most popular guy in the school, and like most of the girls there, I had such a huge crush on him. I know that I shouldn't have sent him those pictures, but I was desperate for him to like me, and besides, everyone did it. He'd said that if I didn't put out, he'd go off with one of the other girls.

When he started blackmailing me, I was distraught and heartbroken. Obviously he'd never cared about me at all, it had all been a big fat lie. When we moved house I really hoped I was free of him. And I was for a while, until Amy led Dale to me. I can't believe she's his cousin. She realised that it was her fault Dale traced me when the police arrested him and discovered he was the one who had been threatening me.

She hadn't meant to put me in danger, I know that. She was just chatting to him about the new friend she'd made, and that's how he found out where I live now. She just made a mistake, like I made a mistake. And Ben, he made a mistake too.

Ben didn't mean to push me. I was sitting on the window ledge, where I'd been trying to get Jacob's attention after Dale

texted. Ben came in and asked if I would play on the PlaySta-
tion with him, and I was so freaked out about Dale coming
round that I snapped. I yelled at him, told him to go away. I was
so stressed, and I didn't want him to see Dale, I thought Dale
might threaten him too.

'You're always too busy. All you care about is those lads
next door!' he yelled. Then he shoved me. He clearly hadn't
thought through what might happen next, he just reacted
angrily, like the little kid he is. I tried to grab the window frame
to stop my fall, but it was too late.

I don't blame Ben at all, that's why I said I accidentally fell.
And I'll always stick to that story. He made up the whole thing
about someone running out of my room because he panicked.
Amy said when Dale arrived the ambulance was already here,
so he ran off. Ben hadn't realised that Jacob and Lucas would be
blamed or all the trouble it would cause. He's only six. None of
it was his fault. It was Dale's. And mine.

Anyway, it's over now. We'll be moving soon and I'm glad. I
want to start again somewhere new, although I will miss Jacob,
Lucas and sweet little Chloe. Jacob has been a good friend to
me. He could have died keeping my secret.

Thankfully, it wasn't as bad as I thought it would be, telling
Mum and Dad the truth. Mum was great, so supportive. And
Dad broke down in tears, telling me he was so sorry I felt too
afraid to come to him, that he'd never hurt me. He's promised to
get help to manage his anger, he clearly feels terrible for how
he's scared me when he's flown off the handle before. He swore
that he'd never hurt me, or Mum, or Ben. And I believe him.
Everything is finally out in the open now, and the photos are
gone.

Now I'm going to make the most of this new chance. I'm
going to start afresh and make sure that I'm never scared to ask
for help when I need it. I'll tell my parents and trust them to
protect me, to love me no matter what I've done.

I was so happy when Jacob gave me back my sunflower necklace. I thought I'd lost it for good. He said they'd found it in the study, it must have broken and fallen off when Aaron was showing me something on his computer. He was so kind to me and I feel bad that he, Jacob and Lucas were suspected of hurting me. Mum's bought me a new chain so I can wear my necklace again.

And I'm getting a sunflower tattoo as soon as I'm old enough. I've always loved sunflowers because they're so bright and cheerful and raise their faces towards the sun. That's how I want to be. The tattoo will remind me not to let anyone stop me from shining as brightly as I can ever again.

A LETTER FROM KAREN

Dear reader,

I want to say a huge thank you for choosing to read *Girl Next Door*. If you enjoyed it, and want to keep up to date with all my latest releases, just sign up at the following link. Your email address will never be shared and you can unsubscribe at any time.

www.bookouture.com/karen-king

The plot of this book is based on the strength of family ties. There are many different types of families, mum and dad families, single parent families, two mums or two dads families, adopted families, stepfamilies all a blend of different personalities held together by love. Often that love is tested and suddenly family members are pitted against each other, how strong is the bond then?

The ties I wanted to explore in particular are the ties that bind a stepfamily together. Many of us remarry or move in together, blending our families, determined to make it work, to treat all the children as equal. But is that bond strong enough when the stepchildren fall out, does it tear us apart too? And what if one of the children is guilty of doing something awful but you are sure your child is innocent and your partner is sure theirs is. Will you work together as a team to find out who is guilty or will you each wrap your arms protectively around your own child and pull up the drawbridge? Is blood really thicker than water? This is the concept this story explores. I hope you enjoy reading about Vanessa and Aaron, and their fight to keep their family together. In many ways though this is Rachel's story and the repercussions of one mistake she makes which tears apart her world, that of her parents, and of the family next door.

I hope you loved *Girl Next Door*, and if you did, I would be very grateful if you could write a review. I'd love to hear what you think, and it makes such a difference helping new readers to discover one of my books for the first time.

I love hearing from my readers – you can get in touch with me on social media or through my website.

Thanks,

Karen

karenkingauthor.com

facebook.com/KarenKingAuthor
x.com/karen_king

ACKNOWLEDGEMENTS

There's a lot of things that go on in the background when writing a book, and a lot of people who help with the process. I'd like to thank my former editor Isobel Akenhead who discussed the initial idea with me and my amazing new editor Rhianna Louise for her support and expertise, also all the Bookouture editing team for their hard work and constructive advice. A special thanks to Aaron Munday for creating yet another stunning cover. And to the fabulous social media team of Kim Nash, Noelle Holten, Sarah Hardy and Jess Readett, who go above and beyond in supporting and promoting our work and making the Bookouture Author Lounge such a lovely place to be. You guys are amazing! Also to the other Bookouture authors who are always willing to offer support, encouragement and advice. I'm so grateful to be part of such a lovely, supportive team. Thanks also to the Facebook Groups of The Savvy Writers Snug and Trauma Fiction for answering my research questions.

Thanks also to all the bloggers and authors who support me, review my books and give me space on their blog tours. I am lucky to know so many incredible people in the book world and appreciate you all.

Massive thanks to my husband, Dave, for all the love and laughter you bring to my life, for being a sounding board for my ideas and for supplying the much-needed logic to some of them. Thanks also to my family and friends who all support me so much. I love you all.

Finally, a heartfelt thanks to you, my readers, for buying and reviewing my books, and for your lovely messages telling me how much you've enjoyed reading them. Without your support there would be no more books.

Thank you. xx

PUBLISHING TEAM

Turning a manuscript into a book requires the efforts of many people. The publishing team at Bookouture would like to acknowledge everyone who contributed to this publication.

Audio
Alba Proko
Melissa Tran
Sinead O'Connor

Commercial
Lauren Morrissette
Hannah Richmond
Imogen Allport

Cover design
Aaron Munday

Data and analysis
Mark Alder
Mohamed Bussuri

Editorial
Rhianna Louise
Lizzie Brien